Advance Praise for *The Legend of Carl Draco*

"A twisted, kinetic escapade through darkness and danger."
— **Mario Acevedo**, author of the Felix Gomez vampire-detective series

"Loyal to oral traditions, the novel's rich prose ripples with poetic imagery, rooted in a specific sense of place. The story's climax was as startlingly original as it was satisfying."
— **Brian Kaufman**, author of *The Fat Lady's Low, Sad Song*

"Gary Reilly was more than a teller of wonderful stories —he was a lyrical, beautiful writer whose words echo with you long after the tale if finished. *The Legend of Carl Draco* is one of those books that I know I'll be reading over and over again."
— **Jeanne C. Stein**, New York Times best-selling author of The Anna Strong Vampire Chronicles and The Fallen Siren series (as S.J. Harper)

"Reilly's Carl Draco is a man of few words, fewer goals, and some wildly powerful juju. Fueled by dizzying magic and moonshine, *The Legend of Carl Draco* delivers a deliciously vengeful yarn I couldn't wait to unspool."
— **Warren Hammond**, author of the KOP series and *Denver Moon*

"A college English professor could spend hours on allegory and metaphor when discussing Gary Reilly's *The Legend of Carl Draco*, but I have a strong suspicion Reilly would laugh and respond, 'It's just a little novel.' A master storyteller in any genre, Reilly excels in this suspenseful tale of good and evil in a magical world."
— **Pat Stoltey**, author of 2018 Colorado Book Award finalist *Wishing Caswell Dead*

"Neil Gaiman meets Flannery O'Connor in this story of a drifter coming home to reclaim his fate. A homespun tale wrapped in spellbinding prose, Reilly's story delivers magic in your moonshine, hope in the sound of bullfrogs croaking from the mudflats, and redemption in every nickel you toss in a beggar's hat."
— **Angie Hodapp**, Director of Literary Development, Nelson Literary Agency

THE LEGEND OF CARL DRACO

Gary Reilly

Running Meter Press
Denver

The Legend of Carl Draco

by Gary Reilly

Copyright 2019 by Running Meter Press

Published by

Running Meter Press
2509 Xanthia St., Denver, CO 80238
Publisher@RunningMeterPress.com
720-328-5488
Cover art: Jim Borgman
Book interior design: Jody Chapel
ISBN: 978-0-9908666-8-8
Library of Congress Number: 2019932563
First edition, 2019
Printed in the United States of America

Also by Gary Reilly:

The Asphalt Warrior Series:	The Private Palmer Series:
The Asphalt Warrior	The Enlisted Men's Club
Ticket to Hollywood	The Detachment
The Heart of Darkness Club	The Discharge
Home for the Holidays	
Doctor Lovebeads	**Standalone Novels:**
Dark Night of the Soul	The Circumstantial Man
Pickup At Union Station	
Devil's Night	

Foreword

You hold in your hands Gary Reilly's thirteenth novel to be published by Running Meter Press. Today is your lucky day. *The Legend of Carl Draco* represents a departure in prose and content from his previous work. Copy editor Karen Haverkamp puts it this way: "Draco is an elegantly written contemporary folktale whose archetypal characters and setting hold all the fascination of good literature in this genre. The protagonist may have supernatural abilities but, in true Gary Reilly style, he's terribly low-key about it."

Mark Stevens and I launched Running Meter Press not long after Gary died in March of 2011. He was our friend. We were both bowled over by the magnitude and quality of his fiction, although none of it had seen the light of day before he left us. It has been our mission to publish his writing. With this book, we've just passed the halfway point on the long shelf full of his manuscripts. Our inventory shows 25 novels so we have a dozen left to publish.

First, there was The Asphalt Warrior series, a collection of comic novels featuring Murph, a Denver taxi driver who vows never to earn more than he needs to keep a bohemian lifestyle afloat. Murph also promises himself to never, under any circumstances, get involved in the lives of his fares. He consistently fails with this pledge. There are ten novels in this series. We've published eight to date.

Then there was the Private Palmer trilogy about life as a soldier before, during, and after the Vietnam War. This character and these novels were based on Gary's own experiences as a military policeman during that conflict. Palmer copes with army life, tries to keep a low profile, and tries not to care about anything or anybody. He's not always successful in blunting his connection with life around him and, to his own surprise, finds himself doing the right thing.

Gary Reilly

In some ways, these acts represent a certain kind of failure even though Palmer feels better for having reached out.

The Circumstantial Man, published last year, was a standalone thriller that told the story of Pete Larkey, a quiet guy who tried to start his car one morning and—you guessed it—failed. Looking to replace the battery, Larkey finds himself at the center of quirky circumstances that spiral far out of control.

In a sense, with *The Legend of Carl Draco*, Gary Reilly comes full circle. His only published fiction before Running Meter Press was a short story called "The Biography Man," which appeared in *The Iowa Review* in 1977. This story was included the following year in The Pushcart Prize Anthology (Volume IV): Best of the Small Presses. In both cases, Gary pays tribute to the magic of American folklore with his own unique spin. With Draco, get ready for a reprise of this rich narrative style.

Mark and I hope to carry on publishing Gary's novels. (All of which, by the way, have received rave reviews from *Booklist*, National Public Radio, *The Denver Post*, and such literary lions as Stewart O'Nan, Ron Carlson, Jeffery Deaver, and others. And countless readers, too.)

But we could not have done it alone. We've had the support of The Tattered Cover Book Store all along and help in various ways from Nick Zellinger, John Sherffius, Sherry Peterson, Jody Chapel, Karen Haverkamp, Anita Austin, Jim Borgman, Dennis Gallagher, Denis Berkfeldt, Michael Goldsmith, and the vast Reilly clan—Gary's brothers and sisters and their extended families.

And now, get ready to meet a fresh new anti-hero. Like Murph and Palmer and Larkey before him, Draco is a guy you're never going to forget.

Mike Keefe
January 2019

chapter one

You could walk down a road you've walked before and not recognize the familiar bleach of neon painting sidewalk slabs at your feet because those fine and freshly snipped and lilac-watered barber-college hairs at the back of your neck are being stroked harder and faster by that old anticipation. The sounds of the city might plunge into silence, in the way air suddenly stands still in reverent preamble to the advent of a plains tornado, making you stop long enough to take a quick look over your shoulder.

No one seems to be following you, but you step into the nearest saloon to take stock of the situation, and the sight of drinking men takes your mind momentarily off your own soluble problems. You ease yourself onto the torn and stitched oilcloth seat of a stool at the far end of the bar and lean forward to signal the bartender for a glass of red wine.

You glance down the long line of seated customers and wonder who among all these Salvation Army discard suits might be contemplating a nightcap of surreptitious stalking culminating in futile assault. But you realize quickly enough that all the schemes and dreams of all the men rooted to stools in this skid-row gin mill could be stacked heel to shoulder and the final tote wouldn't top a three-tiered shot-glass pyramid. They sit with their shoulders hiked high to hide trembling fingers counting coins or pinching cigarettes going up in

1

smoke. Sipping in silence is the only plan of any man in here. The bartender places a glass of red wine in front of you and collects his take, and you finally relax.

On the TV overhead, gloved men in silk trade shots, but the sound is turned down too low, you can't hear the smack of bruised flesh or the rattle of bones decked in the second round. When your glass is empty, you order another for the heat you'll need for the fight you'll win later on, then you place a dollar tip on the bar and walk out.

Alleys are favored places of your enemies, so you approach the upcoming break in the walls slowly, though not out of fear or even necessarily caution. But you have to give it to them if you want to get it over with quickly and put enough distance between yourself and their corpses to lie low long enough to sleep well enough to be awake enough for the next fight. Then a fast black bulk leaps past your head, a tin lid rattles in the darkness like a coin settling on asphalt, and you uncurl your newly balled fists and grin at the sight of a tomcat running up the sidewalk with fishbones in its teeth.

It had been a long time since Carl Draco had laughed at himself, much less grinned. In fact, he couldn't recall even smiling in a long time, but he was laughing now as he watched that scuttling outcast haul his feast.

Draco moved on, making for a building that he'd called home more than once while passing through this part of the country, a twenty-dollar-a-night flophouse complete with bed and no bath. He came to another alley and overheard the drone of bum chatter devoid of malice. The devious ways of his enemies had never taken the form of this masquerade—had always been frontal and fruitless—so he wasn't particularly concerned as he peered into the darkness toward three men seated on concrete near a garbage dumpster with their backs against the wall.

He knew them, had stood all three at different times in different bars. Cadge masters, they licked their glasses

The Legend of Carl Draco

empty and shared day-labor take when they had it, shared wine, shared life stories, and sat down uninvited to beg or offer smokes. He'd spent alley evenings with such men in other cities, drawn from his digs to their brief companionship because even a man unlike themselves needs to sit down once in a while and shoot the kind of bull they shoot best.

He stepped into the alley. The three men went silent and looked up at him, exhibiting that nervous tic of fear that plagues the faces of men at odds with life and the law.

He asked how they were making out tonight, and they said "fine" in unison, possibly recognizing him, and possibly not, outside the context of a bar. One man raised a sacked bottle near empty, but Draco turned down this proffered symbol of friendship and handed him a five-dollar bill. As he walked away, they all said, "Thank you," repeated it, "Thank you," with that slow, deliberate precision of indebted earnest drunks.

There would be no sleep tonight, and though sometimes the heat of Los Angeles alone was enough to keep a man awake, it would be the ritual vigil of listening that kept Draco from shutting his eyes now. He lay on clean sheets in his darkened room beneath a window left open to entice a passing breeze. He hadn't bothered taking off his coat because if he heard the heavy tread of booted feet on the stairs, he didn't intend to stand and fight. His exit would be hasty and out the window. He'd learned long ago that sometimes it takes more than cowardice to run away from a fight—sometimes you just had to be tired of killing.

He reached up and shoved the window open a little further and gazed at his right hand in the alley light. He pondered every pale scar tattooed on every tanned knuckle, and every faraway state, back-road hamlet, and seaboard metropolis where he'd bought those souvenirs hard and fast. All that mottled meathook lacked was the callus shine and crust of heavy labor.

The creak of a stairway slat gave it away. Draco sat up and stared at the hallway light glowing beneath his door. He waited until he saw a shadow darken the light, waited until he heard a sound like the snuffling of a wolf ranging that narrow space, but didn't wait for the click of hammers cocked. He was out the window and down the fire escape before tripped triggers thundered, taking the door off its hinges and sending a swarm of shotgun pellets crashing through the window.

Draco hit the ground and paused only long enough to look up at that lethal black cloud passing overhead fomenting a rain of glass, which danced ringing down the fire escape, then he heard the bawling, braying, mechanical scream of an engine accelerating. He turned and saw a car coming at him.

In the strange way of combat, it can make a man laugh to see an enemy demonstrate a glimmer of intelligence: vertical pincer movement. Draco took off running toward the far end of the alley with the chrome teeth of a black steel beast on wheels bearing down at his back, possibly a Plymouth, but old, he wasn't sure, and was less interested. As he passed the hollow tin cube of a cafe dumpster parked beside a delivery door, he reached out and grabbed the lip and let his weight drag it rolling into the alley.

He let go and ran, and listened with pleasure to the tortured howl of wheels braking too late, and the bass-drum reverberation of sheet metal stove in.

*

The only sound in the park was a tinny husk of teenage voices drifting across a yellow lawn. Draco leaned against a tree and studied the crowd until he was certain that the kids gathered around the dry fountain half a block away were nothing more than curfew-breaking boys and girls upending illicit beers.

The lawn was long and level and would be an open run past an empty swimming pool. The highway was just beyond the edge of the park, and that's where he was headed, toward an arrow of parallel lightposts pointing east. Only the low, flat-topped black shape of the swimming-pool pump house stood between himself and that boundary line.

He moved out at a trot, already certain that these most recent brutes were at least as ill-equipped to kill him as all the others who had tried to take him out, so he was a bit surprised, though not at all shaken, when he heard a hissing liquid squeal of water escaping from a drinking fountain and looked over and saw in the feathered darkness of an evergreen grove a different texture of shadow, a smooth and looming shape, possibly a Plymouth.

The flashbulb burst of a single headlight caught him in midstride. Maybe they thought he was a deer, thought he'd lose the rhythm of his retreat and trip over his own feet, but whatever their misconception, he turned toward the fence that surrounded the swimming pool and leapt with a feline spring and slithered up its steel netting with a reptilian grace.

It was the same car, one-eyed now and fender-dented, tearing a dirt two-track across the lawn and sliding to a stop just outside the gate. Draco edged into the shadow of the pump house, then climbed up onto the flat-topped tar roof and lay low watching two men dressed in black overcoats and high-crowned, wide-brimmed black felt hats emerging from the car.

One man carried a shotgun still warm from its recent flophouse roust. He placed its muzzle against the steel padlock of the closed gate and tugged the trigger. Coiled links burst, ringing into the empty swimming pool. The two men strode in, sniffing chlorine odors and peering into dark corners seeking what they doubtless believed to be a panicked quarry.

Who lay prone peering over the edge of the roof and studying the hunters pacing the pool perimeter like baffled animals stalking weak meat. Not worth killing. Time to go.

As he was getting to his knees in preparation for slipping

off the rear of the building, he heard the thin high-pitched rising wail of a siren coming his way. He dropped flat against the roof and watched the white rectangle of a police cruiser racing across the lawn. A spotlight hit the men standing directly below him.

The car stopped in front of the dented sedan, and a policeman got out and crouched behind his door with a pistol drawn.

"Drop the gun!"

Draco looked at the cop, then looked over his shoulder toward those highway lights growing small in the east. He wanted to make that road tonight.

"Drop it!"

He heard the clean click of a shotgun touching concrete and saw the cop come through the gate kicking links into the pool.

"Hands above your heads!"

One man raised his arms, but the other began edging away with both hands hanging at his sides. The cop pointed his pistol at him, and Draco saw it happen, saw the man with his arms raised reach inside his greatcoat and bring out a revolver and point it at the cop, who looked down at a fresh hole the size of a poker chip punched into his chest. The two men retrieved the shotgun and walked past the cop, ignoring his blind, off-balance, lurching, graceless fall into the empty pool.

Draco waited until the dark sedan retreated across the lawn into a shadow line of trees, then looked down at the spread-eagled shape on the dry swimming-pool floor. He eased off the roof and dropped to the sidewalk, hopped down into the shallow end of the pool, and knelt beside the cop.

A flow of blood was trickling off the chest and worming downslope toward a drainage grate suffocated with weeds. No pulse. He dragged a lid open on a dull lens. The sound of another siren came from a street bordering the park, and

The Legend of Carl Draco

Draco glanced up, then looked down at the alabaster face and had to stop himself from doing what he did best, had to set his shoulders and breathe deeply to keep from running.

He wiped beaded sweat off his brow and opened the cop's shirt and placed a damp palm over the coagulating pot of blood rimmed with torn flesh and splintered bone in the center of the man's chest. He held his hand there until he sensed the bullet tucked deep inside a leather pocket of the man's heart. He closed his eyes and calculated the bullet's lie and gauged internal damage.

Then he took it.

The spent slug rose slowly through a drilled and bleeding meaty straw. Draco felt the chunk of useless lead spill into his hand. He rolled it between his fingers and examined it in the spinning flash of approaching red-and-white lights. Flattened, bent, flecks of scorched blood in the crevices, the soft metal had destroyed itself crashing through the breastbone. Draco chucked the chunk of lead over the fence, where it bounced in the grass with the soft sound of a small animal in retreat.

He placed his hand over the hole and closed his eyes and set his jaws so tightly that his eardrums began to hum, and in this stifling humid vale of LA heat he caught a whiff of cool rain-lashed rock, of thick-treed mountain peaks and fast winds dragging heavy clouds that glowed with silent lightning. He clamped his eyelids tighter and saw a single blue flash of static split a bowl of night, delivering a feast of power and life—and felt the burrowed flesh beneath his palm begin to stir like worms.

A pistol hammer cocked at his back.

"Get away from him!"

The scorched rim of that poker hole shrank with moving flesh-meeting-flesh until it closed with a healing pinhole snap. Draco lifted his hand and examined the seamless rip. The trail of blood no longer stretched toward the drainage grate.

Spit-shined shoes smacked the pool concrete.

"Facedown with your hands behind your head!"

Carl Draco took one last look in the direction of that line of receding lights aimed at the desert east, then intertwined his fingers against those fine and freshly snipped and lilac-watered barber-college hairs at the back of his neck and surrendered himself for the first time in a long time to a decent night's sleep.

chapter two

A match head whispers across the front bucktooth of what might be a pirate's skull perched on the cluttered top of an oaken desk. The waxen wick of a candle is lit. The spent match lands in a porcelain nest of pipes, and the leaves of a newspaper are peeled and shuffled as a scholarly man settles into his leather chair perusing the minor headlines of the day.

"Listen to this," he says, speaking to that mute ball of bone. "Policeman survives mysterious shooting."

The paragraph is tucked into section C, not quite worthy of front-page exploitation. "No blood, no bullets, just a mysterious finger-sized hole drilled into a uniform shirt. Quote: 'It felt as though a line drive hit me square in the chest.'"

A pause as the scholar contemplates the deadly flight of stitched horsehide launched by the ash mass of a Louisville Slugger.

"Says here he believed himself to have been hit by a bullet, and saw blood on his shirt, but the policemen who discovered him lying at the bottom of the pool found no sign of injury to his person."

He smiles at the skull. "What do you think?"

No reply.

A suspect arrested at the scene, but no name given. A drifter, currently being held on suspicion of assaulting a police officer.

"A drifter," the man mutters, folding the paper and setting it beside his mum friend, "and a policeman who believes he was bleeding." A fact worth pondering as he rubs the scored tile of the skull's fixed grin until the carbon scratch has faded into yellow.

"We may have a healer in our midst."

The scholar sets the newspaper aside and settles the tip of his pipe between his teeth. His gaze drifts across his book-walled room, drifts across the city to a university office where once a small boy sat squirming under the inquisitive eye of a spinning disk.

*

The racket of phlegm hawk and demands to "see my lawyer!" woke the unnamed suspect, who opened his eyes and listened to the morning ritual of porcelain vomit and the cement scratch of first-smoke matches being struck.

Carl Draco gazed at the cracked and water-stained ceiling overhead and contemplated the events of the previous evening when a homicide detective had come to his jail cell and asked him questions about the shooting, asked how Draco had come to be standing at the bottom of an empty swimming pool where a cop with a bullet hole in his shirt was lying unconscious.

"Just passing by," Draco had said. "Heard some shots. Found him lying there."

"They found a padlock blown to bits and shotgun pellets in the pool."

Draco had shrugged. "I don't know anything about that."

The detective leaned close then and let a chewed breath mint billow into this lying jailbird's eyes. "Tell me who put that hole in his shirt."

"I don't know. Why don't you ask him?"

"He can't tell us what happened. He doesn't remember."

After the cop had left, Draco lay down and pondered

images of cops in lesser burgs who'd detained him on suspicion of back-door bolts broken and dry goods pilfered, who'd finally shown him out barking threats about unpinned crimes unsolved. But he had always taken them and their hospitality for all he could get, because he had never known such peace as the peace of jails.

"Grab your hat and get outta my cell!"

A deputy yanked the barred door wide, wiggling his thumb in the direction of the nearest exit.

Draco rolled off the bunk and picked up his hat and coat and stepped out. "What are they going to do with me?"

"Don't know, don't care, up the stairs to your right." The deputy wouldn't meet Draco's eyes. He looked above Draco's head when he looked at all. His lips were set with grim aversion to a man held on suspicion of assaulting a brother officer.

Draco walked through the double doors and up a concrete stairwell into the restless noise of an outprocessing sally port where bail bondsmen counted cash while women wept beside their freed men. Within a glass-windowed room adjacent, a deputy sheriff was typing release forms. A door on the far side of the room opened, and the homicide detective stepped in. He walked up and stood close to Draco and spoke softly.

"You're free to go. Our man wasn't hurt, so we can't hold you any longer. We probably couldn't find a reason to hold you even if we wanted to"—then his voice plummeted until, even if the room had been silent, even if the typing and talk and muted, hungover detainee moaning beyond the walls had ceased, no one could have heard his whisper except Carl Draco—"which we do. I know you're lying to me, but I don't know what you're lying about, you sonofabitch." Then his lips thinned into a pleasant smile. "You'll be leaving town, I suppose?"

Draco nodded politely.

"You've got one friend in this town."

"Says you."

The detective pointed toward a man standing next to the door. Draco looked at him. Tweed suit-coat. Briefcase tucked under one arm. Salt-and-pepper beard. Brown pinholed shoes not at all stylish.

"I don't need a lawyer."

"He's not a lawyer. He's been waiting all day for your release. He even offered to make bail."

"Can I go now?"

The detective turned and walked away. A deputy slid a brown paper bag through a hole in the glass. It contained a clip of folded fives, a cracked cowhide belt, and shoelaces, all of it belonging to Draco, who unrolled the belt and began working it through his pant loops. The detective stopped long enough to speak to the man by the door.

"Don't look to him for any thanks, mister. His kind don't know the meaning of the word."

Balmy, there was no sky in the basin, only a white haze dragging its muggy inversion across LA. It would be dark in an hour. Draco stood outside the door of the police building, slapping his hat to give it a little shape and listening to the clicking heels of the man who had shadowed him all the way down the tiled hallway.

"Carl, wait!"

West was end-of-track, an ocean full of fish piss and sunbathers. East was the rest of the country. Draco thought about hiking south to the border and maybe finding a spot where the crossing would be easy. Then he shoved his hands into his pockets and just thought about finding something to eat before getting out of town.

"Please, Carl. Wait up."

Draco walked toward an intersection where the streetlight was about to turn green.

"Wait, I need to talk with you."

Draco turned around and faced the man. "You'd be well

advised to keep your distance, mister."

The man pulled up short, hugging the briefcase across his chest. Possibly a shield—but no, he was just holding on tight, a harried businessman afraid of losing his grip.

"You probably don't remember me," the man said, swallowing hard with what Draco perceived to be unfettered excitement.

"You're probably not worth remembering."

The man removed his glasses and smiled, his cheeks pink and bulging, his nearsighted eyes squinting. "The last time you saw me, I was a little thinner. I've put on weight since."

Draco turned away and stepped up to the curb. The light was back to red. He gritted his teeth with only minor annoyance and sniffed as pipe smoke trapped in tweed approached. But he sensed no particular evil in the vicinity.

"I'm Professor Dunsmore."

Draco hesitated a moment, then turned and looked the man up and down, fitting a memory to the pop-cheeked wrinkled mug peering at him. He stepped a pace closer and tilted his head like a dog getting a new fix on a squirrel. "Professor Dunsmore."

"You've changed too, Carl. You were only seven years old when I spoke to you last. Do you remember?"

"I remember."

Dunsmore drummed the briefcase with his fingertips. "When I read about this incident in the paper last night, I had no idea that the suspect involved might be you . . ." And as he prattled, Draco stripped the fat off that face with his eyes and took a razor to the neat gray stubble. But then he remembered, the young professor who had put him through the wringer back then had sported short black whiskers. So he put the stubble back on and ground some coal dust in and saw again the young scholar with the same inquisitive iron-gray eyes that were probing him now. "I never gave up hope of seeing you again, Carl."

Draco remembered. There had been this one man whom he had liked, and even trusted, out of all those people, right up to the very last day. He smiled and put his hands into his pockets and nodded.

"Yeah, well, it's nice to see you again, Professor." He glanced over his shoulder. "But I gotta get going." He turned to the crosswalk.

"Wait a minute!" Dunsmore said, insulted maybe, trying to haul Draco back with the edge in his voice. "I haven't seen you in twenty years," his voice rising in pitch as if amazed at this singular truth. "The least you could do is give me a few minutes of your time."

"I'd like to, Professor, but that story in the paper was read by a lot more men than you."

"What do you mean?"

"There's men trying to kill me."

"What men?"

"I don't know."

"Why do they want to kill you?"

"I never stuck around long enough to find out." The light turned green. "So long, Professor. I gotta go."

Dunsmore reached out with fingers gathering the thin fabric on Draco's shoulder. "But why won't you come with me, Carl?"

Draco glanced at that pleading fist, then gave up a smile. "Listen, Professor. I don't want to put you or your family in jeopardy. The men chasing me don't fool around."

"I'm not married, Carl, I'm a bachelor. I have no family. Please. It's been twenty years. Won't you come with me? You don't have to stay long. I want only to ask you a few questions."

Draco looked up at the green light, watched as it rose through amber and hit red. Then he shrugged that shoulder and nodded and let Professor Dunsmore, as he had done twenty years earlier, lead the way home.

chapter three

The competition between wood and porcelain was fierce, with domino-sized dragons, unicorns, and similar but unidentifiable critters rearing back on hind legs cloven-hoofed or clawed. In one corner of the room, wood-skinned and clutching a spear with his fists balled at his belly, a life-sized hand-carved African warrior stood guard. Draco waited in the front doorway for Professor Dunsmore to flip the light switch illuminating this museum of the arcane, this abode of a man without a woman in a house containing nothing but his heart's desires.

Dunsmore led his former patient down a dark hallway toward the rear of the house. The room they entered was cavern-like, high-ceilinged and long, and dark until Dunsmore produced a single flame, striking teeth that grinned in the sudden flare—the skull of a man long dead holding down a sheaf of recently typed papers. Draco gazed at the empty eye sockets as Dunsmore took a seat behind his oaken desk and motioned him toward a wood-framed leather-upholstered chair.

"I'm going to have to leave soon," Draco said, and his voice seemed strangely muffled in this large place. He studied the walls, or what little he could see of them hidden in the flickering shadows behind shelves filled with spines made of leather or cloth, books placed in neat tight rows giving the room the faint odor of trees.

"I understand, Carl," Professor Dunsmore said quietly, trying to control the timbre in his voice, which indicated that his excitement was equal to Draco's uneasiness concerning the wisdom of this unscheduled meeting.

"Don't even think about offering me anything to eat or drink," Draco said. "I got miles to make tonight."

"Have a seat, Carl," the professor replied.

Draco removed his hat and sat on the chair, the wood frame creaking like a pleased beast shouldering a familiar load. "Have you read all these books?" Draco said, craning his neck to look around at those hedgerows of dusty volumes.

"Most of them," Dunsmore conceded with unsuppressed pride. He removed his glasses and untucked a handkerchief and began polishing his bifocals, his fingers working unsupervised as he squinted at the shelves. "I even authored a few of them."

Draco nodded. Scholars write books. He'd seen men do less noble things. "All right, Professor. I'm here. What do you want?"

"I want to know where you've been," Dunsmore said, putting his glasses back on. "I want to know where you went the night you ran away from the orphanage. I want to know what you did during the intervening years. And I want to know who these men are who are trying to kill you."

"I haven't been doing much of anything, Professor. I move around. I ride the rails. I'm not a hobo but I live like one. I don't know who the men are that are trying to kill me. I only know they're men like me."

"How so?"

"They can do the things I can do." Draco fixed his sights on a thumb-smudged paperback resting on top of Dunsmore's desk—and as though he had reached out with one hand to pull it toward him, the book began sliding. It teetered on the edge of the desk with its pages fanning open and dropped to the floor. "Do you remember that?"

"I remember, Carl. Oh yes, I do remember. That particular scene was engraved upon the surface of each and every neuron of my brain."

Draco picked up the volume and set it on the desk.

"Are you a healer, Carl?"

Draco sat back and rubbed his thumbs on the threadbare brim of his hat, but said nothing. Dunsmore pulled out a newspaper. "A veteran police officer reported that he was shot in the chest. He insists that he saw himself bleed. Did you heal him, Carl?"

"I had to."

"What do you mean?"

"The men I told you about carry guns. He got caught in the crossfire."

"But you don't know who these men are?"

"I don't know them personally."

"Do you know where they come from?"

"No."

"Do you have any idea at all why they are trying to kill you?"

"No."

"Have you tried to find out?"

"No."

"Why not?"

"I'm not interested."

Dunsmore closed the newspaper, folded it neatly, set it on the desk. As a child Carl Draco's personal brand of obfuscation had manifested itself primarily in silences, and though he was at least talking now, Dunsmore could see that the attitude of the boy-become-man had remained fundamentally unchanged and was just as irritating.

"Do you remember what we did the last time I saw you?"

"I remember." And it didn't take ESP to figure out where Dunsmore was headed. "Forget it, Professor."

"You were only a child, you couldn't handle it back then."

"I'm not a child now, Professor, and I'm not interested in handling it."

Dunsmore's voice had been growing progressively louder, as if he wanted to reach out and grab his former patient by the lapels and give him a solid shake and say not "Tell me what you know" but "Stay."

"I gotta get going, Professor."

The single candle flame gave a solitary shudder, sending shadows dancing up the walls. "Carl," Dunsmore said softly, everything under control now except his guest, "you are the only person I have ever met who possesses true telekinetic powers."

"There are others," Draco replied. "I expect they don't let on."

"After you ran away from the orphanage, I kept a lookout for you," Dunsmore said. "I kept in touch with other people in other states. Long after the authorities gave up, I continued to search for you. I had supposed that someone would find you dead in an alley, but I nevertheless held out hope for you because I had to believe that a boy who could move books with his eyes was a boy who could survive anywhere he landed."

"You were right about that, Professor."

"Why didn't you come to me after you left the orphanage? A child with your powers ought to have had the prescience to know where he would be welcome."

"To be honest with you, Professor, I tried to forget about you the same day I ran away."

"I always thought you liked me back then. I thought we got along well enough."

"I did like you, Professor. But when you put me under that last time . . . well . . . frankly, I held that against you for a couple months."

"That was an unpleasant experience. I'm sorry, Carl. I was

trying to help you."

"I know that, Professor. It's forgotten." Draco sat forward and rested his elbows on his knees. "I really ought to get going, Professor. Those men might show up unexpectedly. They do that."

Dunsmore sat back in his chair and raised a finger. "If they have powers similar to yours, we have nothing to fear." He opened a desk drawer and pulled out a black silk bag the size of a change purse. "A few years ago I wrote an article about a folk hero of Black mythology named Stackalee. During my research I met with a purported witch by the name of Mother Rose who lives right here in LA. I interviewed her three times, and after our final meeting she gave me this bit of sorcery to ward off bad luck." He leaned across the desk and handed it to Draco. "What do you think, Carl? Is it authentic?"

Draco hefted the sagging silk walls in a palm. Sewn shut with black-cat hairs, it contained things once alive: teeth and fern, worm and scale. He raised it to his nose and took a long, deep sniff. He smiled.

"This is a different kind of magic."

"What do you mean?"

"This is good," he said. He nestled the bag hard against a nostril. "This is the real item. But it can't protect anyone from the men who are following me. Their power is different from this."

He set the bag on the desk.

Professor Dunsmore felt a gentle tickle of hair rising on the back of his neck. To ease this taut and tingling sensation, he grabbed the bag and put it back into the drawer.

"Do you know, Carl, after you disappeared I wrote a paper about you. I never published it, but the process was pivotal in my writing career. In fact, that paper was one of the many reasons I am no longer employed by UCLA."

"Did they fire you?"

"Let's just say that my exploration into paranormal

Gary Reilly

phenomena did not meet the university's budget criteria."

"What do you do for a living now?"

"For the past twenty years I have been the sole faculty member of the Dunsmore Institute for Psychic Research."

"Where's that?"

"You're sitting in it." Dunsmore spread his arms wide. "This is the Institute. I make a living publishing books and articles which focus on the occult. However, my specialty, so to speak, is American folklore. It all ties together. In the end, everything ties together."

"Listen, Professor, you can't publish that paper about me."

"'Can't' is the correct choice of word. I had considered publishing it a number of times, but I can't, or that is, I never could. The subject of the paper had disappeared, and writing about the paranormal is a risky enough enterprise without making claims that cannot be substantiated."

"And they never will be," Draco said, rising from his chair. "I gotta shove off, Professor."

He'd heard good-byes before, the professor had, but none so piercing. "Your suit," he said.

Stay.

"What about it?" Draco said, glancing down at the front of his coat.

"Might I offer you something better?"

Please.

Not an unlikely proposition, considering the state of Carl Draco's wardrobe. A man who lives like a hobo entertains a unique relationship with the seasons. Snow and rain saturate threads, which dry shapeless under a merciless prairie sun. Wind unravels what it can, seat of pants, knees, elbows, the places that work hardest and wear thinnest, those that lose their color first.

Dunsmore went to a closet on the far side of the room and opened the door, reached inside, and began examining a selection of cloth-cut corpses dangling on wires. "I never

20

The Legend of Carl Draco

throw anything away," he said as he groped at collars and cuffs, examining the quality of the merchandise. "I keep telling myself that the thing to do is call the Salvation Army and donate this stuff, but then I think that the real thing to do is go on a diet and make these things fit again." He pulled a brown sports jacket off a wire and held it up. "In the end, though, I never do anything. This looks like it might work. I bought this suit twenty years ago. I was a lean hound in those days."

Draco shoved his fists down the arms and worked the shoulders into a loose fit. He nodded his approval and changed into the pants. The fabric felt new, a light material, a man could run fast in this outfit. He took off his hat and looked at the sweatband, held the greasy crown against his new used coat, then shook his head. "This hat won't do now." He crossed the room and set the cap at a rakish angle upon the skull. "I'll pick up another along the road."

Dunsmore studied his guest. The sports coat and pants fit well. A shave, a haircut, new shoes, and he'd be a good-looking young man, could be mistaken for a Jaycee or a go-getter on a Kiwanis committee. "Is there anything else I can do for you, Carl?"

"You've done enough, Professor."

"Money? Do you need cash?"

"No problem, Professor."

Dunsmore hurried to his desk and scribbled something on a business card. "My home phone. The next time you pass through LA, I'd like to see you again."

Please.

Draco palmed the card and slipped it into a pocket.

He led the way back along the dark hallway toward the lit front room where the wooden warrior stood silent watch over their farewell. Draco's grip was firm, but even Dunsmore in his personal despair noted the soft underside of that clasp of friendship, the smooth flesh of a palm making a lie of the tanned and scarred back of the hand. Whatever Carl Draco did to get money to support his scant needs, it did not appear to involve anything directly related to manual labor.

Dunsmore stood in the open doorway and watched his guest, friend, and former patient—the boy-become-man— move down the sidewalk at an increasingly rapid stride and head off in an easterly direction, becoming finally invisible in a darkness that was never quite resolved in this city of endless and intolerable light.

The professor closed the door and stood for what must have been a full minute without moving, unable to think what it was he had planned to do this evening. Nothing seemed to be of any particular significance anymore. His only reason for living had just walked out the door in a secondhand suit.

*

A train rolls out of the station into the night. Draco hops an empty boxcar and sits by the open door watching the industrial suburbs of LA growing small in the distance. He pulls Dunsmore's business card from his pocket and tears it into confetti and tosses it to the wind.

Balling up his coat for a pillow, he lies down and watches the passing lights of the countryside, some of which are homes, and as he drifts to sleep it occurs to him that his life will always be like this and that those men will never quit coming for him, though that part doesn't matter because his moves are too good. They don't have any moves, unless you view dogged persistence as a strategy in and of itself. He makes a vague attempt to tote the number of men he has killed since he was a seven-year-old child, but it's too late. It's been too many years and too many lives, and the numbers got too big too long ago.

And as sometimes happens after encounters with those men, he tells himself: Why not take a stand? Plant yourself and let them come until they understand that they'll never beat you. But after a while he lets that thought go and turns

The Legend of Carl Draco

onto one side and waits for sleep to come, thinking as he always does that in the end he'll continue to go with what he knows.

The line between blue sky and brown earth is speared by a pale lane of asphalt. He's walking along the shoulder of a road toward the outskirts of a distant cluster of unlighted buildings. He believes it to be a town, but as he draws near he sees that it's a shabby, shingled, wood-framed motel set back from the road, fronted by an apron of gravel.

Approaching from behind is a sound of hammering pistons. A pickup truck rushes past him and rolls into the parking lot. It stops outside the manager's office. The driver climbs out wearing overalls shot with red dust and the ash of fallen leaves. Above the door of the office hangs a mangled tube of pink neon flickering with the sound of many flies: VACANCY. The man enters the office, the door closes, the hinges cry like seagulls, and a woman and a boy wait like shadows inside the pickup cab.

Carl is the boy seated beside the woman, who puts an arm around his shoulders because his fingers sting from touching the sun-hot metal of the door sill. She's comforting him, holding him gently and firmly against her side. He can smell woodsmoke caught in the threads of her print dress, can smell the odor of wildflowers trapped in the strands of her loose brown hair. The man comes out of the manager's office with a key in his hand and beckons them into a room.

Carl is seated on the floor watching a black-and-white TV and holding a glass of water in one hand. In the other hand he's crumpling a noisy wad of cellophane, which he had peeled from the glass. He sips the water and watches a herd of silent buffalo blanketed by falling snow, their heads clustered together, their wet nostrils launching steam into the air. They are collapsing one by one in a white field, each death preceded by the crack of a rifle concealed in a tree line.

The man and woman are seated on the bed behind him.

He can smell the beer in the sweating cans they hold in their hands. They are talking quietly but he does not pay any attention to them, too curious about the TV, which he knows is neither a window nor a lantern filled with dying bison, but he cannot say for sure what it is or how it works because he has never seen a TV before.

The rapid tap of a knuckle on wood, the intake of breath behind him, he hears these things but cannot turn his head. Three heavy steps, he knows it's the man moving across the floor toward a chest where the blue steel of a pistol lies hidden.

"Draco."

The voice comes from beyond the door, but it's muffled as if spoken through water. The pistol scrapes wood as the man opens a drawer and gathers it into a shaking hand.

"Open up, Draco."

Massive curly snow-plastered shoulders drop in a field already littered with steaming bodies. Heads hanging, eyes closed against a hard wind, for reasons Carl cannot understand the herd does not stampede. Calves lean huddled, freezing against their mothers' bellies, as the rifle brings another animal to its knees.

"Who's there?"

The muscles of Draco's neck twist in his sleep, and he sees the man in a crouch aiming the pistol at the door. The woman stands up from the bed. The beer can slides from her fist and drops to the floor, drawing a line of foam in the air.

A felled buffalo's bellow rocks the room. Snowflakes spring from the legs of the wounded beast kicking icy hooves at the sparkling winter sky. The dying sound spirals into Carl's eardrums and he realizes it's not the beast but the woman screaming, and as he turns to look up at her his vision is distorted by a much larger sound, that of the motel room door exploding.

Steel wheels clatter across a grade where flashing lights ring a warning to night travelers seated in idling cars. Draco wakes up with the engine horn-blare and crossing bells fading, wakes into the soundtrack of his dream breathing heavily, his neck and forehead damp with the memory of that familiar and tedious nightmare.

He sits up running his fingertips through his hair, regretting now that he had left his hat at Professor Dunsmore's house. He puts on his coat and buttons it tight and shoves his hands into his pockets. The odor of pipe smoke rises from the lining. He feels granules of ancient tobacco driven into the seams, which reek of that same sweet, leafy perfume that he had first smelled as a boy, back when Professor Dunsmore had given him a reason to run away forever.

chapter four

You search for answers buried in leaves printed by sheet-fed offset or the sainted patience of monks whose lives are consumed by gilt, quill, and folio, and then one day your dream blindsides you through a machine-fashioned length of sleek talking copper: "I have a young boy in my charge whom you might be interested in seeing."

The woman identified herself as Edna Helms, matron in charge of an orphanage that accommodated children up to the age of eighteen. Professor Dunsmore cradled the phone on his shoulder, held it with his neck, opened a notebook, and set his pen against a blank page. "What is it about this boy that might interest me?"

"When he gets angry, things break."

Not unheard of. She told him that the boy was seven years old and that his name was Carl Draco. "No one on our staff has actually seen anything break," she said. "However, some of the children claim to have seen it happen, and they also insist that he can open and close doors with his eyes."

"Are these children otherwise prone to exaggeration?"

"Prior to his arrival two months ago, the children never talked about such things. It was one week after he came here that the stories began to circulate."

"Is he a bully?"

"He is a very quiet boy."

The Legend of Carl Draco

"Does he have friends?"

"None that I know of. I can only tell you that some of the children are very afraid of him. They bring me their broken toys and tell me that Carl did it with his eyes."

Dunsmore wrote the boy's name on the tablet. "Do you know who his parents are?"

"No. He was found in a desert by the state police and was delivered into our custody by the Court of the County of Los Angeles. He told them his name was Carl Draco, but he did not know where he came from, or who his parents were, or why he was wandering alone in the desert."

Dunsmore drew three hairlines beneath Carl's name. "I see. I think I would like to set up an interview with the boy. My schedule is open."

"I want you to understand one thing." And a hardness intruded upon the woman's voice, the inflexible subtext of a salesperson about to cut a nonnegotiable deal. "As head of the institution, I am considered by the state to be his legal guardian."

"Of course."

"Consequently, if there is any money to be made out of this, I will represent Carl's legal and financial interests."

"Yes. Well. Why don't you bring him around?"

They made an appointment. Dunsmore hung up and jotted it on his calendar.

Three days later he watched from his window as the woman climbed from a car in the parking lot and beckoned to the boy, who slid reluctantly across the seat and emerged wearing a blue suit, which Dunsmore concluded had been purchased some time during the past two days. A good-looking kid. He was on display. This woman had something she thought she might be able to sell.

He was a quiet child, bordering on sullenness, but there was something in his withdrawn demeanor more calculating than naive anger. He did not betray the silent wariness and

27

watchfulness Dunsmore would have expected to find in a mistrustful and cunning young rebel. Carl Draco, in fact, seemed abundantly disinterested in everything going on around him.

Dunsmore, Mrs. Helms, and the boy gathered in the comforting chrome-and-Naugahyde sterility of a conference room and got to know each other. Coffee for the grown-ups. A Coke for the boy? "We don't allow soft drinks at the institution," Helms explained.

By the time it occurred to Dunsmore to ask Carl if he even knew what Coca-Cola was, the boy had gone away forever.

"Well, I think the time has come for Carl and me to step into my office and get to know each other better."

Helms didn't like that, Dunsmore could tell, but he wasn't doing it to annoy her, although he might have. He had to get the boy away from the "authorities" if he expected to get any straight answers.

They entered Dunsmore's private office. He directed Carl to an oversized faculty-lounge chair dragged in here for the occasion, a soft acre of leather for a boy to get lost in.

Dunsmore took a seat behind his desk to give Carl a bit of distance, then leaned forward and rubbed the short black bristles of the beard he had begun growing six months previously. "Do you play mumblety-peg?"

"No."

Dunsmore frowned with disappointment. "I thought every boy played mumblety-peg?"

"I don't have a knife."

Dunsmore slid a drawer open and pulled out a Boy Scout knife. He handed it to Carl. "I'll teach you. Then you can teach the other boys at the orphanage."

Carl accepted the tool, wrapped his fingers tightly around the plastic grip. With a fingernail he hooked a steel half-moon and drew the buried blade from its slit. Clicked secure. He peered at the honed chrome mirror, a new knife waiting for

The Legend of Carl Draco

a boy to strop a whetstone, whittle a totem, or hack a branch for that legendary splint. Or merely show it to the other boys.

Carl folded the blade home and handed it back to Dunsmore. "Mrs. Helms would take it away from me. The boys aren't allowed to have knives."

Dunsmore placed it in his drawer, shaking his head. "I suppose you're right, some adults do frown upon boys possessing such things." He closed the drawer and looked Carl squarely in the eye. "What do you know how to do?"

Carl shrugged. He intertwined his fingers church-and-steeple on his lap and turned his head to study the furnishings.

"Can you move things with your eyes?" Dunsmore said.

Seemingly captivated by the sight of a battleship-gray filing cabinet, Carl did not reply.

"I didn't think you could," Dunsmore said, sitting back and smiling smugly.

Carl gave him a look that hovered between insult and anger, a face momentarily alive. But it quickly settled into bored resignation. Interviews with adults always came to an end. You just had to wait it out.

Dunsmore dug through his drawer and found a magnifying glass as large as a hockey puck. He held the lens to his eye, which became a saucer of milk with a gray olive fixed in the center. It blinked at Carl. "Big eh?" He held the glass in front of his incisors and clacked them. Monster teeth. Carl's cheeks were lost to an uncontrollable grin.

"Would you like to have this?" Dunsmore said. "It's very scientific. I doubt that Mrs. Helms would take something this educational away from you. It's an excellent tool for studying fingerprints, ants, and things of a minuscule nature in general."

Carl took it and peered through the lens toward the canals of his hand. He inspected the gilded edges of a book, the dusty base of the fluorescent lamp on the desk, then relinquished it to the professor. "One of the big kids would just take it away from me."

"A bully maybe?"

Carl nodded.

"Mrs. Helms tells me that you can handle yourself pretty well in a fight. She told me that you had an altercation with one of the bigger boys. She said you hurt him."

But Dunsmore was competing with the filing cabinet again.

"She said you . . . what was it . . . you broke his lip?"

Something shrill entered Carl's voice—"I broke his front teeth"—but his eyes remained fixed on the cabinet.

"You don't look strong enough to break anybody's front teeth."

"I did."

"How, Carl? How could you possibly do that? You're such a skinny boy. I don't think a skinny boy could do much of anything around a bully except talk."

Carl stared at him.

"I think you're lying," Dunsmore said.

"I am not."

"How could a boy as small and weak as you break somebody's front teeth?"

Carl's eyes dropped a notch. He regarded Dunsmore's teeth like a bowler sizing up a row of standing duckpins. Then he shifted his aim toward the desk. The gilded book began to move.

Dunsmore heard the clothbound shuffle but looked down only in time to see the spine dip into space. When he looked up, the boy was rigid, the muscles of his entire body flexed and shaking. His head began to twitch, and his eyes began to move as if following something roaming about the room, though the two of them were alone in the office. Then Carl began to scream.

That was the end of the first interview.

Dunsmore saw Carl two more times. During the second interview Carl was uncooperative to the extent that he would

The Legend of Carl Draco

communicate only by nodding, or shaking his head no. The professor felt like a man scaling naked rock. No fingerhold here. The boy was in charge.

But during the third and final interview, Dunsmore found an accommodating hairline crack in that vertical stone. The boy's interest was piqued by the mention of hypnosis.

Mrs. Helms was marking time in the outer room. During the previous visits she had borne the attitude of a stage mother confident that the performance of her talented child might culminate in the fulfillment of her private dreams. But the interviews had not been going as well as she had anticipated. She strode about the outer office now moody and tense, frustrated by the potential collapse of her financial fantasies.

Dunsmore locked the inner door to his office and turned to the boy. "Tell me something, Carl. Have you ever heard of the word 'hypnosis'?"

The boy's face had been averted, but at the mention of the word he looked at Dunsmore.

"Do you know what it is?" Dunsmore said.

Carl nodded.

"Can you tell me?"

"On TV, the man swings a watch and the people talk like chickens."

"Do you understand how he is able to do that?"

"Magic."

"No, it is not magic," Dunsmore said.

"I saw it."

"What you saw was . . . well, a performance by a man who was using a scientific method of relaxation to entertain people."

"They talked like chickens."

"I'm certain they did. But hypnosis is a technique also used by doctors, and men like myself, to examine the thoughts of other people. Have you ever been hypnotized?"

"No. Have you?"

"Yes," Dunsmore said.

"Did you talk like a chicken?"

"No."

"What's it feel like?"

"Would you like to find out?"

"But what's it like?"

"Very pleasant. I found it very relaxing. When I came out of it I felt as if I had taken a nap."

A glimmer of new life entered Carl's eyes. Whatever had gone on between them during the past interviews seemed forgotten. Hypnotism. Magic. Dunsmore went to the closet and brought out a black box with a disk on a spindle attached to the side. He placed it on the desk in front of Carl. The boy touched the outside edge of the disk's red-and-white spiral pattern and traced it to the center.

Dunsmore turned on the desk lamp, yanked the venetians closed, and switched off the overhead lights. He dragged his chair from behind the desk and set it next to Carl. He sat down and turned the device on. "Now, I want you to watch the spiral," he said. "Concentrate on the spinning disk."

Carl looked at the disk obediently, eager to do his part in this performance. Dunsmore crooned his instructions, watching the boy's eyes, which never left the infinitely inward drilling of the crimson graphic. After a few minutes Dunsmore raised his tone of voice. "I am going to ask you a few questions now, Carl. But first I want you to return to the desert on the day the policeman found you."

Carl's eyes stayed fixed on the disk, but his chin lifted a bit, as though he were craning to view a distant horizon.

"Can you see the desert?"

Carl nodded.

"All right. I am going to ask you to go back to the place where you were before you came to the desert."

Dunsmore didn't notice—he was peeking at a palmed notepad of scribbled questions—when Carl suddenly held

The Legend of Carl Draco

his breath.

"Where are you?" Dunsmore said.

"The motel," Carl whispered.

"Is anybody with you?"

Carl's lips moved. Dunsmore leaned closer. "I can't hear you, Carl. Is somebody with you?"

Carl nodded.

"Who is with you?"

The boy shook his head no.

"Are your parents with you?"

He nodded.

"What are they doing?"

It was a repeat of the first interview. When Carl began screaming, Dunsmore shut off the spiral and gripped the boy's shoulders. He planted his face in front of Carl's eyes until the boy came back from wherever he was, a motel somewhere in a desert.

Carl stopped screaming then. There was a moment of silence, followed by a gut-wrenching sob of hopelessness so devastating that it stunned Dunsmore, which is why he did not hear the pounding on the door for nearly half a minute.

This time it was only Mrs. Helms and the janitor. The remainder of the office staff had already departed for spring break.

chapter five

Engine cut and gliding, a black-painted, fender-dented, one-eyed sedan pulls up to the curb in front of a modest Tudor house within walking distance of UCLA.

A shaman's shape in the wind tells the men seated inside that Carl Draco has already come and gone but has made a stopover in this house, which is dark but for a candlelit glow filtering into the backyard, which these particular men can see in the way a dog can see with his snout the passing of an enemy or a long-gone bitch in heat.

They leave the sawed-off shotgun on the front seat and climb out and walk with an unhurried stride up the sidewalk toward the front door, which swings open of its own accord. The two men enter the house unnoticed by any neighbors.

The man in the lead pauses for just a hairsbreadth of a moment at the sight of a black man bearing a spear in one corner, but before his hackles rise he smells wood and walks on past, leading his partner down the hallway toward a soft clicking sound coming from beyond a closed door underscored by the yellow flicker of wick-fed flame. The musty odor of libraries hangs in the air, so the leader knows before he even enters that he is in the home of a learned man.

Who sits slouched at a keyboard feeding words into a word processor, transcribing his thoughts in a state of such intense concentration that he fails to leap up startled as the door swings open with two men shouting, "Where is he!"

The man seated at the computer glances with a disinterest bordering on aplomb toward the men who have shattered his academic peace. The shorter of the men walks across the hardwood floor with his arms spread like a wrestler prepared for the grim business of a street-brawl takedown. He slams his fists onto the desk and shouts, "Where is he!"

The old man sits back with apparent calm and looks him in the eye. "Where is whom?"

Without hesitation, without even looking at the glass face of the machine's glowing monitor, the man reaches out with one extended finger and plunges its tip against the last two typed words—Carl Draco.

"I do not know," the seated man replies, his innocence both feigned and obvious.

The intruder's head suddenly snaps to one side to study a hatted ball of bone. He takes a careful hold of the rakish headgear, in the way a man might latch onto the loose skin at the neck of a sleeping wildcat cub, and raises it from the skull. Apparently satisfied that the thing is not going to bite him, he jams the threadbare felt against his sunburned nostrils and gives it a sniff, then flings it aside. "Draco," he hisses.

His partner too sniffs something familiar and begins tracking scent along a wall toward the door of a closet, which he yanks open. Gabardine and tweed, racked coats hang stinking of cleaning fluid but for one recent addition slightly rumpled on its wire. The man drags it out of the closet and holds it up and shakes his head. "He's wearing a new disguise." He drops it to the floor. "Make him talk."

The shorter man rolls the cuffs of his coat up forearms white as ivory and spreads his arms wide, then makes a quick motion with his fingers generating a flicking, gritty, rattling sound, a minor insult engineered not only to infuriate but to educate his victim. Posters, maps, drawings, photographs, all the handwrought trash of a man who feels the need to plaster his walls with paper, begin popping from each tacked and scotch-taped perch.

When this show of force doesn't elicit the desired response, the man shapes a less subtle dumb-show glyph that launches bound volumes off the shelves. Books both new and ancient fly across the room and collide with shelves, their spines cracking, their machine-stitched binding splitting, raining leaves of scholarly debris.

Professor Dunsmore rises from his chair and shouts, "Stop that this instant!"

"Where is he?"

But again the victim chooses not to cooperate. Trembling a bit, possibly out of fear, possibly simple rage, he sits back down ignoring the uncollated pages of his library fluttering to the study floor, which makes the intruders wonder whether there might not be more to this room than discard Goodwill costumes and one aloof academic. Might this man be protected in some way unfamiliar to them? Carl Draco has been here. Carl Draco, who has killed too many of their own ilk. The shorter man brings his fist down without prologue on top of the grinning skull, sending teeth, jaws, and cranial dust cascading across the desk.

Uneasy now, the taller man reaches out and places a restraining hand on the shoulder of his partner, indicating that it's time for this fruitless interlude to come to an end.

But before the two men turn to leave, the taller one pulls his coatfront aside and reaches into a deep pocket in a lining of fine animal fur. He pulls out a small bag like the udder of a cow, tanned and knotted at the neck with a leather drawstring. He opens it and dips his hand into the bag, withdraws his hand revealing the tip of his thumb coated green like the wet topside of new leaf.

Executing a jab of sucker-punch speed, he plants his thumb against the flat bone fronting the seated man's brain. He yanks his thumb away leaving a coin-sized tattoo, concentric whorls

The Legend of Carl Draco

of green, a souvenir punishment and warning to the resident of this newly cursed place that he must never again make the mistake of giving aid and comfort—and disguises—to their enemy and running prey: Carl Draco.

chapter six

The white-lettered black belly of a water tower rose on a thin blue wash of noon horizon, but Draco couldn't see the name printed on the far side of the tank as he sat at the open door of a boxcar. His body swayed as the linked energy of the train slackened for a whistle-stop. Draco shoved off and hit the ground at a trot.

The railroad station itself, further along the track, was little more than a redbrick shack slapped with jigsaw adobe flaking off in chunks. No one was on the platform, only steamer-trunk baggage stacked on a cart. The houses nearest the tracks were shacks too. Chained within the boundaries of one particular picket perimeter, a rising German shepherd with fur bristling on its hackled back targeted Draco with dangerous eyes. Its nostrils flared once as it sniffed his passing odor, then it relaxed and the snarl went away. The sentinel paused to take a leak on the rusted tubing of an abandoned trike before returning to its crouched watching posture in the weeds.

No shadows on the main street, the walls of the shops open for business were whitewashed clapboard, burned whiter by the sun. A pickup truck parked at a hardware store backed away from a curb and rolled alone up the street, heading out toward plains so flat and empty that Draco wondered where the driver could be going with all that feed and seed.

In a junk store advertising its wares as antiques he found a

The Legend of Carl Draco

shapeless hat in a bin of discard clothes and paid one dollar cash for the bargain. He bought a pint of scotch at a liquor store on the far edge of town. He trashed the sack in a sidewalk barrel and put the bottle in his hip pocket and started walking the asphalt shoulder toward a lone cluster of distant prairie buildings that began to grow familiar as the town grew small behind him.

The motel was a bad green made pastel by the sun, but in his dream it had no paint at all. He stopped and studied the long concrete walk fronting the seven available rooms. Shuttered venetian blinds hung on the office windows, ice machine standing by the door, and on the wall above the door was a place where rectangled red tubes might once have buzzed, but that spot was now bare. He read it as VACANCY though, with no cars in the graveled lot. All the potential customers were passing along a new interstate further south.

He went to the manager's door and heard beyond the dusty screen the muted mumble of a TV above the rattle of a fan. He opened the door and stepped inside. Through another doorway leading into a back room he saw a woman in a print dress seated on a Naugahyde chair watching soap operas and drinking grape soda and keeping a silent tempo with a wire flyswatter in her fist. Draco tapped a bell on the counter. The woman looked over at him with thick bifocals that gave her the eyes of a startled owl. She set the pop down and rolled forward out of the chair, a woman made big on pop and chocolate, a woman almost as wide as she was short.

"I didn't hear you drive up," she said, setting the swatter on the counter like a loaded pistol.

"I got no car, but I got cash," Draco said, reaching into his coat and pulling out a brass money clip pinching folded twenties.

The woman's blue irises floated down the thick lenses of her glasses and settled on the long green.

"I'd like to rent that last room at the end of the row for

tonight, if I could," Draco said, sliding a twenty out of the clip and placing it on the sign-in book. "I been walking all day."

"It's twenty-five dollars," she said, and as she spoke, the twenty disappeared into the pink folds of her pop-chilled palm.

Draco flattened another onto the book. "I'd just as soon not sign anything, if that's okay, and why don't you keep the change there, ma'am?"

The second twenty went wherever the first one did, and the woman smiled. A tiny bulbous worm of grape worked itself from a corner of her mouth, and Draco smelled the friendly odor of vodka. The woman handed him a key.

"Your room's made up," she said, lifting the flyswatter and moving back into the sounds of her soaps.

Draco stepped outside and walked along the line of rooms and stopped at his door. He poked the key into the lock and gave the knob a quick twist. He reached inside and flipped the lights on and studied the decor. A double bed near the door, in his dream twin beds sat against the far wall. No black-and-white TV, a color job now on a low chest of drawers below a big mirror. He stepped inside and shut the door, punched the lock, and latched the worthless chain.

Jammed into the far wall was a small silent air conditioner. When he turned it on, an odor of clean metal came in with the chilled flow. He set the liquor bottle on the dresser and looked at himself in the mirror. Already his gift of clothing was filthy. The stubble on his cheeks and chin was longer than usual. He touched it and thought vaguely about shaving it off.

In his dream he had sat cross-legged staring at a picture of toppling buffalo, but the old carpeting had been covered over or ripped up. A new worn shag camouflaged the spot. He looked at the wall above the doorway and saw the telltale ragged edges of painted plaster, which had been spread long ago to cover a strange place for damage. The room had been stripped, cleaned, painted, refurnished, and sprayed with an

The Legend of Carl Draco

antiseptic chemical that permeated the woodwork and erased forever an odor that he believed he ought to be able to smell.

Drapes yanked tight blocking out the sunlight, he sat on the bed and broke the scotch cap, tipped the rim, and took a drink. Only after the tasty heat had seared his throat and settled simmering in his belly did he give a moment's thought to an odd sensation that he interpreted as an unhealthy manifestation of sentimentality. He might not have been able to turn his back on Professor Dunsmore had his habits not been so ingrained. When he walked out of that house in LA, it was not because he wanted to, and in doing so he had shown as much concern for the professor's well-being as his own.

But indulging in this brief reflection was as far as he was willing to surrender his fate to emotion. He took another solid sip and got up to check out the bathroom facilities. The small room had the chlorine stink of old age, but the tub was clean. He stripped down and plugged the drain. With the bottle clutched in one hand, he cranked both faucets and watched the water flow.

*

Ordinary darkness wielded an ordinary magic of its own. It reshaped redbrick, mocked memory, and turned familiar streets into mazes. Professor Dunsmore told the cab driver to make one more pass along Ambrose Lane before he spied the familiar twist of a broken handrail on the staircase of an abandoned building that he had visited long ago but only in the daytime. He instructed the driver to pull over.

Black men passed by, ducking momentarily to look inside the taxi stopping at the curb. Dunsmore climbed out of the back seat, and the leery cabbie barked, "Do you want me to wait or what?"

Dunsmore said it wouldn't be necessary, and the back door hopped out of his hand as the car lurched away. Dunsmore peered at the upper windows of the building that he was certain he recognized, although he wasn't entirely certain of

41

much of anything anymore.

Halfway down the block, blue neon light and loud music burst from an open door as a black man ran or stumbled or maybe was only tossed from the cigar talk and jukebox haze of a members-only after-hours dive. He came to a stop beneath a streetlight and tugged a wine bottle from his coat pocket and upended the neck. Slaked and humming, he looked up the block and saw a lone white man wearing a long overcoat and an ugly high-crowned, outrageous, outdated, righteous hat. He tucked the bottle into a pocket and held it against his thigh and stepped out hollering, "Hey old man, what are you doing here?"

Dunsmore tugged his hat brim low and peered in the dim light toward the man. "I'm looking for a woman."

The man scratched his breastbone and smiled. "Who isn't? Say man, that's a bad hat you're wearing. Where can Davis get himself a hat like that?"

Dunsmore shook his head. "I doubt if they make them anymore."

The man reached for the hat, but Dunsmore stepped back. Shaking his head, the man said, "Please, I got to try that hat on. I want the ladies to see Davis wearing that hat."

The odor of wine drifted like smoke from the man's lips. Dunsmore realized that he was drunk, and thought it best to explain.

"The woman I'm looking for is named Mother Rose."

Though the man had been reaching out eagerly to pluck the hat from Dunsmore's head, his groping hat-hungry fingers curled into a fist and the toying grin disappeared from his face. He lowered his arm and pulled erect his shambling gait. "What do you want to see her for?"

"Do you know where she does business? I thought she operated out of this building."

The man turned and peered along the avenue, as if to make certain that nobody was listening in on this troubled conversation. He looked back and examined Dunsmore shoe to hat-top, and when he spoke, the wet chords of wine were gone from his voice.

"She's gone. Mother Rose lives down by the river now."

"Where is that? Could you show me?"

"Listen, old man. My name is Davis. You best listen to Davis." He pointed a serious finger at Dunsmore's chest. "You got to go home."

"I need to speak with Mother Rose."

"Naw, you need to go home right now. This is no place for you to be."

"I have business with the woman."

"What kinda business you got with Mother Rose?" Davis said, his eyes slitting slyly. "You gonna buy some black-cat bones?"

"Not tonight."

"Love-potion?"

"If you could just point the way."

Davis lifted an arm and pointed west. "That's the way! If you want to get out of here with your hide intact, that's the way!"

"It's important that I go the other way."

Davis cranked his head to one side, then snapped it hard as if to shake from a clogged ear a plug of water or a white man with no sense. He rose to his full height half a head above Dunsmore and took a deep breath. "If I show you the way, it's going to cost you."

"I'll give you ten dollars."

"Twenty."

"All right, twenty." Dunsmore reached into a pocket and pulled out a twenty. He slapped it flat onto Davis' outstretched palm, the deal shook and done.

*

A sliver of light slips between the curtains from a gibbous moon moored at the horizon and slides across Carl Draco's dreamless eyes. He turns his head away.

Sand and weeds beside the access asphalt vibrate with the passing of semis slowing near the main highway. Window glass rattles with their passing, and Draco's eyes move restlessly back into that light which opens up a dream.

Of moon-reflected sunlight shining on a car so bent upon evil that particles of raining light are trapped in the black tar of every metal body part exposed. The front door of a house that he recognizes opens. He expects to see Professor Dunsmore step outside, or maybe even one or two of those black-hatted bastards who can't bring themselves to give it up, but sees instead the shape of a woman whom he does not know and has never seen before. From his perch wherever it is that a man stands inside his own dreams, he watches her watching him curiously. She looks tired, wearied, there's some sense of hard effort coming from her, but more than that, the thing he senses most strongly is the total absence of malevolence emanating from this stranger, this woman. Instead, there's a sensation of beckoning that makes him wary. She raises a hand and opens her mouth and says something that he cannot quite understand, although he is certain it concerns the inhabitant of this house, but before he can make sense of it, his damp and frowning face wrests itself from the bright ball of that peeking moon.

*

The wine-bottle-littered asphalt road ended at the base of a hill. Davis led Dunsmore up a trampled weed path to the summit, where the professor looked up to see the hard, cold fire of a Milky Way that he had never quite seen before. He could no longer smell the smog of LA, as though during their climb they had broken surface on that reek. But more peculiar than that, he could not see the notorious glow of highway lights spanning the LA basin. He started to speak, but Davis held up a hand for silence. Dunsmore listened—and out of this rare urban silence came the hiss of moving water and the

The Legend of Carl Draco

dim-keyed notes of a distant piano.

He looked down the far side of the hill and saw, tucked beneath the spread branches of a singular and unfamiliar species of high-topped tree, a two-story house gray in the moonlight, its windows lit yellow. At one side of the house, a slowly flowing river fed the thick sprawled roots of the tall tree.

Davis motioned Dunsmore forward. The two men began descending the hill, and as he took care with his footing down the steep path, it occurred to Dunsmore that there was no river in this area of Los Angeles that he knew of.

Torching tobacco and laughing, three men—decked out in spats, hats, and sharkskin with gold watch chains dangling— stood on the front porch watching the pair coming down the hill. Alongside the men stood a woman in a short green sequined thing, which sparkled in the light leaping from a porch window. The trio heard one of the men say, "Now you just wait here a minute. Davis will go inside and speak for you."

Dunsmore touched the man's sleeve. "Tell her that Professor Stackalee wishes to speak with her." Davis yanked his hand away—"I'll do that"—and climbed onto the porch where his audience showed friendly smiles and allowed him to open the shut screen door.

With chilled fish fog rising around him, Dunsmore took a deep breath and exhaled, and heard a scratching, dragging sound above his head. He looked up and saw an owl seated on a tree branch. The bird manufactured a contemptuous "hoo" and disappeared behind a curtain of leaf and vine.

Dunsmore raised a hand to touch his forehead but diverted that wretched habit to caress his unclipped beard. The woman in sequin green poked the white length of an unlit smoke between her lips. She eyed Dunsmore standing out there alone on the bare mudflats, then sucked flame proffered by one of the men. She stepped to the edge of the porch to get a good look at the white stranger. A blue smoke-shot halo rounding her head, she descended the stairs one step at a time, toe on plank, heel and toe, she took it slow approaching the old man.

The fisted twist of a bartender's rag inside a pitcher slows as Davis leans across the countertop. The bartender checks out the room as he listens, watching cut decks dealt to serious men and laughing women, his face impassive but his hand bearing down on bubbles as Davis whispers an absurd request.

Neck rolling as if to purge a crick, the woman in green stood hip-cocked and curious in front of Dunsmore, eyeing his attire. She blew smoke aside, chuckling sweetly, and fingered his lapel. "What are you doing out here, old man?"

"Good evening," Dunsmore said with a brim pinch, with a smile on his only slightly unnerved face.

Red painted nails tickled his top button. "You cold, honey?"

Dunsmore cleared his throat, at a loss for dealing with the subtle nuance of salty social protocol. "It's a bit crisp out tonight, don't you think?" he said, shrugging to ease a sudden binding in his armpits.

"I think it's hot out tonight," she said, dragging a single finger down the length of one coat sleeve and poking him in the palm. "You afraid to go inside?"

"I was told to wait here. I've come to see Mother Rose."

The woman's eyes grew wide. She choked on uninhaled smoke, and spoke. "Mother Rose don't see no one."

Davis approaches a raining multicolored fall of cheap plastic curtain-beads nailed over a doorframe, hiding the room beyond. At his back, bettors heed the piano man's traveling key-roll, refusing to acknowledge Davis' approach to that forbidden door. He leans close to the balled strung straws and listens for one moment, hesitant to rap and make his presence known, then knocks on the doorframe quickly, not wishing to appear impolite.

The Legend of Carl Draco

"What do you want?" replies a quick, throaty, sullen voice.

"Mother Rose. This is James Davis. I've brought a man who wants to see you," he said, delivering his message softly and with due respect and awkward, reverent courtesy. When he hears nothing from the other side, he frowns and listens harder.

"Why are you wearing that long overcoat?" the woman said, toying with Dunsmore's breast pocket. "Are you naked under there?"

"I've come on business," he replied, embarrassed to have such a beautiful woman playing with his accouterment.

She pondered the cut of his shoes, shifted her weight from one hip to the other, and blew a ring of smoke. "I've never seen a white man around here before. This must be some serious business, 'cause Mother Rose don't see nobody, and she especially don't see no white men."

Davis cocks his cautious head, afraid of missing or misunderstanding a single word. He leans so close to the plastic hanging beads that they tickle his ear. "He's a white man, Mother Rose."

But hears only the same deafening silence as before.

Worried now about the wisdom of having undertaken this paid favor, Davis swallows hard and makes one last imploring effort. "He said for me to tell you that . . . Professor Stackalee wishes to speak with you."

Pink-nailed black fingertips part the strings of rattling beads, and Davis sees her eyes, only her eyes, peering out at him.

With a spring twang and frame bang of the screen door, Davis stepped outside and signaled with a waving hand for Dunsmore to quit bird-dogging that waitress and get up here. Another hat-brim tweak and a smiling nod, Dunsmore took his leave. "A pleasure talking with you, ma'am." He headed for the porch, hearing at his back a feminine giggle.

Davis held the door wide—"I'll wait for you out here"—

and stood back as Dunsmore stepped into the eye-stinging smoke and beer-suds tang of a living room transformed into a gin-mill cabaret crowded with gamblers seated at poker tables. A ceaseless tack-hammered ivory background music came from an upright at the far end of the room, where a vested professor in his own right collected tip take in a mason jar. But nobody looked at the man who'd sent Davis knocking on that curtained frame. They read fanned cards and fed chips to the kitty as though nobody at all had just walked in, even though he bumped backs squeezing between tables and offered unacknowledged apologies.

He felt rude wearing a hat indoors as he plowed past high rollers toward the mahogany bar, but he didn't remove it. Though his own intrusive presence didn't seem to impact the customers, the joint went suddenly silent at the soft rattle of strung beads parting at the back of the room. Dunsmore looked around wondering if some subtle signal had been given, for his was the only hearing in this room not attuned to that part of the house.

A woman wearing a black blouse and a wide red skirt stepped through the beads with her arms spread wide. "Professor Stackalee!" she squealed, crossing the room and embracing his buttoned girth. She pressed her cheek against his chest.

"How do you do, Mother Rose?"

She pushed him away with teasing fingers and studied him with a skeptical eye. "Did you come all the way down here just to ask me more college-boy questions?"

"I need a consultation," he said quietly, that he might keep his business private from all the slack-jawed and wide-eared curious customers at his back.

But she only smiled and stepped away to let her audience in on it. "We got us a college professor here! He writes books on the hoo-doo!"

Laughter ranged around the room. Shuffled decks fluttered

The Legend of Carl Draco

as Mother Rose took her preferred customer by the hand and pulled him toward the back room.

Dunsmore ducks through the beads, and Mother Rose shuts out all the cigarette-strike and pitcher-clink of fresh orders delivered with the door bumping closed and locked. Dunsmore keeps his hat on as he looks around the candlelit dim lodgings furnished with a chest of drawers and a coatrack bearing a shawl, and a single table in the center of the room decorated by a burning candle and a dealt solitaire hand abandoned.

Mother Rose stands back with her fists socked on hips hidden beneath her wide red ankle-length skirt. Fine links of neck-chain gold shake as she shakes her head grinning. "Now tell me why you've come to this part of town this time of night, Professor Dunsmore. Do you need more stories about Stackalee that badly?"

"I have very serious troubles, Mother Rose."

She looks at her former student stuffed in an unseasonable overcoat beneath a ludicrous hat and recalls his visits to Ambrose Lane, recalls sober, serious, though insignificant, questions probing Black Folklore, which was not folklore but history. Sober and serious in those days, he now looks like a clown in that silly hat and heavy coat.

She leads him to the table where they sit down opposite each other. She looks into his eyes and cocks her head, and says softly and sweetly, "Tell me your troubles, Professor Stackalee."

But words are weak and cannot bear the weight of what he has to say, so Dunsmore removes his hat and sets it on the table.

Mother Rose sees that patch of plant green glowing on his forehead and kicks back her chair rising. She reaches into a skirt pocket for a hex-packed powder bag, which she yanks out and shakes in retreat, shaping incantations and pointing fingers to fabricate a desperate whammy defense.

Stunned by her response, Dunsmore remains seated as a churning crab of fear kicks inside his gut. He hadn't expected this from his former mentor, this chanting of indecipherable language as she backs away sprinkling clouds of blossoming white powder. He had envisioned a quiet examination and consultation, and perhaps the prescription of some esoteric sorceress balm. But that's what a university education does to a man—fills his mind with simplistic textbook solutions.

"Can you help me, Mother Rose?"

She stops stepping backwards and leans from the waist to study that green concentric wound, her head turned slightly to one side as though listening, her nostrils flared seeking lethal odors, her lips silent but mouthing unspoken words: Who did this to you?

As if satisfied that the evil that has wormed its way into her house is contained, and will remain, inside this man, she begins stepping toward him. "Who did this to you?"

"Two men who broke into my house."

"What did you do to these men that they would put that mark on you?"

"I helped a man they are searching for."

"What man?"

Working open the top button of his overcoat, Dunsmore reaches in and drags from a tucked place above his heart the crumpled ball of Carl Draco's hat.

Mother Rose leans toward it slowly, mindful of evil's mercurial ways. She touches the hat with the tip of a finger, then takes it and lifts the crown to her nose for a thorough bewitch-conjure-snuffle, seeking smudged sweat and skin-flake residue. She lowers the hat and says softly, "Who is this man?"

"His name is Carl Draco."

"He is a powerful man."

"I am certain of that, Mother Rose. I met him briefly twenty years ago when he was just a boy. I didn't see him again until

The Legend of Carl Draco

two days ago. He visited my house, and after he went away those two men came looking for him. Carl told me that men like them have been following him ever since he was a child. They want to kill him."

Mother Rose places the hat gently on the table. "You found Carl Draco in a jailhouse."

"That is correct. He was arrested on suspicion of shooting a police officer. Carl is a healer, Mother Rose. After the policeman was felled by a bullet, Carl healed the wound."

Mother Rose nods, then peers closely at Professor Dunsmore's forehead. "How do you feel?"

"Afraid."

"Your body. Does it hurt?"

"This thing on my forehead . . . it stung when they put it there. After the men left I tried to wash it off with soap. There's no pain, but . . . it feels as if . . . there's a crawling sensation beneath my flesh, as if this thing is putting out roots."

"Do you see things?"

"What do you mean? What sorts of things?"

"Things that should not be there."

Dunsmore swallows hard. "I have not experienced any hallucinations, Mother Rose. Nothing like that."

Something in her eyes, her cheeks, her heart, goes slack. She sits down on her chair and leans forward and takes his hands in hers. "That mark is going to get worse."

"Can you help me?"

She sighs. "I know this kind of curse. It is different from ours. There is nothing I can do to remove it."

Upon hearing this, Professor Dunsmore asks the only question he has left in his arsenal of desperate moves. "Can you bring Carl Draco back to me?"

Mother Rose picks up Draco's hat and examines the soiled nap and stitch, sniffs the crown, and turns it inside out. She slips two fingertips beneath the hatband and slides them around searching until she pinches three strands of hair. She holds them up for Dunsmore to see, then puts them on the table. "Give me a moment."

She retrieves from the knickknack clutter on the chest of drawers a flat-topped black stone lava-textured incense burner purchased in an LA five-and-dime. She sits down at the table and places the object in front of her, and from a skirt pocket lifts a pouch, opens it, and plucks a pinch of black granules. She twiddles her fingers letting the material cascade onto the altar stone, then strikes a match and passes the bursting flame across the stone. Blue sparks sputter as the granules take the flame.

She picks up a single plastic strand of Carl Draco's hair and lets it drift with a feathery slip-slide fall spearing the fire, curling, balling black, and becoming white smoke, which she inhales quickly.

She sits back shivering with quick tears rolling down her face, her hands grabbing hold of the edge of the table. She closes her eyes and shudders once, and when the lids open, the sockets are hollow, blood-walled, and empty of eyes.

Dunsmore slides his chair back, barely able to stifle a groan of revulsion, certain that Mother Rose has succumbed to some pitfall in an incantation gone awry. Spittle dribbles from her breathless mortal remains going limp before his eyes. Too stunned even to feel helpless, or to wonder how he might get out of this house alive, and gripped by an unshakable certainty that he is now seated across the table from a corpse, Dunsmore simply stares at Mother Rose until he hears an odd chirp pluck her vocal cords and sees her lids close rounded. When they open again, two dazed and unfocused eyes return his alarmed stare.

She speaks, breathing hard like a woman exhausted from a hard run. "He's traveling east," she says. She rises from the table and crosses to the coatrack and grabs the shawl and throws it around her shoulders, hiding newborn gooseflesh erupting on her arms.

The Legend of Carl Draco

"Will he come back?" Dunsmore says.

"I called to him. But my magic cannot make a man like that come back if he doesn't want to. I cannot promise you that he will return."

Dunsmore nods, and gazes for a moment at the hat on the table, then picks it up and stuffs it inside his coat. "In that case I had best be getting home." He rises and puts on the ridiculous hat, which he had worn only to hide his forehead curse. "Thank you for trying, Mother Rose."

She tells him not to leave just yet. She unsnaps from her throat a fine gold-chain necklace and sets it on the table and proceeds to knot a single strand of Carl Draco's hair through a link. She steps behind Dunsmore and drapes the chain around his neck. "This might help keep you from harm. It is a part of him."

Professor Dunsmore gathers the chain and pours it inside his shirt, where the pure element rests warm and comforting against his flesh. "Thank you, Mother Rose."

The jawboning ceased as the quartet looked to see who was coming out onto the porch. They had watched through the window as Mother Rose emerged from her room to welcome this unexpected, uninvited, and unprecedented visitor, and now here that white man was again, walking out alive and looking no happier than when he'd gone in.

Davis escorted him down the steps and back up the hill toward LA. The woman in green swayed to the piano beat. The men listened to the manic buzz of Davis questioning the professor, who didn't seem all that interested in answering. An oddball sight to be sure, but not as odd as that of Mother Rose coming out onto the porch and stepping up to the railing.

Her audience sank back against the wall and stood silently staring at their shoes. Mother Rose touched her neck, caressing the fine links of a single gold chain. She tugged gently at a strand of knotted hair and whispered, "Carl Draco." She watched in silence as the silhouette of her favored former student crested the hill and hiked head-bowed across the face of the rising gibbous moon.

chapter seven

The earth turns. Moonlight crawls across a pillow. Carl Draco's eyes are found again, struck, lit, he sees a single headlight spiraling into his eyes like a spray of knives, a light so bright that it carries its own sound, a radiant trumpeting louder than hammered black powder spitting lead.

His opening eyes erupt that dismal scene. He lies in bed staring at the cracked ceiling, wiping dream-wrought sweat from his heated face. That old anticipation had not lessened in spite of his quick trip out of LA, and he knows now that he should have killed those men the first time he saw them. Men like that cannot grasp the lessons of mercy.

The sudden crunch of gravel hauls him out of bed for a confirming look out the window. The black bulk of a familiar car, with its fender dented and one light cracked and dangling like a damaged eyeball, is rolling across the parking lot toward his door. Foolish to think for a moment that they would give up, or that others wouldn't step in to continue their pointless mission. But they won't do it here. If those demons are hell-bent on destruction, he'll accommodate them in a hell of his own choosing.

He turns and crosses the room, steps into the bathroom and squeezes through a thin window and drops to the ground. He takes off at a sprint toward the night horizon, knowing that those hunters will pick up his scent quickly out here on fallow land so flat that there's no place where even a man of his survival instincts might hide.

He makes thirty yards before he hears the rattle of steel racing around the corner of the motel in the lowest gear available to the driver, who shifts into second with the pedal floored and the grille aimed at a lean shape out on the prairie falling into a trot spotlighted by a single headlamp closing in.

Draco listens to the rising whine of the engine as he leads them toward their graves, leaving the motel as far behind as he deems appropriate before he turns and kneels on the ground in the path of the accelerating sedan (Plymouth, yes) and wipes his hands in the loose surface dirt until they're filthy with soil. He raises his arms and holds his palms out flat toward the bumper, and the driver and his passenger remain conscious long enough as they fly through the windshield to wonder if they had plowed into a brick wall.

Draco feels the thwarted velocity travel up his arms like an electric current, which surprises him and makes him wonder what new form of magic these vermin have acquired, or else had been bequeathed, before setting out in search of him. He shakes out his hands and releases the car, which now rests motionless except for liquids leaking from a flattened radiator, with smoke rising from a twisted engine, with shatterproof glass dropping from gutted frames.

He stands up and looks out at the prairie, which is now lit by a single cockeyed headlight slowly fading to orange but still bright enough to spotlight the bloody, sand-frosted bodies of those two hunters lying belly to the stars.

He turns his back on them and looks at the motel, satisfied at the distance he'd made. Nothing to do now but keep moving east, then north, maybe so far north that the spawn of the devil might just find it too damn frigid to bother tracking him. He hears a rustling sound in the vicinity of the recently deceased and is surprised, but not frightened, to see those two conjure-decreed husks of cooked flesh exchanging their

The Legend of Carl Draco

shredded fingers for lupine claws.

Something new and strange is taking place here. These are the first dead men who have ever come back for seconds—but then he realizes that he hadn't confirmed the kill. Something to remember the next time he takes them out, which ought to be in about thirty seconds as the shape-shifters sprout bristled mats of fur on the bull-shoulders of wolves working themselves unsteadily upright.

He watches with something akin to amusement as the two reborn beasts find their footing and begin a slow sidle in his direction, their almond eyes glaring, their jaws dripping, their vocal cords vibrating as thick as thunder.

He drops to his knees and grabs earth to coat his bruised palms—there's still that ache, which doesn't worry him although he does note its peculiar presence. He stands and crouches with his arms spread and his fingers splayed awaiting their assault which, unlike true canine divide-and-conquer tactics he has witnessed in the wilderness, is applied head-on, launched by hind legs sending those razor teeth toward the sunburned flesh of his waiting neck.

He raises his hands, and something unseen meets the wolves in mid-air, something that stops their ballistic flight and holds them like fireworks timed to ignite in stages. Hanging poised and snarling with muzzles shining black, with battling claws swimming in the air, the beasts explode like paper lanterns rising toward the moon.

Draco lets go and squeezes his fingers the way a frostbit man might massage a throbbing winter ache in summer. New weaponry. That cast spell took too much energy out of him, which is irritating because he has never before suffered physically after a slaughter.

Brains, spines, and extremities barbecued, an alkali flat further out catches the scraps falling from their orbit. He hears two brief hollow thuds like cordwood tossed, and sees in the cast light of the moon two wadded heaps plastered flat

Gary Reilly

against the earth.

Another night's sleep wasted. And for all he knows a new pair might already be traveling some distant highway seeking the scent of this most recent duel. Maybe it's time to cut south, clear to Argentina. But because he's pondering his next move, he doesn't notice the twitch of those charred bundles changing skin again.

Reptilian their tack now, bodies elongated and shovel-headed, they plow across the ground toward Draco, who hears their surreptitious slither and glances around to observe them, wondering just what it's going to take to dispose of these two pests before sunup. He has miles to cover.

The lead beast strikes his right leg like a bullfrog's well-aimed lick, curling itself around his ankle. Its partner lunges for the left leg, and Draco bends down fast and grabs hold of their scaled bodies just behind the skulls. But as he lifts them they tie his torso with muscular hugs that he cannot unwind, not only because his hands are busy but because his magic doesn't seem to be able to get a decent grip on those thick whips choking his chest.

There's something truly wrong here. It's as though each time he sends the hunters to hell they come back resupplied with armaments of a greater caliber, and for the first time in his life he begins to feel a thread of doubt dangling at the back of his brain as he digs his fingers deeper into those cold shingles, which begin to splinter beneath the charm-driven muscles of his hands.

"Quit," he says, but then stops abruptly, encountering a new sensation, a force fighting back nearly as strong as his own, matching his grip with new resistance and threatening to break it, as though these twins aren't at all snakes in his hands but the arms of some singular devil with venom-slick fangs for fingers. Their jaws open wide, and their darting tongues begin tickling the tender flesh at his jugular.

Never before has there been a moment when he has

The Legend of Carl Draco

doubted his ability to kill his enemies, not right up until this very second when he feels his arms beginning to weaken even though his tapped magic continues to drive his drilling fingers into the bases of their bone-sheathed brains—and for the first time in his life something like an ice-cold ball of fire, something tainted with the odor of fear, passes near his heart, because his magic isn't doing it, isn't taking these beasts out.

Snake breath stinging his eyes, he plants his feet firmly in the soft sand and inhales deeply for one last heave and strain against all this wrapped reptilian brawn . . . and it doesn't work. His final squeeze, engineered to send his tormentors to their graves, falls so short that the only thing of interest occurring in this struggle witnessed by every lurking desert creature startled at sleep disturbed is a sound of despair, a crude cry of limits met, which even as he sends it flying toward the blind eye of the gibbous moon, "GRACE!" strikes a bell in his memory. Once before in his life at a moment of near despair he had shouted this incomprehensible plea "GRACE!" and though there's not a rock or a cactus of respectable size within a hundred yards, that single drawn-out howl echoes across the windless flats back and forth like a tire-swing affixed to a naked branch—"GRACE!"—and at that precise moment the two scaly necks become the unshaven throats of two black-hatted men pleading "don't kill us."

Surprised, but used to the vertigo of surprise, Draco tightens his fists on their necks. "Why not, you sonsabitches?"

But all those squeaking throats can produce is feeble supplication. "Please, Draco, no . . . ," and finally, "You win."

An old truth, but he'd never heard it stated aloud before. He eases off his choking hold to let them take a few last breaths before their final dispatch, and to tell them something he'd never had time to tell any of the men who had come to him to die.

"That's right," he says. "I win. You fools keep coming and keep trying, but you've never beat me and you never will."

Then he shoves them away, disgusted that their ilk hadn't understood years ago that this must be the only outcome of combat with Carl Draco.

Pointing a finger at men like these and changing them into chunks of carbon-black is protocol by now, but he holds off. He knows that, were Professor Dunsmore here to witness this encounter, there would ensue a college-educated interrogation the likes of which would fry the brain of any sensible demon. The professor would be kneeling in the sand scribbling frantic notes and demanding answers to the most obtuse questions. Thus, though the answers hold no particular interest for Carl Draco, he suppresses the desire to wipe these two demons off the face of the earth long enough to ask, "Where did you come from?"

When they don't answer, he steps up to the men and stands so close that they could grab his legs and drag him to the ground. Stands close to let them know they're beat.

"I asked you a question."

The taller man raises his head and rubs five coin-sized bruises on his neck, and glances at his partner. "He's right. We can't do it."

"Shut up. Baxter will kill us," the sidekick whines.

But the tall man knows exactly whose hands cradle his life now, or thinks he does. He looks up at Draco with the sort of weary resignation you see on the faces of men sent to fight battles they don't understand, peering up at him as if to speculate upon how much mercy this victor might be willing to barter for information. "We come from a town called Chuckney."

"Shut up!"

"It's in the Appalachian—" A quick movement at the man's side. Something in the pocket of his greatcoat begins shivering and kicking like an animal, and from that slit falls a bag like an udder, which tumbles to the ground and bursts, spilling green powder that flows around the knees of the two men.

The Legend of Carl Draco

Draco barely has time to step back from a sudden eruption of sand, both men lifted by the speared growth of needled branches driven by the trunk of a black tree rising. Faces, lungs, guts forked by unfathomable vengeance generated to unleash at treason, the howling impaled hunters fly skyward kicking blood across the face of the moon.

Draco turns his back on this scene and begins walking, and as he listens to those diminishing sounds of remorse braying in the branches, he considers three important things that he had learned on this vexing night: One, the man who wants him dead is named Baxter. Two, Baxter lives in the Appalachian Mountains. And three, Baxter cannot kill him.

Draco knows that the last item must be true, because if Baxter could kill him, this business would have ended badly long ago.

chapter eight

"I remember Professor Myerson," Professor Dunsmore says, panting with every mud-clawed stroke in a rain so unexpected that he believes it's not really there at all. "The earth is usually dry in the summer, and now, beneficent, this non-rain was made just for me," he pants, clawing at mud in the garden in the back of his house in the dark near a green hedgerow sparkling with rain.

Its thick leaves are bulbous, dripping and tickling his exposed neck bent into this mortuary work at the corner of the garage. "Red brick," he sighs, hard red brick softened by non-rain, but it never rains in LA. He encounters the cement foundation and leans back on his tucked muddy calves sunk in a downpour pooling around his knees as a pleasant thunder mumbles through low clouds above his garden. Garden. Well. No flowers ever grew here, remembering pea plants tied with kite string on sticks, pitiful withered shoots brown against the wall. You bury seeds in LA, they stay buried.

Satisfied with the plumbed depth, he reaches for a shoebox at his side, unlids it, lifts and peeks at eyeholes, teeth and jaw, yellow dust and chin, tapped by raindrops dripping from branches overhead.

"What was your name?" he whispers, and tenderly takes them one by one and ponders with each placed piece the man who once had lived inside that skull. Who was he? You get a degree and end up toying with human beings, but then that's what universities are for, to probe, pick, examine, classify, label, box, and publish. Who cares if this man skinned and stapled and poised upon a UCLA pathology-class rack might once have seen his children suffer, or lost his faith, or died without ever seeing a single one of his dreams realized. Let's varnish his bones and give them away to jolly men with pipes!

He taps the upturned box until all the dust has fallen into the tomb, then sets it aside and fills in the hole gently, and with each handful of mud thrust onto that shattered head he whispers a prayer of apology. "I'm sorry, friend, whoever you were. Rest now."

He rubs his muddy hands on his thighs. His robe is clotted and wet with weeds clinging like so many tiny bones. He looks around, adjusts the thick-lensed glasses perched on the bridge of his nose, and speaks aloud. "I remember a sergeant I once knew, a dedicated man . . ." of military bearing who instilled his war-won values into his green troops insisting that by god when you leave a campsite the enemy must never know you've invaded his territory. Bury your refuse, douse your coals, take no prisoners, and eat the dead.

He pats the grave firmly as the rain comes harder. No enemy will ever know I've trespassed upon his territory except perhaps a savant slug mewling among these fingered furrows.

He stands up reaching blindly for branches that dance in his hands and offer no support. His thighs ache from sitting folded for so long. A Boy Scout at twelve, forty-three years ago, camped in the low brown hills surrounding the San Fernando Valley. How strange, I've never been back there since. Where have all the years gone?

He looks down at the trowel on its back like the sinking hull of a steel boat. Forgot to use it. Spent ten minutes digging through kitchen drawers for a trowel, then forgot to use it. But this is better. A grave fashioned by hand, a grave that has

Gary Reilly

been—rain rolls off his nose, rain tickles past his ears onto his neck, he cannot make sense of his burgeoning thought—a hand-fashioned grave has . . . more sincerity perhaps.

My only job now is to hang on, he says to himself, scouring his mind for the names of people he once knew, places and events, to make certain it's all there and will remain there always, because it will take someone with less love of life than himself to take the coward's way out. He trudges back along the sidewalk inch-deep in water to the brick rise of his back porch. Rest in peace, whoever you were.

He enters blinded by kitchen appliance glare, Christ, what is the theory behind porcelain? Illusory cleanliness. It means something. Probe and categorize. Get to the goddamned bottom of everything and then you'll see, we'll weep no more.

He closes the back door.

I remember the phone call from Mrs. Helms. I remember the Boy Scout knife Carl would not take. I remember the black woman who sat in my class scoffing at my theories and then introduced me to Mother Rose. I have not lost track of time during the past seventy-two hours. I remember everything I ever said or did during my entire lifetime and therefore I am not yet insane.

He touches the profaned spot on his forehead. Surely it must have blistered from all this wretched rubbing.

Sergeant Jarvis, that was his name. Disciplined man of war, he taught us to prowl the woods in silence, study the terrain, and take mental notes because a soldier can't write with his finger glued to a trigger aimed at shadows in the cold tree-line rock of South Korea. Too young for Korea though, merely a drafted youth counting on GI Bill benefits to get him through college, where he studied folklore. Well, you paid for your war, now take it.

He goes into his study and switches on the word processor. The rising whine of chips heating up briefly halts the ceaseless mental patter that has driven his every move for the past . . .

64

The Legend of Carl Draco

seventy-two hours? Monitor graphics spring amber onto the dark screen, and he seats himself comfortably on his reliable swivel chair and calls up a file that begins:

"I have met with Carl Draco again. The last contact I had with him was twenty years ago April, when he was a boy of seven . . ."

Twenty years ago last April.

He rubs his thighs, which are chilled and dirty from the hedgerow dig. Twenty-five years of writing academic notes based on the objective study and observation of . . . of . . .

He rises and goes to the kitchen in search of a bottle of brandy that had been given to him by a fellow professor whose name was . . . whose job anyway in the pathology department was to teach young pre-med students the structure of the human body, the very wellspring of history itself—start with the mulch of marrow and move outward in concentric circles of time and space until the poetry of Shakespeare is nailed like a dead butterfly to velvet!

Have to go with wine. That precisely remembered bottle gathering dust on the white tin shelf in the kitchen cupboard was in fact poured empty on the day my services were no longer required by UCLA.

He hears a scraping sound, a sort of soft kicking. He closes his eyes until the sound creates an image in his mind, that of a person whittling a stick with a sharp knife, a stroking, chuffing sound of friction. Out in the backyard. He flips the kitchen light switch off, and the white shape of the back door remains on his retina for one moment. When it fades into darkness, he still can hear that sound, louder now. He crosses the room and looks out the door.

The rain has stopped, the clouds have parted. Each red garage brick is outlined by a paler line of gray cement that creates a web of rectangles against which a form is emerging from the ground, spotlighted by the moon. The noise is the sound of soil being disturbed, a tomb from which a creature groaning with the effort of twisting ribs and hips struggles from the garden earth with the rebirth contortions of a split cocoon. Fingers grabbing handfuls of grass, the fully fleshed, fully clothed, full-bodied corpse drags itself onto the lawn and kneels for one moment to catch its dead breath before raising its grinning head to stare into the eyes of Professor Dunsmore.

The spear in the living room is a separate item from the statue itself, though seemingly a part of the stiff-cupped hands of the African warrior, the blunt end plugged neatly into a drilled hole hidden between two polished veined black feet. Only wood though, but long and heavy in Dunsmore's grip as he wrestles it from its bedded stand and lifts it and hears the first rattling twist of the locked kitchen door.

Blood drains from his head to feed his racing heart as he hears the scuff of shoes shuffling along the flagstone sidewalk that fronts the house. He sees the shadow of a manshape moving along the curtained picture window.

The balled brass front doorknob begins to turn. Dunsmore backs away with the spear held at his side like a bayoneted rifle. "I remember the drill instructors who had survived human waves of Korean combat"—even as he wonders how could they stand it, how could they face such mortal danger, didn't they realize what a bullet must feel like tearing through the flimsy tissue of your body—and the lock fails and the front door swings open revealing the owl-eyed specter of a head so white that Dunsmore's upheld spear is cast black against its startling brightness, a white head slightly flattened on one side as if hammered by a shovel laid flush.

The teardrop spear-tip rolls spinning to the floor as the last of Dunsmore's strength leaps from his throat with a fear-freighted wail of despair. But just before he falls, the cosmos shifts, and order is snatched out of chaos, as a suddenly familiar silhouette blots out the bright lopsided face of the glowing gibbous moon.

chapter nine

Carl Draco knelt where Professor Dunsmore lay unconscious on the floor. He sniffed the skin-rich planted curse as Dunsmore's heart pummeled the fabric of his sweat-soaked shirt. Draco placed his hand on the green graphic to judge its depth, and at his touch the roots began to wither, releasing their bone-drilling clutch. The whorled green thing came off in his pinched fingers like a guitar pick. He put it into his mouth, no more flavor than a leaf, and swallowed it whole.

He carried Dunsmore to the couch and rolled him outstretched onto the cushions, then sat on a chair and waited for the windows to begin glowing with pre-dawn pink. When Dunsmore's nasal breathing settled into the normal cure of sleep, Draco got up to find something in the kitchen to eat, to eradicate that evil leafy taste.

"How do you feel?"

Professor Dunsmore's lids fluttered as if dust were cascading into his eyes. He turned his head and saw Carl Draco slouched in an easy chair rifling an open bag of potato chips. Draco chewed, nodded hello, and repeated his question, palming a handful of crumbs into his mouth.

"Carl!" Dunsmore said, sitting up and pawing at his forehead. "My God, Carl, after you went away two men broke into my house and put this mark on my forehead. I began seeing things!"

"I got rid of it," Draco said. He dug for a last handful of chips while Dunsmore hurried to the bathroom to see for himself. Draco rolled the sack tight and set it on the coffee table. He looked up as Dunsmore came back in. "Sit down, Professor, before you fall down."

Dunsmore sat on the couch and leaned toward his friend. "Why did you come back, Carl?"

Draco worked a last fleck of chip from between two teeth and looked toward the picture window. "I came back because I want your help, Professor. I know now who's been hunting me all these years. I found out from two men I killed out on the desert—probably the same two men who put that curse on you." He paused to see how this news took. The professor sat transfixed. "The man trying to kill me is named Baxter. He lives in the Appalachian Mountains, in a town called Chuckney."

"What can I do to help you, Carl?"

"I want you to put me under, Professor. There's a door inside me that all my powers can't open. But you can open it. You've done it before."

The book had been published ten years earlier, a tall thread-bound illustrated tome of the earth's face, but when Dunsmore studied the pages open to the Appalachian map, neither he nor Draco could find the name "Chuckney."

Dunsmore dragged a fingertip down the index columns, but the town wasn't on the roll. "Perhaps those men were lying?"

Draco shook his head no and took a seat on the leather chair. "Those men were facing death and they knew it. They didn't have lying on their minds. 'Chuckney,' they said. One of 'em. The other told him to shut up."

"Chuckney," Dunsmore whispered, then suggested "Shuckney" as an alternative, but the town wasn't there.

"How come you buried your friend out there in the

68

garden?" Draco said.

Dunsmore looked up and sighed. He resumed his hunt as he spoke. "One of those men broke the cranium with his fist. I was subsequently overcome by the sheer indecency of using a human skull as a paperweight." He told Draco about his hallucination in the backyard.

Draco nodded. "When I got here I tracked that bone smell around to the garage. I thought maybe they'd planted you in the garden, Professor, and I was puzzled because that's not their style."

Dunsmore crossed the room and took from the shelves an atlas twice the thickness of the first, its cover missing, its pages age-browned and brittle. He set it on the desk and hoisted open the back cover, the rotting spine cracking. "This was published in the nineteenth century."

Draco got up to take a look. Dunsmore scoured the index columns with a magnifying glass until the ballooning black letters spelling the word "Chuckney" spilled into his eye.

"Chuckney," he hissed, as if to drive a nail through it. He set the glass aside and turned the pages until he came to the Blue Ridge spread. He picked up the glass, calculated the crosshairs of the designated meridian, and zeroed in on a point located between two long gray-shaded ridges high in the Appalachian range—and found a dot labeled "Chuckney."

He compared it with the other atlas, examined the same section of runneled earth, but the later edition displayed only a vague drawing indicating the terrain of a wide mountain, no valley at all. "I find it hard to believe that the U.S. Geological Survey could overlook an entire populated valley." And this made him think of Mother Rose.

Draco gave a noncommittal cough and put his finger on the map. "The Blue Ridge Mountains," he said.

"Pretty name, isn't it?" Dunsmore said. "The folklore of the Appalachians is rife with legends of magic. In fact, I have a volume on the folklore of that region, which was written by a scholar in the early nineteenth century . . ." But as he turned to his shelves, Draco cut him short.

"Professor, I'm not interested in looking at any more books. If you're up to it, I want you to put me under right now."

Dunsmore's academic enthusiasm fell like a wounded sparrow. "I'm willing to do that, Carl, but I have to warn you—"

"I'm beyond warnings."

"I only wanted to say that I can't guarantee anything."

Draco set his hat on the desk and sat back down in the leather chair. "I've never had much truck with guarantees. Let's get started."

*

The stale smell of rotted fabric, the tin rattle of a primer-black hood eating up the horizon, seagulls cry, and a twisted, red, unreadable snake of light buzzes above a door. Dust drifts into the unrolled window of the parked truck. When he touches the metal window frame the sun's heat stings his hand like a wasp. His mother kisses his spread fingers as he cries out from surprise rather than pain. Her hand is nut-brown, callused and cool, and gently cups his balled fist. Buffalo drop like pitched bales on a TV screen as he rests the curved edge of a water glass against his bottom teeth and listens to the sharp report of a rifle propped on a log in the shadow of an ice-crippled forest.

"Draco."

The voices of his mother and father are like the droning of flies. They sit on the bed behind him and quietly plan their next move, but he's no longer interested, he's heard them prepare their plans so many times before, had heard their muted murmur and felt their quick glances in every motel room they had holed up in. Even when they look him square in the face, their eyes seem furtive. They will not tell him where they're going, or why they left their mountain home.

"Draco."

The Legend of Carl Draco

Knuckles rap against the door. He hears the shuffle of his father's pant legs moving toward the chest of drawers. "Who's there?" His father grabs a loaded pistol, a snow-salted bovine topples, a trail of foam hangs beside the bed, and his mother's jaw stretches as if to take a bite out of something monumental. Though he knows she is screaming, he cannot hear her because the report of the shotgun destroying the door fills the room with a noise that renders inaudible both his mother's scream and the ineffective shot squeezed off too fast by his father's trembling hand.

Two men with black coattails flung wide step through the devastation. They aim twin-barrels, and his father is lifted by a gnat swarm and carried across the room. His body slams against the wall and slides to a sitting position on the floor.

His mother's scream mingles with white gunsmoke boiling along the ceiling. Carl sets the glass on the floor as a shotgun blast carries her body across the room and dumps it into a narrow space between the wall and a bed.

Carl stands up and feels the water of the fallen glass spilling across one leather shoe. He looks down at the dark stain on his foot, then looks up at the approaching men bearded and tall, with faces dark beneath the brims of hats like his own father used to wear. Mud-caked hobnailed boots bear down on him. Gun muzzles still ringing with the sledgehammer stroke of hand-packed shells hover before his eyes.

He takes them both at once.

Lifts them off the floor and drives their startled bodies high against the wall above the open door. He reaches inside the cradled guns and brings the shells to life.

They explode in place, bolt, pin, trigger, stock, and barrel spiking guts through drywall like smokehouse meat slaughtered and hung. People down the sidewalk open their doors and come out bathrobe-clad to see two dead bodies pinned with legs dangling inside the doorway. White-haired men keep their women back as the manager runs across the lot shouting "what the hell's going on" as Carl closes his eyes so tightly that he can no longer hear the shouts of "oh my God," hears only a thin high-pitched voice screaming the word "GRACE!" —and hears the gentle flinch of grasshoppers springing above rustling weeds. When he opens his eyes, the color of hell has become a bowl of blue, and a high sun begins drying the dampness on his shoe.

He walks until he comes to a road. A car approaches, and a man with a badge and a holstered gun gets out.

"Carl?"

"What's your name, boy?"

"Carl?"

"What are you doing out here all alone, boy?"

"Wake up, Carl."

The rims of his lids were wet and his eyeballs were red, shot through with the dismal passion of that memory revived. He turned his head and looked at the worried frown on Professor Dunsmore's face.

"Are you all right, Carl?"

Draco eased himself out of the creaking leather chair and crossed the room toward a window that gave a view of grass springing upright losing the residue of last night's rain.

Dunsmore dropped his eyes from the silhouette at the window and turned his attention to the atlas.

"My name is Carl Draco."

Dunsmore looked up to see the man moving back to the leather chair, rubbing at an eye with a knuckle dirtied from the road. Draco sank in and slapped his hands on the arms and gripped them tight, as if testing the frame's give.

"I remember the mountain valley where I lived as a child," Draco said. "My parents took me out of there when I was seven years old."

"Why?"

"I don't know. A couple of months after we left, my parents were murdered by two men in a motel room."

The Legend of Carl Draco

"But . . . why?"

"Professor, you got as many whys as I do. But I do remember where I lived, in a house made of white stone set on a hillside overlooking a town."

"Chuckney?"

"It must have been. I remember leaving that place one night wrapped in a blanket in the back of a buckboard. Sometime after that, we got a pickup truck."

"Where did you go?"

"All over. We were always on the move, for the same reason I've been on the move for the past twenty years. Someone named Baxter wants me dead." He got up slowly, a young man not yet thirty getting up like a man bone-joint weary and sick of rising every time an enemy wrestles him down and dies. "Thanks for everything, Professor. I gotta get going."

"Where?"

"I'm going to Chuckney, Professor." Draco lifted his hat off the desk. "I got some business there."

Dunsmore stared at Draco, his lips shaping unspoken words as if he could not bear to ask his question because he could not bear to hear the answer. "Let me come with you, Carl."

Draco looked down at the floor and pursed his lips. He shook his head no. "This is going to be bad business, Professor."

Dunsmore reached up and ran his fingertips across his profaned forehead, then held out an open palm.

"Bad business? I've devoted my entire life to the study of bad business. I've suffered the indignity of personal assault and survived the terror of a malevolent curse and I'm still alive to talk about it. Do you really expect me to be frightened off by the prospect of bad business?"

Draco raised his eyes and studied Dunsmore's flushed face. "I don't know what I'm going to be up against when I get there. Every time Baxter sends men after me, I believe he gives them a little more magic of his own. They always get better at tracking me, and nearer to taking me out. When I get to Chuckney I'm going to be working on his turf, and I expect I'll have enough trouble looking out for myself without trying to guarantee your safety."

A melancholy smile spread among the gray roots of Dunsmore's beard. "Don't give me any slippery talk about guarantees, Carl. I'm fifty-five years old. In ten years I'll be dying on the rack of unfulfilled ambitions. But I'm not afraid of dying, Carl. I'm not afraid of anything except failure. If you don't take me with you, I swear to God I'll track you clear to the Blue Ridge Mountains. I'll crawl on my hands and knees if I have to. I am not afraid."

Draco nodded, then smiled. "I've never been afraid either, Professor. I've been annoyed, pestered, and disgusted, and there were a few times when I actually felt close to being whipped, but I can't say I was ever really afraid." He took a deep breath. "But then I always had good reason not to be afraid. I've never been beat and I never intend to get beat. But . . . if you want to come along, I guess I got no objection."

"Thank you, Carl. We can use my automobile."

"You're welcome, Professor. Let's shove off."

chapter ten

Tar Heel battle-descendants pumped gas while Cherokee children squatted grinning at the blue out-of-state plate screwed to the bumper of Dunsmore's car. The professor frowned studying elevation contours on the cache of maps on his lap describing the Appalachian range, which dipped down into Alabama and rose northeast along the St. Lawrence River all the way through Maine, shattering on the pug-tipped peninsula of New Brunswick and Quebec.

Draco drove north through the hills of the Carolina mountains while Dunsmore traced their steady and watchful two-lane trek. He marked the map with ink and looked at his watch. He tapped the crystal and listened, then shook his head.

"My watch has stopped." He popped the stem and gave it a few cranks. "It's broken."

Draco glanced at the machine strapped onto Dunsmore's wrist. "Toss it."

"What?"

"I doubt you'll need a toy like that where we're going."

Dunsmore unstrapped the watch and gave it a futile mending shake, then slipped it into a pants pocket. He slapped a new map open on his lap and read silently the names of towns hidden along roads that snaked through the river valleys on this ever-rising Appalachian spine.

Gary Reilly

A settlement came into view tucked below heavy trees at the base of a mountain, wooden buildings blown silver by wind and rain. Dunsmore suggested they stop to get something hot to eat, but Draco shook his head no and said if it's all right with you, we're not that far from our destination. So Dunsmore chewed stale packed sandwiches to sustain himself on the last leg.

Another hour on the main asphalt, then Draco slowed and took a right turn onto a dirt road that hairpinned up into a patch of woods. A steep climb, they drove in silence, with Dunsmore glancing again and again at Draco, who was watching the rutted road with its close growth like a man paying attention to landmarks.

Dunsmore didn't see anything of note, but Draco suddenly braked to a stop. He began studying the weed-grown side of a hill. "I've been here before."

Dunsmore looked out the side window at the innocuous dirt slope.

"I know this road," Draco said.

Dunsmore looked at his map to get a fix, but all he could see was the blue trickle of a road, which may or may not have indicated the dirt track they were on.

Draco shut off the engine. The silence tugged unpleasantly on Dunsmore's eardrums until he broke the pull with a crackle of his map. He traced the thin blue line north, then Draco nudged his hand. Dunsmore looked over at him. "What?"

"You're looking in the wrong place."

"What do you mean?"

"I mean throw that paper away, Professor, and look out the window." He aimed a finger past Dunsmore's nose. "I recognize this road. I once saw it from the rear of a horse-drawn wagon when I was seven years old."

Dunsmore could see only tall grass flooding the incline, but he supposed a four-wheel-drive vehicle might successfully negotiate that rise of earth. And as Draco guided

76

the car around and aimed the hood at the hillside, Dunsmore supposed that this man could negotiate it too. Draco brought the car up against the base of the hill and forced the one-wheel drive to make the climb.

This brought them onto a shoulder of the mountain where the angle of ascent was not as pronounced. The front end of the car came back down far enough to allow Dunsmore to see a pine tree line in front of them, with white peaks beyond. When they entered the trees he rolled his window down until he could smell the odor of hot lichen affixed to sunbaked rock, wildflower on the wind, and the bug-drilled core of dead log long gone to rot.

They came out into a meadow walled off further ahead by the old growth of a darker forest. Draco guided the car across the meadow, mowing high grass and flowers flat beneath the front bumper until the wheels began to lose traction on the final gentle grade and began slipping. He let up on the gas and the car rocked to a stop.

"That's as far as she goes," he said, hitting the emergency brake.

The car now parked on a high windblown wilderness saddle, Dunsmore slowly rolled his window up to shield himself from the sheer magnitude and raw charm of all this untrammeled nature. Draco held onto the keys dangling from the ignition and studied a dark gap in the tree line ahead, a space giving way in the pine-topped wood wall through which his invisible road doubtless ran. "We're going to have to walk in from here," he said. He unplugged the keys and handed them to Dunsmore.

They got out, and Dunsmore popped the trunk to retrieve a duffel bag that he had filled at home with clothing and books and sundry scholarly debris. He tucked his briefcase into the canvas bag and fastened it closed. Draco slapped his hat on a thigh and tugged it snug onto his scalp. He had no baggage. Dunsmore rolled the car windows tight and locked the doors.

"I don't mind telling you this," he said, "but I feel somewhat leery about leaving my car unattended out here."

"Don't worry about it," Draco said, slapping a hand on the thin metal hood smeared with milky rolls of spider webbing. "Your car will be safe."

Dunsmore shrugged and slung his duffel bag over a shoulder, and as they started toward the tree line Draco glanced at his friend hunched and hiking head-bowed, and said, "Want me to carry that thing?"

"Oh no, I'm quite all right."

"Did you really serve in the army?" Draco said. "Or is that just a surplus item?"

"Oh yes. In my youth I was drafted into the army a private and came out a private. I was not much of a soldier, although I did see some action in Tijuana." He smiled at Draco. "At any rate, that's what my drinking companions told me afterwards. But I do not remember her name or her face, for I was drunk on tequila the entire five minutes."

They came to the gap in the tree line and stopped. "I don't know the route," Draco said, "but I expect there's only one road into Chuckney." He stepped into the shadow of the woods. Dunsmore shifted the luggage already tiring his shoulder. And here, unweathered, untrodden, rutted but weedy with disuse, was that road which began, or ended, just inside the trees.

Through a pine maze of rising switchbacks, they hiked for an hour, Dunsmore growing bent like a fishwife hauling catch, studying the toes of his dusty shoes and feeling the first twinge of hip-socket ache. He had not hiked this far since his army days.

"Let's make it to that rise," Draco said, pointing at a level turn in the road ahead. "We'll sit for a bit."

Dunsmore nodded and felt impolite because his gasping lungs were unable to grab enough air to fire more than a brief, "Okay."

The Legend of Carl Draco

When they reached the curve, Draco raised his chin and took off his hat and breathed deeply. "Smell that?"

Dunsmore sat down on the road and breathed in the same thick pine air that they'd been plowing through for the past . . . he looked at the white band of flesh around his wrist and wondered how long they'd been hiking.

"Chimney smoke," Draco said. "A couple miles further on. Be an hour before we get there."

Dunsmore began exploring the pockets of his coat, then realized with a heart-clutch of dread that he'd left his pipe, tobacco pouch, and matches back in the car, tucked in the glove compartment where he'd put them specifically so that he would not forget them.

"Damn," he whispered, running his splayed fingers up and down his coat.

"Chiggers?" Draco said.

"I left my goddamn . . . I left my pipe and tobacco in the car."

Draco made a sympathetic clucking sound against a back tooth and shook his head. "Tough break," he said. "I like a smoke every now and then myself."

Dunsmore spent a few irritated minutes massaging his hot feet and sore calves, then said, "It's strange, but I haven't heard a single bird since we came into these woods."

Draco nodded, then stood up stretching, his fists balled red and his face pinched in a soundless screaming grin of energy renewed. "One more hour, Professor. Let's hit it."

Dunsmore worked himself up off the road, adjusted his glasses, and shook a sleeping foot. "I can handle the duffel bag . . . ," he said as Draco grabbed it and slung it over a shoulder and started up the road.

Dunsmore wallowed for a moment in the guilt of being a burden, but better to feel guilty than to carry that bulk any further. He wondered now what was in that canvas sack so important that he felt the need to lug it along anyway. Papers and pens, books and notes and clothing. But he would trade it all right now just to feel his favored pipe clamped between his teeth.

After the calculated hour, Draco veered off the road and hiked up a slope, motioning Dunsmore to follow him into the forest itself. As they made their way up the incline, the trees thinned, and they saw between the trunks of younger pine the smoke-blackened redbrick tower of a chimney balanced on the steep shingled roof of a two-story house.

They came out of the tree line onto a long slope of barren front yard, which led up to the porch of the house where a white-haired woman was seated on a rocking chair chewing the stem of a knife-whittled lit pipe bowl. Her shoes looked factory made but ancient, pressed flat against unpainted plank flooring as she shoved the rocker in a gentle rhythm.

Draco set the duffel bag on the ground. "I know her."

"Who is she?"

"Wait here." Draco climbed the final twenty yards and stopped at the bottom of the steps.

The woman took the pipe out of her mouth. "You've come back," she said.

Draco took off his hat and held it at his side. "Who are you?"

"I'm your Aunt Grace."

Draco took this in and considered it for a moment, then said softly, "Who am I?"

"You're my nephew Carl."

She pointed her pipestem at the door. "Come inside. I've been holding supper for you." She eased up out of the chair with a delicate groan and knocked a stray gray hair away from her eyes. "Tell your friend the table's set."

Draco looked back down the hill, and the angle of the slope pulled from his memory a dawn where a sledge hoof pawed fogged ground and the champing lip-flared head of a plow horse hitched to a buckboard bobbed eager to strain against

The Legend of Carl Draco

buckled traces and haul its human load downhill.

He knew this house, knew its wood-shingled gables and deep root cellar and the candlewick-lit rooms and the stairway that led to the finished tiers of an attic furnished with the trunk-clutter storage of decades. And beds, his bed, standing against a wall below a window where he'd sat up one night and looked down this same slope toward the edge of the property and saw steam rising off the rippling flanks of a horse asleep upright, its lungs rumbling like a bellowed blacksmith fire, where Dunsmore stood now, stooping to pick up his duffel bag.

Draco turned and saw Aunt Grace slap the bowl against her palm and catch smoldering ash and fling it off the porch, knocking the pipe against her thigh as he himself might slap shape into a hat. She stood small and framed by the dark mesh of the screen door, which he knew led into a kitchen, a house built so that the kitchen was the first room you entered, a room where the fire roared in a hearth fitted with squared blocks of hand-chiseled hillside stone.

Dunsmore hiked the slope, climbed onto the porch and set the bag down and wiped his brow. "How do you do, ma'am?" Short of breath, he nodded and smiled, extremely pleased to have encountered at last a bivouac.

"Aunt Grace, this is Professor Dunsmore."

The woman pocketed her pipe and stepped up close to Dunsmore and squinted at that forehead spot once cursed. She raised a veined and spotted hand and dragged a finger across it once, twice, and again, as though measuring its breadth and depth and danger.

Satisfied, she gripped both of his upper arms for a moment, then turned away, pulled the screen door open, and pointed inside. "Fresh cornbread, fried chicken, baked potatoes, green beans, sweet peas, pie . . . ," reciting a menu conceived at dawn, chickens caught, killed, and cleaned, garden foraged, wood-burning hearth stoked and put to work for the divined homecoming of her kin and welcome guest.

And finally Dunsmore remembered that he was hungry. When he took his place at the table, the seat and chairback crafted by hand buoyed the ache of his tendons and joints, its support seeming to draw even the heat and blister heel pain from his feet. Like the chair, the table was planed wood, unpainted, and dowel-fitted with not a sign of glue or nail. He looked at Carl seated across from him, whose form suited these bare wooden walls varnished by hearth heat and stove steam, suited the line of his unshaven jaw and the tilt of his squared shoulders waiting politely as his aunt daubed food onto pewter plates and dealt boiled greens, her hands at ease with the ritual of a spread.

They ate. Dunsmore felt the pocket of his belly, where so many forms of fear had resided in so short a time, filling now with fowl fried, with milk that had been squeezed ringing into galvanized tin, felt the fear drowning in a benevolence of labor. There was something in this place, in this building, these walls, floors, furniture, the product of tools braced shaving raw wood bringing order to the wilderness. Something in that labor which drove all of his fears out of his gut and off this claimed and cleared parcel of land.

And best, throughout the meal, no one spoke.

The shadow of the mountain across the valley moved up the front yard. Dunsmore watched its dark rim rising like a tide. Draco dragged two more chairs out onto the porch, and the men listened in the failing light to the hand-pumped splash of water in the slate sink in the kitchen. The sun gone, the shadow completed on the hillside, Dunsmore ran his tongue along his lower teeth reviving the taste of a pie he thought might be rhubarb but hadn't asked. He worked at letting go of his embarrassment at Aunt Grace's refusal to allow him to help wash, towel dry, or stack the plates. But then he had never allowed anyone to perform his own scholarly labors. Work is a fortress.

The Legend of Carl Draco

They sat silently in the dark, and after a while the light of a match struck inside flickered yellow through the screen door. Hearing the ringing scrape of glass clamped into place, Dunsmore looked around and saw through the doorway Aunt Grace arranging a lantern in the center of the kitchen table and cranking its flat wick high.

She balled a drying rag one last time, then hung it on a wooden rack above the sink and picked up a coffee tin. The screen door opened and both men arose and waited until she had settled herself on the rocker between them.

Dunsmore felt that any human voice at all would intrude upon this evening's peace, but when Aunt Grace broke the silence and spoke, her voice became the night air, as pleasing as a trout-leapt creek surface burst. "Either of you men care for a smoke?"

Dunsmore leashed his craving for his own blend and allowed Draco to accept one of three clay pipes before he reached out eagerly.

"Grow this tobacco myself," Aunt Grace said, passing the tin around.

Dunsmore remained politic, plucking a pinch and stuffing the bowl and packing it with the tool of his thumb as he inconspicuously sniffed the reek of fertilized earth and leaf insect-chewed and sun-cured without the benefit of science. Aunt Grace passed around wooden matches. The porch planks were scratched, and sulfur flared as the bowled leaf took.

Dunsmore inhaled slowly, a cherry-blend addict heedful, a new flavor is a trial. But the taste was not that of tilled earth nor bug-dung unwashed, it was sweet, and not unlike the flavors of his own lost pipe and pouch.

"Do you know about the men who've been following me all my life?" Draco said.

And here, for Dunsmore, was that intrusion. He took the pipe out of his mouth and looked at Aunt Grace's face half-lit by the kitchen lantern.

She drew a long sip of smoke and nodded. "I do."

"Do you know who Baxter is?"

"He's the man who chased your family out of the valley twenty years ago."

"Why did he do it?"

"He was afraid of you."

Dunsmore leaned into their conversation and spoke. "Where is the valley?"

Aunt Grace waved her pipe indicating the hillside behind the house. "Over the ridge."

"Is the town of Chuckney there?"

She nodded.

Draco spoke. "You saved me from those snakes."

"You asked me to. You called to me that night, just as you called to me the night your parents were murdered."

"Why didn't you help my parents?"

"I couldn't. Your parents were not like you."

"I've helped people who are not like me," Draco said. "Why can't you?"

"Because I'm not as powerful as you are."

In Dunsmore's cupped fist the red-rimmed leaves went out and ash fell. He felt it and heard the pop of twig sap cooked, the bowl cooling as he took this in, this revelation.

Neither Draco nor Aunt Grace spoke until Dunsmore could no longer bear the silence. He leaned forward.

"What is it about Carl that this man Baxter is afraid of?"

Aunt Grace turned to him. She raised her chin and looked off toward the woods as if to indicate something out there, something high in the trees. Dunsmore peered at the vague skyline but could see nothing. Aunt Grace knocked the inverted bowl gently against the arm of her rocker. Dying ash scattered on the boards. "There's some things best not spoken of in the night," she said with a casual finality that brought the conversation, and this pleasant sit, to an end.

The Legend of Carl Draco

She led Dunsmore through the kitchen into a small high-ceilinged guest room furnished with a frame bed and night table where a lamp cast shadows on the naked walls. Dunsmore set his duffel bag on the floor as Aunt Grace pulled back a down-thick quilt and smacked the pillow with the back of her hand.

"Clean sheets. Sleep well." She walked out of the room.

"You are very kind, Aunt Grace," Dunsmore said as the door softly closed.

He sat down on the bed, surrendering to his weariness and draping the duffel bag on a bunk post at the headboard, which brought a pleasing tactile memory, this motion a habit in the army, in-transit among bleak outpost barracks and bunkhouses, securing the kit bag of a peacetime soldier.

He undressed and slid beneath the cool fabric of the blanket and tried to reckon the extent to which this journey might be analogous to a trip overseas, traveling toward the unknown and possible danger. But sleep came so fast that his mewling GI nostalgia was interrupted by a dawn that seemed to break the moment his head hit the pillow, a military phenomenon to be sure.

Draco knew the way up the staircase, which was more narrow than his memory allowed, steep, solid steps that did not creak, and at the top, two doors. His was on the right.

Aunt Grace carried a lantern behind him as he entered a room also smaller than that of his memory, but the gabled ceiling, the single shuttered window overlooking the front yard, and the bed big enough for a big man and fitted with a sewn-square white-bordered quilt, brought his childhood finally back full circle. "I've slept here before."

"Many times," Aunt Grace said.

He ducked below the angled ceiling and stepped to the window, leaned across the bed to look down at the yard.

"There was a tire-swing strung from that high tree," he said. He looked around at Aunt Grace. "When my parents and I first came here, I had never seen one before."

She nodded.

"I feel safe in this place," he said.

"You are safe."

"I've never felt safe any place in my life."

"I know it," Aunt Grace said. "Sleep well." She left the room.

Draco took another look out the window and remembered this view, the long drop to the ground, the tall tree with that long naked branch, which had supported that swing that he had played on when his parents were still alive. They had come to this house in those days for the reasons that all families congregate, to feast and sing, to share news, to meet new babies, and to dance.

This had been his room in those times. And he stayed here, too, during the last night in this part of the country before they ran.

He kicked off his shoes, and grinned removing both his shirt and trousers thinking how many times they'd served as his bed and blanket. He blew out the lantern light and lay on top of the quilt examining the patterns of the angled night-shadows on the gabled ceiling, which fit into his childhood memory with an immediacy that seemed to deny every evil thing that had happened to him since he lay here last.

While letting go, his mind drifting asleep believing in the safety of this place, the soft thud of wood on wood brought him wide awake sitting up.

He heard the tread of a shoe on plank. He pressed his face against the cool window glass. In the crisp light of the risen moon he saw someone wwwalking away from the house. It was Aunt Grace, bowed under the weight of a shouldered shovel and a burlap bag slung across her back. She was heading toward the woods.

She stopped and turned and looked up at him, and Draco moved back from the window feeling foolish and discovered.

"Go to sleep," she said, and turned away.

chapter eleven

Slab bacon, cracked eggshell yellow and slime poured onto a fired griddle, pan bread singed over open flame, odor became image as Dunsmore opened his eyes in a quilt balled tight around his chest and thighs.

The good ache of calf muscles exercised, the bruise of a duffel bag strap deep in his right shoulder, he stretched his body, shooting blood through dull flesh past bones revamped by that mountain hike. He hadn't awakened this refreshed in memory. His one thought as he rolled sitting up with the quilt spilling at his feet: the air of Los Angeles alone could take ten years off a man's life.

He dressed but left his coat on the bed, pocketed a notebook and pencil, and opened the door to the stove odors that had drilled into his dreams making his stomach muscles tug and twist him awake. He saw heated food on the stove. Through a mask of steam on the kitchen window he could see Draco prowling among the trees at the edge of the property, coatless, hatless, head bowed with his hands on his hips like a Sunday gardener eyeing the reach of a dog-run plot.

Aunt Grace opened the screen door and stepped inside. "Morning."

"Good morning, Aunt Grace. I must tell you, I believe that was the best night's sleep I've had in years."

"Breakfast is ready." She moved to the table and dished

up eggs and strips of bacon, spooned tub butter, and poured milk from an enamel pitcher. Dunsmore ate recalling something he'd once read: mountain air gives a man an appetite. He swallowed milk and forked fried yellows and bacon bits, which slid thickly down his throat. All of this uninspected, freshly slaughtered, laid, and udder-hung food truly underscored the dominion of nature.

Aunt Grace began carrying plates and pans to the sink, and Dunsmore felt awkward, as he had the night before, uncomfortable letting a woman wait on him. But when he carried his own plate to the sink she snatched it and released him from his guilt by telling him to get out of her kitchen, she had work to do.

He stepped onto the porch and shoved his hands into his pants pockets inhaling a cool mid-morning breeze, which caught the screen door and bounced it shut behind him. He closed his eyes to dissect the odorous air: pinecone, porch wood, and the fishy reek of a hillside stream. For the first time in memory, he did not crave a first draw upon a first pipe of the day.

He watched as Draco reached up to touch the flat bark of a tall tree while craning his head back to look at a branch outthrust overhead.

Dunsmore walked down the hill to the leaf-blown territorial border where Draco stood.

"Good morning, Carl."

Draco nodded, squinted the sun from his eyes, and pointed up the tree. "Look."

Dunsmore stepped closer and sighted along his arm.

"I don't see," Dunsmore said.

"Rope."

And saw a twisted shank of knotted rope binding the long arm of the lone branch, a woven bracelet ingrown with bark bulging around it like gripped flesh. But the rope had been broken off close to the knot, a stub of hemp hanging useless

The Legend of Carl Draco

in a tangled spray of fiber.

"What is it?" Dunsmore said, pondering the sudden, unpleasant prospect of a noose.

"A tire-swing," Draco said, lowering his arm. "I played on the thing when I was a kid."

He led Dunsmore to another spot further along the hillside and pointed out a natural cornice of rock jutting from the earth. He said he'd played on it as a kid, but remembered it as being a boulder the size of a buckboard, though it was no larger than a wheelbarrow sunk in the weeds.

"I've been up since dawn," Draco said, his fingers slicking back his sweat-flattened hatless hair. "I walked the property behind the house and down near the creek, and with every step I took I found some small thing I remembered as clear as a snapshot in a photo album. There's a barn back there with a carriage parked in it with a stink of rotting upholstery that I can still remember. I've never smelled anything like that anywhere else in my life."

The rattling of pans and the squeak of the pump ceased in the house. Aunt Grace came outside and called for the two men to come up the hill for a sit and a smoke.

They fired packed bowls and drew on coals until tobacco and silence and the tree-line bird-chirp and chipmunk-tossing of husked food put them into the proper mood for talk.

"Professor Dunsmore asked a question last night appropriate only to daylight," Draco said.

Aunt Grace nodded. "Baxter's afraid of you because you're the one written about. Legend says that a righteous child of the Draco family will return to the valley one day and take over."

"Where is this written?" Dunsmore said.

"It's not in a book," she replied. "It's in the story of our people." She pointed the stem of her pipe at Draco. "Carl was born with a caul. At the age of seven he grabbed a bolt of lightning and held it in one hand."

Dunsmore nodded, appropriately nonplused. He frowned. "I don't quite understand, Aunt Grace. Does that signify some sort of archetypal folk symbolism?"

Aunt Grace gave him the fish-eye. "I mean to say, it was raining one summer night twenty years ago in the valley. Carl walked outside his house into the storm, and when lightning struck a tree, he took hold of the bolt with his fist and held it up like a candle."

"I don't recollect doing that," Draco said.

"I expect you wouldn't," Aunt Grace said, spitting a fleck of tobacco from her lips. "You were laid low for a week." She put the pipe between her teeth. "You lived."

"Who is this man Baxter?" Draco said.

"He's a bad man. He rules the valley. No one to come along in a hundred years has been as powerful or as mean as him."

"A hundred years?" Dunsmore said. "How old is he?"

"Same as me, hundred-twenty."

"Have you ever met this man?"

"I married him ninety years back," she said. She glanced at Dunsmore. "The union didn't take."

"Are you as powerful as Baxter?" Draco said.

"No, but I was powerful enough to get away from him and come to this side of the mountain."

"Has this man Baxter ever come here and . . . harassed you?" Dunsmore said.

"This ain't the valley," Aunt Grace said. "He doesn't care what goes on outside his valley. But if he came onto my land, I would very likely have more power than him. He knows that. He has no cause to come to the outside world."

Dunsmore pulled a spiral notebook from his pocket and began writing.

"What does he think killing me will get him?" Draco said. "I don't want his valley."

Aunt Grace looked him in the eye. "If he is able to kill you, it will prove that you are not the one spoken of in the legend."

The Legend of Carl Draco

"What does Baxter do in this valley?" Dunsmore said.

"Runs moonshine. Owns everything. People come from all over to barter and trade. He's got saloons. Women. Gambling. He's rich and he's a hard man. People are afraid of him."

"Why don't they leave?" Dunsmore said.

Aunt Grace smiled at him. "He takes care of them. They wouldn't stand a chance down in the flatlands." She raised her chin and looked at the far ridgeline. "When we leave these hills, we go to work in factories. We die yonder."

Dunsmore penned a few lines in his notebook. "Does anybody else in the valley possess the sort of power Carl has?"

Aunt Grace looked at the notebook. "What are you scratching on there?"

Dunsmore held up the pad. "I'm making a few notes."

"To what end?"

Draco spoke up. "Professor Dunsmore is a writer. He's published books."

"Concerning what?"

"Folk legends, superstitions and myths," Dunsmore said.

The wrinkles on Aunt Grace's forehead increased twofold. "Do you intend to write about us?"

A fleeting sense of rudeness crept over Dunsmore. He placed the notebook on his lap and smiled beseechingly. "I would very much like to record all of the things I see and hear on this journey. It's a standard practice in my profession."

Aunt Grace drew back her lips, showing a mouth full of teeth all hers, and bit down hard on the pipestem as if to gnaw on the standard practice of a flatlander's vague profession. "That's not advisable," she said.

Dunsmore discreetly closed the notebook and placed it into his shirt pocket.

"What you need is a turn at the woodpile," Aunt Grace said.

"I agree," Draco said.

"I'm sorry," Dunsmore said, looking from one to the other.

"I don't understand."

"The axe," Draco said, rising from his chair. "Wood for the winter!"

He hopped off the porch and headed for a side yard motioning Dunsmore to follow. The professor climbed down from the porch and went around to the side of the house where he found Draco standing over an axe sunk in a debarked tree-trunk chopping block white in the forenoon sun, surrounded by cloven stumps and curled shavings.

"A man's got to earn his feed," Draco said, grabbing the long handle and yanking the blade out of the block. He picked up a short thick stump and stood it upright on the block. He chopped it in two.

Dunsmore mused, "Wood for the winter. You know, except for a few times in Boy Scouts, I do not recall ever having chopped wood."

"Boy Scouts," Draco said with mock scorn. "Around here people chop wood to stave off frosty death!"

He offered the axe handle to Dunsmore and pointed at a scattering of sectioned stumps.

Dunsmore rolled his sleeves to the elbows and took the axe. He chose a decent candidate for a winter's hearth and set it upright on the chopping block. He gripped the pleasing machine-milled handle and slid his hands up and down its palm-polished length.

"Feet apart," Draco said. "Pick your spot."

Dunsmore raised the axe high and felt the iron head adding momentum as he followed through with a determined heave and chop. A passable slice of kindling spun into the weeds.

"Busy yourself here," Draco said. "This kind of labor cures a man."

"Of what?"

"You'll find out," Draco said, heading back to the porch.

Dunsmore reset the cordwood and picked his spot.

Labor—it wrings out sweat, pumps arm muscle, and puts

The Legend of Carl Draco

a plastic shine on hands where tools move, like a badge, like pay. It steals sunshine and deals shadows, it puts to sleep that thinking, useless bit of a man's brain not involved in the next saw, heave, dig, twist, or yank.

Dunsmore wiped his forehead with a reddened wrist and picked another log and took another swing. Cooling perspiration leaked into his ears and salted his eyes as the sun walked unobserved west.

The shadows lay long up the front yard when Dunsmore came around to the porch disheveled and weary. Draco was seated on the edge of his chair, leaning close to Aunt Grace as she spoke of things Dunsmore was not meant to hear. But when the professor's feet kicked leaves rounding the corner, Draco sat up and looked at his friend's pleased, overheated, grinning face. Dunsmore climbed onto the porch and dragged his chair a little closer to the edge where a breeze was running. He flopped down on the squeaking wood and set his heels bouncing.

"You probably chopped enough cord to keep Aunt Grace warm into February," Draco said.

Dunsmore rubbed the moist hollow of his neck and gazed at the sky. He nodded slowly, and this made Draco smile.

"Thirsty?" Aunt Grace said.

Dunsmore tried to speak but his stale throat cracked, and for one moment Draco feared his friend might hawk a loogie right in front of Aunt Grace. But Dunsmore merely coughed politely and said that a cup of ice-cold water was all his soul required, and that he would get it himself.

"I got something better," she said rising and going into the kitchen.

The two men waited silently, looking at each other. Dunsmore's lips were fixed with a cheek-blown self-satisfied smirk that made Draco nearly burst out laughing. Labor can cure a man, but can inflict a man too.

Aunt Grace came out carrying a glass filled with a liquid as

Gary Reilly

clear as water. "Home brew," she said.

Dunsmore sniffed the draught with doubt. Injecting alcohol into his heated system seemed like a risky proposition, but when he took a sip it spiraled into his mouth as clean and quenching as spring water with a pale liquor undertaste of distilled corn squeezings. He had to stop himself from taking a second bigger swallow.

"This is wonderful," he said, looking up at Aunt Grace. "I expected something a bit harsher."

"Brew it myself," she said, taking her seat. She went to work stuffing a new pipe and firing it, and after she blew a cloud she looked at Dunsmore. "Carl and I got business to attend to tonight. You'll be staying inside while we're gone."

Dunsmore nodded and looked at Carl, who volunteered no further information. Uncertain whether to pursue it, and feeling already light-headed from the drink, he asked if he had missed dinner, for he could not say for certain how long he had been at the woodpile. Already the sun was near the horizon. He knew only that there was not a single impatient thought chattering away in his brain as there had been, it seemed, for the past fifty-five years.

"Dinner's about ready," Aunt Grace said. "We'll eat as soon as you've recovered. I expect it takes a college professor a little longer than the average fellow to recuperate from the rigors of real work."

Dunsmore glanced at her but said nothing. He had always known in some small corner in his heart that he would one day pay for his diplomas. He put the glass to his lips and saw through the warped wall a wide grin on Draco's upturned sky-studying face.

Aunt Grace unlidded a stew made of leftovers from the previous night and dished it onto plates. She offered Dunsmore another cup of brew, and poured one for herself, but didn't offer any to Draco. Dunsmore took a sip and concluded immediately that two cups of this distillation was

94

all he could handle. The alcohol seemed to sweep through every part of his body like a soft rain.

"Let's go look at the evening sky," Aunt Grace said when Dunsmore had finished his meal.

They took their cups onto the porch and sat in silence. No one spoke or felt the need to speak, until the last sky glow fled the far range. Then Dunsmore set his cup on the floor half-finished and told Aunt Grace that one and a half cups of this potent libation apparently was his limit.

Draco stood up and looked at Aunt Grace. "This is as good a time as any."

She arose and took the two cups inside and left the men alone.

"Aunt Grace will be taking me into the woods tonight," Draco said, stepping to the edge of the porch. "You'll be staying here alone. We'll be back around sunup." He turned and looked at Dunsmore. "I want to tell you something important. When I come out of the woods, I will not be the same man I am now. I want you to know that."

"How will you be different?"

"I don't know. This is what Aunt Grace has told me, and I'm confident she knows what she's about."

"What are you going to be doing out there?"

Draco smiled. "Still taking notes, Professor? I thought you'd be cured of that by now."

"I simply wish to know whether you're going to be in any danger, Carl."

Draco shrugged. "Aunt Grace doesn't seem to think so."

Aunt Grace came out with a lit lantern gripped in one hand and the hand-knit wrap of a gray shawl over her shoulders.

"When we leave here, you stay inside the house," she said to Dunsmore. "Don't go outside alone as long as we're gone, regardless of what you hear."

"What might I expect to hear?" Dunsmore said.

Aunt Grace twisted the wick high until the flame glowed

brightly on the porch. She shrugged. "Raccoons root around. They won't come inside."

Aunt Grace and Draco went down the steps, and Dunsmore stepped into the kitchen. Through the screen-door mesh, which smelled of rust, he watched them enter the woods, the fine crosshairs fragmenting the swinging lantern light, which dwindled to a pinpoint and finally disappeared.

He closed the kitchen door and wriggled the bolt locked tight. He looked once more out the window at the wall of night, then went into his room and lit the bedside lantern.

He felt as though this day had passed in an instant, the hours at the woodpile compressed into brief turns of steady chopping that had driven away all previous concerns, ambitions, and desires, their lack of substance now evidenced by their absence. He drew back the covers of his bed and blew the wick flame dead.

chapter twelve

The glow of Aunt Grace's lantern swung up bark alive with insects and danced back down. Draco followed her shawled hunched back, black against the rocking light, trusting her step along an unfamiliar path. She paused and pointed whenever the trickle of a grass-overhung stream or crippling gully cut across the trail. Draco measured his pace evenly against hers and walked where she walked.

The light grew brighter against trees growing so close their trunks began to look like the stripped timber walls of a cavalry fort. He recalled how the previous day Dunsmore had brought to his attention the absence of all the bird flutter and song, and it was absent here too with the sun gone. The expected hectic motion of furred things curious or frightened of the light was absent too. The only sound in the woods was the slip of shoes and the occasional muted commotion of a close creek.

Then the light spread, captured and rising in a large clearing, which took Draco by surprise. It might have been a room but for the circle of pine-rimmed sky and stars overhead. In the center of the ground was a square hole three feet on each side. Next to it lay the shovel and burlap bag that he had seen Aunt Grace carrying into the woods the night before. A shallow trench ran from the hole to the far side of the clearing and passed between two trees. He heard beyond the trees the rapid flow of water. Aunt Grace set the lantern on the ground and pointed at the trench. "Take the spade and clear away that dam."

Draco picked up the shovel and followed the trench to the trees and saw now between the trunks a hand-packed earthen berm that kept a stream two feet wide and no deeper than his hand from spilling through. He stabbed at the berm, and water began trickling into the trench. He walked alongside the flow and watched the dirt-rimmed foam-white crest tumble into the hole.

Aunt Grace squatted on the ground with her back to Draco and began gathering twigs and dry pine needles. "Strip and get into the hole."

"Ma'am?" he said, scraping a rogue stream back into the trench.

"You heard me. Strip and get."

Teeth lathed by a tight-lipped skeptical tongue, Draco pulled his hat off and tossed it onto the shore of the hole. He stripped bare and sat down in the icy lake and heard above him the chopping of wings guiding talons onto a high tree branch.

Aunt Grace stacked kindling into a tent-shape. She picked up a long, thin, dry-weed taper and poked the end down the lantern chimney. She took some flame, touched it to the kindling, and blew coals until an even blaze licked the teepeed sticks.

She stood up and grabbed the shovel and scooped loose earth onto the blade, sprinkling it into the hole as if spicing a soup. She set the tool aside and gathered mock herbs in the form of leaf and weed and tossed them in.

"Lower yourself beneath the water," she said. "Your head too, everything."

Nostrils pinched, Draco lifted his feet and let his weight pull him down along the silky mud bottom. It was not that deep, but there were no root or rock outcroppings to grab

The Legend of Carl Draco

hold of to keep his lung-filled hulk from rising, so he rolled to stay under, and felt tossed earth splashing above his head, felt damp clods sinking along his back, felt the weed and dirt spice become a thickening sludge slowing his roll.

The sidewise scrape of clawed feet creeping for a better view, the twitch and ruffle of dusty neck feathers, beneath the water he heard these sounds in the tree, heard the click of a beak grinding a field mouse into bonemeal, heard the hollow hornpipe "hoo" of his audience owl.

He rolled sitting up, for he could no longer hold his breath, which was strange, and when his head broke surface and cranked back whipping hair out of his eyes he felt a pressure on his neck, like a collar starched stiff and tight against his Adam's apple. Too tight in fact—and that gut spot that blazes when caution begets action pulsed once against his ribs. The short bristles on the bone of his chin brushed earth as dry as concrete. His squatting legs and balled fists wrenched but did not budge. Aunt Grace hadn't spoken of this earlier, hadn't hinted at a cauldron dupe snare dug into the earth tree-walled and hidden.

And only now, in his first flush of startled and burgeoning unease, did he realize that she was no longer there. His clothing had been folded and stacked neatly by the fire, his shoes heel-locked alongside, but the burlap bag and shovel were gone.

His fighter-cocked arms shivered but could not break the earth's hold, and concentrating, he realized that the power that had always sustained his every conflict no longer resided within him. His strength now was only the strength of an average man, and as such he had no more power to burst out of this prison than a muskrat leg steel-jaw bit and chained to the earth.

An emotion began to grow in that spot beneath his ribs, an emotion he had never known before, wormlike, squirming, and gaining size. He had seen it in other men, and had wandered near its neighborhood, but had never met it in the flesh. But he met it now, a spine-jelling full-blown animal fright racing like a wind around his heart. Wrath rode in its wake, a stricken remorse at what he took to be his blind, deluded trust in Aunt Grace.

A booted punt, a sledgehammer leveled fierce, could take him out now, and he began flexing every foot-calf-thigh-back-shoulder-and-fist muscle pressing to stand up, but the earth held him. Blurry-eyed and dizzy with the unfamiliar thoughts of an average man set in concrete to his neck, he did not hear beyond the lantern-lit wall of trees the slow and steady crush of leaf and tumble of pebbles turned aside by a padded foot.

His heavy breathing blowing the dust beneath his chin prevented him from hearing the slinking trot of four furred legs, and because he no longer had his power he did not smell the panting breath blown across sharp white spit-bubbled canine teeth, did not suspect a thing until a lurking burrow-born chicken thief hopped between two trunks into the circle of firelight.

A fox with a red tail flame-erect paused and lifted one black-ankled forefoot to wipe at an eye, as if to knock out a speck of dust or disbelief at the sight of a man's neck rising from the earth like the base of a barkless tree.

Damn! Draco thought of Dunsmore, kind Dunsmore, silver-tongued Judas goat accomplice of Aunt Grace, leading him every step of the way with his prattle of scholarly research. Twenty years of evasion and head-on conflict, Baxter knew what he was doing, Dunsmore was his boy, and Aunt Grace an arachnid spinning webs around his memories, ah but she had pulled him in and bundled him well. He knew that this colorful carnivore could strip meat from a downed carcass and come back for seconds, could chew skull skin as fast as a vulture tearing leftovers from the abandoned nest of a lion kill. His own snarling lip-curled pose was useless and he knew it. He was down and he was meat.

The Legend of Carl Draco

The fox swung its head low to the side sniffing, then trotted toward Draco on thin legs quivering until its scavenger breath blew hot against Draco's cheeks. It set its scrawny haunches on the ground blocking the view of the fire, and Draco's thoughts dwindled to a single savage defense of teeth. When this beast bit he would bite back howling curses at his kin.

The fox's clown face broke, panting as if with laughter, as if it could hear this helpless planted man-head scheming dogfight-death stratagems. Its furred face muscles drew its cheeks up to the base of its ears pointing at the silent big-eyed audience above. Grinning, tongue-drip beading dust, the fox studied Draco's eyes as its twitching snout browsed the random odors of the place. Its tail whipped once, moved slowly, whipped again, and its rapid breath cooled the sweat sprouting on the stretched flesh above Draco's eyes. But the fox didn't lunge, didn't snap its jaws. It just sat grinning until it seemed satisfied.

Then got up, arched and stretched its skinny spine, kicked a little hind-leg dust, marched across the clearing, and hopped between two trees.

The walls wouldn't let the sound of Draco's frightened breathing dissipate into the woods. It caught it, cupped it, and let rise that misted hush of fear given voice and growing louder, let him hear it, a moaning sound he had never heard from his own throat. He braced his feet against the earth, set his shoulders, and held air tight in his lungs, heaving until exhaustion launched a howl of rage from his open aching jaws.

So that the snake made a good distance toward the fire before he noticed it. It was as large as a python, and Draco looked fast for diamonds on its back but saw only shiny, tight-seamed, shingled yellow fire-lit scales. He looked for a pearled whip rattle but saw only a tapered tail drawing a thin S in the dust. Black fork tasting the trail, it wove its liquid path toward the fire, then turned its smiling ground-skimming chin his way. A country of smiling critters. In the wild they always skulk amused but let their smiles drop at the approach of soft-clawed men armed.

Draco's breath began to blow fast as that hinged jaw plowed at him hissing. He felt every rooted scalp hair spring erect as he envisioned it, not with prescience but with fear driving an imagination wild: the spreading triangular head opening, the jaws parting revealing a red sheath of stretched gums, palate and throat gobbling at the side of his face and sliding over the top of his head like a mask dragged fast, the slippery wet reptilian mouth walls pressing against his cheeks and nose and blinding his eyes, and finally lying rubbery and tight against his screaming lips blocking his air and squirting digestive acids amid the stomach stink of rodent rot and bugs nabbed on the run.

Choke you bastard, Aunt Grace, Dunsmore, choke!

The shark-eyed bone head slid underneath and lifted Draco's chin. The tongue fork pricked his neck with kisses while scaled ribs wrapped around his throbbing throat.

He closed his eyes to stifle a scream as the cool, thick, yellow, slithering length pressed gently against his jugular the way a mother might wrap her arms around a sleeping infant to let it know inside its sleep that she's here, sweetheart, right here, caressing a neck as fragile as a paper cup.

Behind his closed eyes he searched like a man kicking empty boxes in a pillaged armory for a scrap of that magic he once had wielded, thinking crazed thoughts of revenge while awaiting the final throat implosion, the things he would do, the things he should have done, blinded by confidence and suckered solid. He was fair game licked fair.

But the thick coil thinned. He felt the tail sliding around his neck in departure. The snake began plowing toward the wall of the woods.

Reddened with fear and shame, mortified at the shape his thoughts had taken scrambled by emotion, he knew now

The Legend of Carl Draco

that Baxter was having his day, was taking his revenge at his leisure.

The snake passed through the same trunk space where the fox had gone, its tail scattering last dust and disappearing. Draco looked at the sidewinder path, which backed up to his neck and drew toward the fire and turned toward the space in the trees where the snake had come from and from which he heard now the certain sound of human feet flattening twigs.

His breath came fast and not from fear but manic victim joy. He had met the fox and serpent, now he would meet the man. He grinned knowing he had lost, and craned his head and worked his lips looking up six feet awaiting the kicked boot or swung sledge. He would spit high into Baxter's grinning victory leer.

The thrust hem of a simple skirt and a factory shoe came from between trees set so close that a fox might squeeze through if he sucked in his gut, and a snake would have no problem, but there was no room for a woman. But a woman stepped from the dark crack and entered the clearing followed by a man wearing leather rubbed oily-black at the elbows and knees, wearing a wide-brimmed hat tugged low to the brow. The man took the woman's pale arm and, elbows locked, they walked through the fire. Their solid surfaces were drained by the light, the man's legs and the woman's skirt bleached to the refraction of a soap bubble as they walked without kicking up wood or ash.

Teeth bit to stifle and swallow a singular ache of grief restless on his tongue, Draco looked up at the crystalline faces of his mother and father moving above the fire and heard in the silence a buzzing like the sound of many flies. He could see their lips moving. That buzz was their whispered conversation, saying something that he believed they wanted him to hear, though they did not look down at him as he wished they would as they strolled across the clearing with their color now returned. He could see creases on the back

Gary Reilly

of his father's coat and red dust paling his bootheels, could see every strand of his mother's brown hair firelit as the two passed arm in arm, going the way of the fox and the snake.

Draco closed his eyes to dismiss the treachery of sentiment, but a sky-racked clarion hammering clouds took his mind off that move. Distant thunder rumbled among tree roots as though the sky had settled like a collapsed tent unleashing its kept clutter of violence along the forest floor. The stalking thunder approached, but without electric flare, to the place where the fox, the snake, and his mother and father had appeared, and just before the new apparition arrived, Draco, reassured by the odd nature of these visits and believing now in their conveyed benevolence, nevertheless allowed his imagination one last leap, a hideous notion: the snuffling steel-clawed hulk of a grizzly on the scent.

But this visitor was a man, mountain bred and black-hatted like the others of his breed. He came into the clearing at full stride, vested chest outthrust with massive muscled arms held away from his sides with hands poised as if prepared to draw pistols from low-slung holsters, though he bore no weapons.

Draco cocked his head back an inch to take in the complete sight of this man a head taller than his father. A big man, wide, but his girth wasn't gone to fat, it was brawn, his arms and thighs thick and fitted tight in dirty leather. Feathers dangled from hat and vest and black boot top. There was animal tooth and claw hung where some men wear silver. There was a bone necklace, and bone rings on thick fingers, and fine-carved, hollow, subtly beaded threaded bones knotted in his hair.

But it was the face, lit white by the fire, a face that had not seen the sun in ages, that drew all of Draco's attention. Cheekbones like granite blocks and a jaw jutting with lips spread wide revealing teeth like tombstones in a grinning mouth, grinning at his absolute right to range these hills unchallenged.

Baxter.

The Legend of Carl Draco

Or his spirit bewitched and charmed forth by an incantation known only to Aunt Grace. Draco looked into the man's eyes shining black above that rimrock cheekbone in the fire flicker and waited to see if the man would notice his imprisoned presence. But Baxter only made for the fire and looked down at it seemingly pleased.

Draco tugged his landlocked fists instinctively so near a battler of this magnitude. For all he knew, Aunt Grace had brought them together to settle their long-standing differences this very night.

Baxter grunted, as that imaginary grizzly might have, lowering his flanks to the ground with a warbled groan of pleasure. He began working at his boots, peeling the tops down and yanking them off his ghost-pale feet. And as he did this, Draco saw something catch a length of light, something thin and gray and falling. It spun from a wooden heel and hit the ground beside the fire, bouncing once. But Baxter's wrestling motion buried it, and Draco could not tell what the thing was lying beneath the scattered earth.

Baxter stretched his legs full-out flat at the knees and pushed his naked feet into the fire like a man splaying frostbit toes near the mica window of an iron stove. He leaned back, arms buttressing his trunk as his toenails plowed ash and dug into sticks aglow. Rainbowed flames curled ankle hair and popped heel calluses, and from Baxter's belly came another groan of satisfaction.

He took whatever pleasure this offered for less than half a minute, then dragged his smoking extremities from the fire and put his boots back on. He hopped up, his bulk made a lie by this lithe leap, and strode across the clearing toward the exit.

No sound of thunderous footsteps departing, Draco turned his head and cocked an ear and listened with the feeble hearing of a mere man. Breathing lightly, certain now that he had no need to fear, he waited for the shuffling signal of the evening's next entertainment but heard nothing, not even the sound of the wind bending treetops across the face of the now full moon.

*

Draco awoke with an intake of startled breath. Cratered dust popped before his eyes. He looked up as raindrops poked his face and battered firewood embers, making cool dark hissing spots on the wood.

A low cloudbank, a fog, drifted among the trees, and the air tingled with the gathering tease of electrons. He had experienced this hair-lifting weather above timberline and knew what was coming. When the first forged blue bolt lit a powder keg near his nose, he turned his face away from the tossed clods and closed his eyes. Another spidery split blue delta danced around his head blasting the binding earth and baring his rigid shoulders, and he felt his chest loosen as the lightning broke open his hexed hold at last.

Deafened, tired, cold, and leery, he struggled out of the pit as the brief storm drifted away. Naked, he moved on his hands and knees to the warmth of buried coals still alive. He blew ash off the sticks until the flames rose again with pine sap snapping its sleepy disapproval. Seated, he dragged his clothes over his shivering skin and put on his shoes. He held his hands over the fire glow for a moment, then looked up at a sky still black, though white with stars. He tried to calculate the time, but in this clearing there wasn't enough sound or light to gauge against the shape of nature when a man might be.

He lay down facing the fire with his head pressed against the pillowed flesh of an elbow crooked, and the lulling heat of the coals pushed him toward sleep. Somewhere outside his sprouting dreams he heard the windy sweep of wings and a sullen "hoo," the warning or celebration of that lone attendant owl cresting pine tops home.

chapter thirteen

"Get up."

A shoe toe poked the small of Draco's back. He opened his eyes smelling the black ash of spent wood.

He rolled and squinted in the morning light at Aunt Grace, who stood studying his prone form with a fresh pipe in her fist. "Did you have a good night?"

Draco levered his stiff, cold limbs and rubbed at an eye. "I've had better."

He got to his feet as Aunt Grace squatted and socked the pipe between her lips and began dragging furrows in the loose earth. She pawed the ground until she struck the thin gray length that had spun from Baxter's boot.

She picked it up, stood erect, and peered closely at it. "That's what I was looking for."

Draco tugged at his clothing, yanked the twisted leg fabric, and worked the arms of his coat into place. He leaned over to study an ordinary boot nail pinched between Aunt Grace's fingers.

She looked him up and down as if to ascertain whether he was any the worse for wear, then reached up and brushed a tangled forelock from his eyes.

"You got all your powers now."

As she led him out of the clearing Draco noticed that those old-growth trunks did not, in daylight, seem set so close together after all, that a man could pass easily between any of them.

As they retraced their steps back toward the house, where Dunsmore no doubt was snoring oblivious, Draco could not recall these twists and turns nor the sounds of particular streams along the path, and though he had dealt poker decks and risked thin odds against gamblers, bums, and thieves, he wouldn't care now to wager that he was leaving the same place where he had cowered the night before.

*

Waking, wondering if the hammer of that moonshine would render his day wasted like recalled undergraduate bacchanalian morning-afters, Dunsmore opened his eyes.

His lips might never have touched drink. His head was devoid of frantic hangover chaos, and he got up pleased. On the kitchen table he found only a thick slab of bacon, which he doubted he could manhandle properly. He wondered where the chickens were whose eggs he had eaten with such flatlander relish the day before. His hunger now seemed robust rather than desperate, as it sometimes seemed in LA when he would drive to a burger joint just to drown that gremlin in his gut with soft drinks and fatty slag. He heard the crackle of leaves outside. He pushed the screen door open and stepped out onto the porch.

Aunt Grace and Draco were hiking the front-yard slope at a stroll. Dunsmore studied Draco, looking for those implied changes in his face, size, or gait, but Draco looked no different now than he had when he'd gone into the woods the night before. His borrowed clothes and brown hat were newly freckled with leaf and dust, but there was nothing in his loping walk or face creased against the morning sun to indicate a transformation.

They climbed onto the porch. Aunt Grace looked at Draco and pointed at the screen door.

"The trunk is upstairs."

The Legend of Carl Draco

Draco stepped past Dunsmore, nodding at him as he went inside. Aunt Grace settled on her chair and struck a match against the boards. Pipe fired, she rocked back and looked at Dunsmore. "Sleep well?"

Dunsmore eased himself onto a rocking chair. "I slept better last night than the night before, Aunt Grace. I cannot recall ever having slept so well or awakening so refreshed in my entire life."

"How old are you?"

"I turned fifty-five last March."

"Fifty-five," she said. "I recall when I was fifty-five. I left the hills and resided one year in the state of Massachusetts. Have you ever been there?"

"I'm afraid not, Aunt Grace."

She puffed and nodded. "I stayed with a niece who was married to a man in the shoe-manufacturing business. I have been out in the world and I have seen it." She spat a fleck from her lips.

The trod planks of the narrow staircase thumped with a thicker sound than before, and Dunsmore looked around at the screen door. Draco shoved it open and came out dressed in new skin, his borrowed machine-stitched city garb tossed. The leather pants retained the folds of their steamer-trunk packing in the attic. So too the coat, and its sleeves, and the shirt of a plain brown fabric so coarse in weave that Dunsmore had to lean close to ascertain it wasn't burlap. Draco's boots were like all cracked, caked footwear worn by men who labored out of doors.

Dunsmore stared at the boots. The cut was familiar. He had seen wood-heeled clodbusters like those before, on the shod feet of the men who had invaded his home.

And in Draco's hand, the canvas strap of a bedroll packed for travel.

Aunt Grace stood up and removed from her pocket the metal sliver of Baxter's boot nail. She placed it in Draco's palm. "Keep this on your person, and Baxter will not know you until you choose to reveal yourself to him."

Draco nodded and slipped the nail into a pocket of his loose dull leather pants.

She placed a hand on his coat over his heart. "I will not be able to help you once you enter the valley. You will be on your own."

The flooding feeling of a burden acknowledged, Dunsmore's face grew heated and pink with surprise and panic and a stinging sense of shame. "Carl. You're going into the valley without me."

"I'm sorry, Professor. I got to go this alone."

"I'm not afraid to go with you!"

Aunt Grace stepped between the men and gripped Dunsmore's arms.

"Professor Dunsmore, we know that you are not afraid." She touched his forehead. "You have already crossed one threshold. But you are not ready to cross this one. You cannot go into the valley with Carl. He has work to do. "

Truth—unassailable, sour to the ear, it wilts a man's will, foments vile resignation, and breeds ungenerous cynicism. Dunsmore turned away from the tranquil pale blue of this woman's honest eyes and looked out across the tops of the trees that flowed green-to-blue unbroken to the ragged horizon west. Perfect walking weather. A shame. He held out a hand without looking up and waited until he felt Carl's grip. "Good luck, Carl," he said softly.

His back to Draco's exit, Dunsmore stood on the edge of the porch listening to the rhythmic shuffle of footsteps treading leaves growing faint up the hillside behind the house until it was lost beneath the squeal of rocker wood, until he smelled pipe smoke. He turned and took his seat next to Aunt Grace, who proffered a bowl freshly lit.

*

Wildflower and erosion hid the long roadbed engineered

The Legend of Carl Draco

for wagon wheels winding toward the gap in the ridge above. Draco walked the abandoned path toward a summit once hacked by dynamite and shovel, its skyline composed of two overhung grass-topped cliffs leaning into each other like sleeping sentries. He walked between the cliffs where the funneling wind accelerated. He stopped at the crest to look ahead at the valley bottom miles downslope but hidden from view by old-growth pine creeping close to a road gone to rack and ruin.

He looked back the way he had come and saw the blackened brick hole of the chimney leaking idle smoke on the peaked roof of Aunt Grace's home. Dunsmore's nettled grief. The stymied scholar vexed by that vulgar nuisance called danger, his pencils sharpened and useless.

Draco took his hat off and slapped it on a thigh and slicked brow sweat back into his hair. He put on the hat and shrugged the packed bedroll higher onto his back and noted that the air here, like the air deep inside that tree line near the spot where they had parked the car, was silent. No birds, no small critters scattering into the brush, the place where he was standing was a piece of the world demarcated by something not on maps.

Seven, eight miles distant stood the slag ramparts of the south end of the valley, their steep slopes blue in a morning shadow not yet touched by the rising sun. And somewhere between this gate and that dark horizon—whether he knew and was prepared, or knew and didn't care, or did not know at all—a man was waiting.

Carl Draco stepped down into the valley.

chapter fourteen

You could walk down a road you've walked before and not recognize the familiar depth of a nearby ditch, or the natural and necessary path around a tree too thick to fell or uproot. You could go around that forgotten squat bark, and the steep drop of the road behind it might knock loose a crust like bark overgrown on your memory, so that you recall something about that slope: it was a tough go for a wagon once. You could walk down a road you've traveled in both directions, but because your eyes were on the sky with the games its silver breezes were playing above your family's heads, you do not recall that chore of gravity as a horse lurched loosely, allowed to find its own foothold up or down the slope. You weren't watching the road. Your eyes were on something else, and now you have to look hard to see anything at all.

The lurking abrupt scoot and pause of a four-legged shadow was the first sound that Draco heard. He saw a bird dive into the green-fanned top of a tree, heard the wind tumbling leaves or shoving branches with a soft-drawn sound as that padding, pausing, loping rush of now eight legs continued, one above him and one downslope, the matted-furred stink of Baxter's sentry wolves carried on the wind.

Draco left the road and cut south along the mountainside,

following Aunt Grace's directions. The wolves began walking flank, and he judged that there were now six. He could hear their heaving lungs, could hear bushes being nudged aside, and at one point saw a pair of white-ringed almond eyes regarding him from a clutter of boulders overhead.

"Ignore them," Aunt Grace had said. "They won't approach you. They let Baxter know when a trader or a stranger has come into his valley, and they keep people from leaving who need to be kept."

He stepped into a ring of trees, unslung his bedroll, and set it on the ground. He knelt and shoveled a hand between the rolled layers and pulled out an empty burlap bag. Bushes further out shivered with a circled gathering of canine eyes hidden. Draco glanced around, a man down, and began picking up twigs and tossing them into the bag.

He filled it half full, then spread the rim wide and reached inside. The twigs lay tangled like bird bones, useless scrap, but when he touched one fragile length, the contents began to glow like silver coals.

He knotted the top closed and stood up. With his pack high on his back and the burlap over his shoulder, he broke trail south through scrub and vine with the windy sound of bushes moving and twigs breaking ahead and behind and port and starboard. The wolves stayed with him until he came to a rimrock free of trees, a panorama point overlooking the town two miles below, spread out on a bottomland scarred north to south by a dirt road running parallel to a creek flowing past clustered settlement houses, past stores, and shacks, and tents.

Looking at this bowl with its geometric smear of human structures, a memory kicked in, for he knew this scene, it was as familiar to him as light-struck light-sensitive paper passed through liquid chemicals and held in his hands. It had always been in his memory, had welled up now and then, but he had never thought anything about it, had given it no more consideration than you would give a recalled photograph in a forgotten book.

He backed off the outcrop and began making his way downhill and realized that, so close to the boundaries of what passed for civilization below, the wolves had ceased their footpad escort.

An unnatural shape appeared between the trees, the dark brown rotting frame of a glassless cobwebbed window below an angle of roof without shingles, a mass of bushes growing wild against teetering brown walls. A cabin uninhabited, its doorless entry black, and where a path might once have led to that door, knee-deep bushes blocking the way. He saw no reason why anyone should not be living there. Clear the clutter and shore the walls, but further along and higher up the hill he saw another structure like it, abandoned, windows and doorway empty, a fence fallen where once a garden had thrived. Disease, he supposed, could have driven them off this hill.

He looked skyward to gauge the angle of the sun's hot light on his left shoulder, observing that it would be about 9 a.m. in Professor Dunsmore's clockless day.

Battling through a hedgerow, grabbing hold of the soft wooden snake of a creeper vine and holding it away from his face, Draco came upon a cleared shelf of earth-buried flat rock outthrust from the mountain's ribs and big enough to be built upon and inhabited.

Close by he saw the rotted rails of an enclosure filled with high weed. Thirty yards distant and set back against the hillside stood the house, within which he had been born among fitted blocks of hand-quarried native stone.

He stepped out of the hedgerow and released the vine, which slapped back rustling and rocked silent. He was surprised to find the house in such good shape, expecting it to have been overtaken by jungle, a ruin like the others. He stood motionless, quiet, wary that it might be occupied

The Legend of Carl Draco

because the shelf of land had the cleared look of caretaker labor. Aside from the wild green interior of the nearby fenced rectangle, the property hadn't succumbed to nature's tasteless narcissism. It looked, in fact, no different than it had on the night they had run.

He reached over his shoulder and tugged the sagging bedroll higher on his back and began walking toward the fenced rectangle, his eyes on the ground like that of a weary, harmless wanderer trespassing without malice, a hobo maybe looking for a cup of water or a slice of bread, just passing through and glancing occasionally toward the dark glassed-in windows of his silent home.

The sun lit a chipped granite arch bulging from the bordered bushes, he saw it from the corner of his eye and looked over at it. There were others buried beneath that green sea, and he recalled now, though it had seemed in his childhood a place much further away from the house, safely distant, the family graveyard.

He dropped the burlap bag from his hand, lowered his shoulder, and let the canvas strap slip off. The rail fence along this side was whole, but two rails on the far sides had fallen into powdered sawdust. The fourth was split in the middle with its ends still poked into the chiseled holes of knee-high cornerstones carved out of the same white rock as the house.

He stepped over the railing and kicked a path between the graves, kicked sleeping insects buzzing awake. A quick beast, maybe a mouse, darted from beneath a bush. Draco squatted before a tombstone and batted branches aside until he could read the simple screed of the buried. "Mary Draco, 1799–1874." He jabbed a fingertip into the carved letters of her name and wondered who this woman was to him.

He stood up and kicked another path toward another tombstone, and knelt. "William Draco, 1819–1901." Uncle maybe, or grandfather, farmer maybe or teamster or blacksmith, dead and buried twice, once beneath the earth

Gary Reilly

and once beneath weeds so high that no passerby could see to note these names.

He followed his path back through the weeds and stepped over the fence. There was no one in the house. He would have felt their threatening presence by now, and they would probably have seen him prowling among his dead and stepped outside to inquire.

He picked up his bag and bedroll and walked toward the house, his eyes darting to each fragment matching a memory. Leading up to the front door, the throne-like stone stairwell that had loomed so large in his childhood now a matter of four innocuous chiseled steps. The eaves of the roof where wasps sculpted riddled nests—his elders had taught him the universal and comprehensible insect wisdom that a child can grip like a stick: "Don't pester them and they won't pester you." But that tree. He looked to the front door and followed random paths out across the yard but could not see the trunk of any tree split by night lightning. He expected it to be somewhere near the edge of the plateau overlooking the town a quarter mile below, but there were no trees at all in the front yard, and no place of sunken earth from which such a thing might have been uprooted and chopped for the hearth or hauled away.

He approached the house with its rear foundation driven into the rise of the hillside. There's a cellar you get to through a hinged door in the kitchen floor—he remembered thick fingers gripping a rusted ring, there was laughter, the floor opened up and worm-tilled basement earth and strung-pepper smells invaded the crowded kitchen where women were cooking meat. Down below were fruity things preserved in thick mason jars in ordered rows on plank shelves. He remembered smelling the mushroom mildew basement odor while squatting by the open floor.

The town was in plain view from this spot near the front steps, so he went around to the side of the house because

116

minions below might be watching for strangers nosing around this place. Up the hillside and around to the back where the steps were built of thick boards anchored in the mountain itself, he stopped at the bottom step and looked at the closed wooden door, the entry to the kitchen. This was where people walked in and out. The front door was opened primarily for visitors, but the back door was where men entered tired taking off coats and gloves, and women walked out carrying baskets of steaming laundry, the door where kids ran out to wrestle on the backyard hill.

He climbed the steps, which were so solid that his boots barely made a sound. The door gave way to his touch, swung in without a creak from its bolted iron hinges, opened on a kitchen unfurnished, with unbroken dusty windows making the inside of the house only a little less light than day.

Cleaned out as if by thieves. Not a stick of wood for a table or chair, just a big empty room with that hearth still smoke-licked around the fitted stone arch edge.

He sensed that it wasn't thieves though. The place felt cleaned out as if by malevolent design. The only sign of occupancy was a woven tangle of twig, hair, and colored rag in one corner, the tattered nest of a critter long fled. Cracked shells of nuts lay scattered about the stone floor, nibbled by squirrels, or lizards, or birds drawn by the dark cubic mystery of a chimney, the only animal entrance or exit from a place with its windows strangely intact.

He looked at the wooden square of the cellar door near the far wall and recalled that the iron ring was not hinged permanent, they kept it on a high shelf hidden from reckless kid hands.

He carried his bedroll like a suitcase across the kitchen to a doorway and paused beneath the arch, a house of arches and solid right-angled stone, and looked at the front room, a big room empty but for a small plain wooden table with two chairs shoved up against the front wall beneath a large

Gary Reilly

picture window. Curtainless, it gave a pleasing view of the ridge across the valley and the town below. On the center of the table stood a kerosene lamp.

He crossed the room with the soles of his boots scuffing the dusted floor, a room big enough for echoes, but there were no echoes. He set his bedroll and burlap bag on the table and looked at the flaked red paint of the lamp's fuel well and glass chimney frosted evenly with dust. The lamp had not been lit in a long time yet did not seem so dusty that it had sat untouched for twenty years. The table and chairs too had not gone unused that long.

He looked around at a doorless arch that led to the bedrooms. That of his parents. His own. He pulled out a chair and sat down, tossed his hat onto the table, and looked out the window. The view was closer, clearer here than on that earlier rimrock promontory, the town now sliced into biscuit squares, thick in the central business district, the highest buildings two-story, but only a few of these. The rest were mostly low flat-fronted boxes of commerce with alleys tucked in between. Outlying from the central cluster of wood frames sprang tents staked between temporary booths with paying customers crowded all around.

The traffic and barter appeared to be taking place on this side of the crooked trickling ditch that ranged the valley north to south. On the far side of the stream were a few travelers hiking in from the east, but they gave wide berth to a house nestled up against the mountain, a mansion fronted by a long, wide, fanning sweep of naked earth sloping down to the wooden hump of a single footbridge spanning the creek. Three stories in the center, wooden-roofed with rambling wings tin-shingled here and there, its walls were black as if damp, as if fabricated from the same species of monstrous arbor launched a hundred feet out of the earth at the front corner of the north wing.

A tree familiar in shape, girth, color, and malevolence—

118

The Legend of Carl Draco

Draco had seen its twin before in miniature, bursting from white sand silencing the foolhardy confessions of two hunters, its black thorned branches raising those bested bodies penalized by Baxter.

Whose house seemed a thickened creeper root born out of the base of the tree, a house grown wild with doors and windows sawn and framed but lacking the plumb-bob science of a carpenter's educated eye. There was something else odd about the place, something that he was not concerned enough about now to ponder seated at the front window of his family home studying the terrain and memorizing the length of the town by the number of random laid-out blocks, and getting a feel for how close the outermost tents stood from the creek, recalling the things that Aunt Grace had told him while Dunsmore was busy transforming a tree trunk into twigs.

As the sun dipped toward the west range and shadows sprouted in hillside depressions and spilled down to the creek and up across the dark mansion, that odd something, a subtle play of light, which had registered vaguely on his eyes, finally emerged. The windows of Baxter's house, the dozens large and small planted across walls low and high, were bright yellow from a light so strong that—even as Draco had sat in this place a quarter mile up the mountain at high noon— his eyes had sensed but not really seen an ethereal shimmer too strong to be doused by something as subservient in this valley as the bounty of the sun. These were the windows of a house lit night and day, and the only kind of men Draco could recall having encountered on his travels who had kept their lights on night and day were men for whom the party never stopped, and men who lived in fear.

chapter fifteen

The moon, gibbous when it had been tracking him during all these recent decisive days, hung full now and white-cheeked, its chin resting on the eastern ridge above Baxter's mansion. The light of the gone sun bounced off its ashen fields and entered the room as a rectangle, where Draco sat working his tongue between two teeth, tugging at a thread of meat chewed from a sandwich packed by Aunt Grace at dawn.

He opened the burlap bag and looked at the nest of twigs glowing silver inside, that tangle of luminescence that constituted his ticket into the lives of strangers. He closed the bag and stood up, put on his hat, and considered the bedroll for a moment, then chucked it beneath the table and headed for the back door.

He found a path at the edge of the plateau where the property line ended and the forest began. There was a wagon track that hairpinned slowly down the slope, but this other path was an easy hike a quarter-mile drop to the town below, a remembered beeline route to the stores. Eroded, weedy, stone-tumbled, and uncleared, it hadn't been hiked in a long time. As he slipped and picked his way down through the trees, the town sounds grew louder. The odors, which mingled with and then overwhelmed the fragrance of pine, grew richer: kerosene fire and barbecue, hot bread, cider, and the shaved-wood and axle-grease stink of a boomtown crowded with customers.

He came out of the tree line at the north end of town and walked a gentle rocky slope down toward the central road which, he now realized, led to the gap cliffs above Aunt Grace's house. He looked north where the road ran into the woods. Tree trunks grew across its centerline. The road died there.

He glanced up at the moon, which had lifted a bit off the ridge. The black sky shot full of shining holes, in all his travels he had never seen stars so large and close. There was not enough light in this town to diminish that show, only flames at the tops of grease-soaked poles posted at intersections all down the main drag and its offshoot alleys and aisles.

Pedestrians crowded the aisles. There were no cars here, no mechanical means of transportation other than the blacksmith-fashioned frames of carriages and wagons, and the soft leather machinery of bits and traces and cinched saddles on horses fabricating their own farm-sweet, benevolent, earthy pollution. No trucks. No diesel. No stop signs here.

He slung the bag over his left shoulder to keep his right hand free and headed toward the flap-roped stake-driven outskirt tents where hawkers plied their wares displayed on weathered shelves of sawn and balanced plank. Braided into all the talk and tang of cooked meats were notes of music plucked, strummed, thumped, or pucker-blown by leather-hatted young people draped in blanket robes belted at the waist, alone or in groups with their hats upturned on the ground for a coin tossed by a passing pleased audience.

The long arm of mercantile ballyhoo grabbed at Draco's ears crying, "Potent elixirs!" and pointing at clay bowls heaped with colored powders blended to increase the bounty of crops, of cattle, of children, or to heal the afflicted infirm. Cries of "Eats!" spit-cooked and sliced for your inspection, roast beef, chicken, smoked ham, beets, corn, carrots, cherry pie, and pumpkin di-rect from the vine! He mingled with the moving stream of men carting shouldered long rifles accompanying bonneted women hugging sacked purchases, hill people as well as men who looked like they might have wandered in from the river bottoms of outside industrial cities seeking a brew to cure disease or embellish some secret-tended desire.

There was magic in the food too—Draco's mouth watered with a whiff of some leavened treat as he passed a wooden booth, thinking that a man could ride in here flush and walk home bust if he didn't have a little magic of his own to put some backbone into a spoken "No thanks."

Permanent buildings began appearing as he drew closer to the center of town, shack booths with front walls raised revealing countertops, and small shops glass-windowed with doors that shut and locked. And further up, stone-founded buildings, hotel, saloon, and hardware, the old town where Mary Draco and William might have shopped shoulder to shoulder with Valley Forge vets of the Rebellion, before Baxter was even born.

The swinging doors of a flat-fronted unadorned two-story building creaked with the exit of a drunk stumbling into the street singing a mountain serenade. A gripped hat rose up at the flash of his unsteady passing, its sweat-soiled brim upturned and empty in a shaking hand. "Charity, neighbor?" But the voice booze-tuned with lyrics and laughter blended with the endless mumbling stroll of street traffic, and the hat dropped back down to the cross-legged lap of a small man seated on a wood-plank sidewalk outside the saloon door where a beggar might catch a customer made newly generous by the product sold therein.

Draco stopped on the street and looked down at the shabby-suited man, hair gone white at the fringes, stubble unchecked on his cheeks and chin, one hand holding onto the empty hat on his lap and the other clutching the crudely carved struts of a pair of wooden crutches padded with rag tops. The man leaned forward to stroke the ends of his legs, which were stretched out dangerously into foot traffic, to massage flesh cupped in hand-crafted leather where his missing feet ought to be.

A silver dollar hit with a soft pat in the center of his hat, and the man pulled his legs in and grabbed the coin quick. He lifted his face grinning and nodding and hoping to prime one more token out of this stranger. "Thank you kindly, sir," he said.

Draco squatted and looked into the watery vein-reddened eyes of this old man with the facial features of a boy smiling rings of wrinkled flesh onto his cheeks. "Evening, brother," Draco said, rolling the burlap bag off his shoulder and setting it on the sidewalk. The beggar leaned to look as Draco drew wide the top, letting a silver glow sparkle onto both of their faces. "Would you be interested in buying some dream root?"

The beggar leaned his face into the burlap and took a deep sniff, then sat back shaking his suspicious head no. "What is it?" he said, quickly shoving the silver coin deep inside his pants pocket.

Draco dipped two fingers into the bag and plucked a single twig and held it up. "Herb," he said. "You boil it into a tea and drink it to cure hangovers."

The shaking no slowed, but those watery eyes stayed fixed rather forlornly on that lit curing stick. "I could use some of that, I guess. But I use all my money to buy hangovers."

Draco spread his fingers and let the twig drop into the man's hat. "Free sample," he said. "Tell your friends about it."

The man lifted the twig out of the hat and squinted at the silver glow that accentuated the once youthful blue of his booze-bleached eyes. "Thank you, brother."

"What's your name?"

"Parker."

"Tell me, Parker. I'm new in town. Can you recommend a good saloon around here?"

Parker started chuckling, his squat body rag-tattered like a tossed bag on the sidewalk shaking. His mirth inexplicable, he shook his head as his right hand touched the pocketed rim-bulge of that single coin. "Take your pick," he said, pulling himself together. "They're all the same. They all serve the same stuff." And he spat out his final comment like a reflexive hawk of derision: "Baxter's moonshine."

Draco nodded and looked the man over, looked at the leather cuffs and white hairless ankles bound with dirty cotton wrappings coming loose. "Are you all right?" he said.

Parker grinned, and something like a wink started up in one eye, but fell apart unrealized.

"You take it easy, brother," Draco said, standing up.

The small man nodded, scooted back against the wall of the saloon, and picked up his hat.

Draco moved on down the sidewalk toward the crossroad, the heart of the main drag where the buildings were highest and oldest, unpainted planks split here and there where ancient foundations had shifted and settled, though the yellow windows still shone brightly, delivering their womanly shadows and songs to passersby.

"Plant 'em wet and bury 'em deep!" barked a voice from a frame booth erected on a corner of the intersection, four shuttered walls open to the wind, its low shelves stocked with things growing green in clay cups. A man and a woman were examining a buy as they listened to the top-hatted vendor in black.

"They grow best under the light of the planter's moon," he said, and they nodded as he wrapped it up, a sack of seed. The couple trudged away, farmers hunched beneath the thick fabric of their sensible clothing, peeking satisfied into the bag.

Draco approached the booth and looked up at a sign painted with a bad brush on the marquee board overhead,

The Legend of Carl Draco

DELGADO'S, said vendor wiping the dust of his latest sale off his hands and pulling from a vest pocket the thin stick of a black cheroot. He examined the crisp wrinkled leaf and slid it under his nose, poked pockets for a match, and watched out of the corner of his eye this new customer, a tall road-dusty plough jockey setting a small sack of burlap on the counter.

"Are you open for barter?" Draco said.

Delgado revived the same grin that he'd used on the farmers, a fine black wash of short bristle stretching across his chin and upper lip as he slipped the cigar unlit into his shirt pocket. "Always," he said. "And how are you tonight, sir?"

"Tired," Draco said. "I come a long way today."

"New in town?"

"That's right."

"Where do you hail from?"

"Mount Shasta, California."

"Well now . . . and what did you bring to barter from the land of milk and honey?"

Draco made a slow show of untying the drawstring, working the knot and allowing a little impatience to simmer in the mind of his potential customer. He spread the neck wide and tilted the hole toward Delgado, who frowned at the pretty tangle, then took off his top hat and leaned in and gave it a sniff.

"What is it?"

"Dream root," Draco said. "It's an herb. Keeps a woman faithful to her man."

Delgado placed his hat on his head smiling, his tongue caressing a back tooth as he pondered this curious piece of information. "Love-potion, huh?"

Draco nodded. "Gaar-an-teed."

Delgado folded his arms and puckered his lips and made a wise sucking sound with his tongue. "I deal in elixirs that improve the abundance of crops, so I wouldn't have much use for your herb . . . neither commercially nor personally." He

125

cleared his throat and raised his eyebrows, and Draco braced himself for the slap of a fastball wink. But the swain merely made another wise sucking sound and pointed east down the road. "However, there is a woman you might want to talk to. Her name is Melanie. She has a little storefront yonder dealing in love-potions and suchlike. She might be interested in what you have to offer."

Draco glanced down the street and nodded. He clasped the sack closed and tied it off and slapped it over his shoulder.

Delgado tapped him on the sleeve. "Before you shove off, friend, how about taking a look at a special that I'm offering tonight only."

"Fair enough," Draco said, setting his bag back on the counter.

Delgado reached down and came up with a small square-bottomed clay cup but held his free hand above it, hiding the main attraction from view.

"You got a girlfriend?" he said and kept right on rolling before Draco could answer. "I would expect that a man who deals in love-potions probably breaks more than his fair share of hearts in any given week. But do you got one special lady?"

"One or two," Draco said.

Delgado grinned big as he set the cup down and ground his front teeth lightly, waiting for Draco's reaction to the unveiling of a stem four inches high bearing six leaves, the stem itself drab green but the leaves veneered with a fine frost of gold that sparkled in the torchlight.

Delgado held a finger beneath a leaf as if he intended to raise it, but did not touch it. "Twenty-four-carat harvest."

"Handy item," Draco said.

"It won't make you rich. In a year you might scrape off a hundred dollars' worth, if you tend it careful."

"Does it do anything besides look pretty?"

"It's strictly ornamental, but the ladies love it. Makes a fine gift for engagements, weddings, anniversaries, and

The Legend of Carl Draco

surreptitious rendezvous in general."

Draco whipped his head once to the side, properly awed, and made a wise sucking sound of his own, then picked up his bag and tossed it over his shoulder. "Sorry, friend, but it looks like neither of us is buying this trip."

"Fair's fair," Delgado replied, setting the item back down beneath the counter.

The four directions out of the intersection were packed solid with bodies finding their own natural unimpeded pedestrian currents along the boot-rumbled sidewalks. Draco entered the flow east and walked among men dressed like himself, anonymous, his head bowed in a crowd that didn't shove or push, people who seemed to know exactly where they were headed, exactly what mercantile establishments they had come to this valley town to visit again, in no particular hurry to get anywhere, a crowd made friendly by the ironclad promise of satisfactions gaar-an-teed.

The shop was no more than a shack, but its checkerboard-paned wood-frame glass lit by colored candles made it seem larger, a glowing jewel shooting colored lights painting passing faces. Draco looked up at the marquee, pink paint stroked with care forming block letters doing business as MELANIE'S. Through the squares of glass, beyond squat cylinders of window-dressing wax and fired wick, sat the proprietress, high on a stool behind a cash-register counter, fanning a deck of playing cards in her hands. Cheek beauty mark, red lipstick, red hair brushed high and combed in flowing curls, her pale green dress was high-waisted with a split-revealing dance-hall-madame blouse. At her back, cups clay and glass bedecked shelves heaped with rainbowed powders. Beaded lapidary art hung strung on gold display-board chain.

Chimes overhead danced as Draco pushed the front door open. Melanie glanced up at him with a smile of experience manufactured to warm and welcome the nervous lovesick

127

braced to seek her help. "Good evening," she said, and the fan of cards in her hand fluttered and clicked square and disappeared up a wide sleeve.

"Evening," Draco said, closing the door tight and removing his hat. Amid hot candle odor, punk coals, and the honey-sweet reek of a flower garden run riot, he breathed in through his nose—and unbeckoned memories of warm, soft bodies embraced at dawn rolled over in his mind. He shut it off and grinned at the woman and walked five steps to the counter.

Melanie leaned toward him, casting a dizzying perfume of her own. Her deep blue eyes took his measure, as might a cop or an undertaker. "Whom . . . ," she said, "may I help you with?"

Draco set the burlap on the counter and tapped it lightly. "A man named Delgado recommended your place of business. He said you might be interested in looking at what I got to sell."

That sort of transaction. The smile remained fixed on her face but lost a layer of light. This man was only a salesman seeking his earned commission. But everyone falls in love, even salesmen. "Happy to take a look," she said.

Draco yanked the drawstring loose and batted the top open. He picked up a single twig and held it toward Melanie, who only glanced at it, her head motionless and ladylike. She did not dip to sniff. "What is it?"

"Dream root," Draco said. "For lovers only."

Faint fish-eyes rolling up amused, she latched onto Draco's eyes and studied him a doubtful moment before reaching out and letting him drop the product onto her palm. Her fingers closed over it, wrestled it gently, felt its length and texture, then she raised her hand and lightly passed it in front of her face for a dainty silent inhalation of essence.

She held it between thumb and forefinger, rolling and compressing the curved knotted sprig. "I'm not familiar with this root," she said.

The Legend of Carl Draco

"Grows in the Orient," Draco said. "Young lovers place it under their mattresses. It hides private conversations from listening ears."

Melanie cocked her head back and chuckled openmouthed with a glance at the ceiling, shaping that scene in her imagination. Then dropped her head and fixed him with one eye opened, one eye closed, as if seriously considering taking offense at the vivid boudoir intimacy implied. "Now who would be listening in on a thing like that?"

Draco shrugged. "I hear it's mighty crowded in China."

Her fabricated glare softened and she stood up off the stool and made a simple pirouette holding the twig high until its silver veneer seemed to grab hold of the light from the candles. Lowered again, it glowed briefly like the bulbous tail of a lightning bug fading.

With her back to him she passed it unseen beneath her nose and inhaled deeply, gazing vacantly for one moment, unable to attach a memory, a name, a place, to this scent.

She turned to Draco, leaned across the counter, and looked down at his boots, at the pants puffed out a bit at the knees, at the coat that didn't look cut to fit him, like it might have once belonged to someone else. "I've never seen you around here before," she said.

"This is the first time I've ever been to Chuckney."

"Is that so?" She folded her arms and squinted at him. "I'd say those clothes were bought in this town."

Draco dropped his eyes to look down the rumpled length of his coatfront. He brushed at a housefly that wasn't there. "Maybe," he said. "They once belonged to another man of my family. We're fairly footloose. I hail from Mount Shasta."

Melanie nodded, and rotated the twig with all its contained and unfamiliar magic, turned it this way and that like a lepidopterist mystified by an unfamiliar butterfly pinned and framed. "Interesting item," she said, then held it out to Draco. "But I do not believe there would be much call for dream root

Gary Reilly

in this valley."

"You never can tell who's listening."

She let the twig drop onto his palm. "It ain't that crowded here."

Her irises, blue when Draco had entered, were green now, pale like the color of her long high-waisted skirt. She could change the color of her eyes, but whether willful or dependent upon a mood, Draco could not tell, until he put a question to her gaar-an-teed to change her mood.

"I'm told there's a man who runs this town with a short leash," he said. "A bully, goes by the name of Baxter."

The green drained, leaving in its place a cold, dispassionate, and distancing gray, matching the faded smile and the sudden and peculiar disappearance of her pleasing perfume. She crossed her arms and raised her chin, studying this stranger anew. "I like living here," she said slowly. "I always have." Frost didn't shoot out of her mouth—it merely coated each spoken word.

Draco nodded and busied his hands clasping closed the burlap, busied himself as if refusing to acknowledge the significance of her reply. He tied it off and slung it over his shoulder, reached up and pinched the brim of his hat. "I'm new in town, just got in this evening, and consequently I'm unfamiliar with the lay of the land. By any chance could you recommend a hotel or a rooming house where I might spend the night?"

Arms akimbo, her right hand toying with a thread on a sleeve, Melanie gave him a good study hat-to-toe and everything in between. "We have a half dozen hotels in town," she said. "Bachelor quarters, and places for families. Anyone on the street can point one out to you. Are you married?"

"Not yet," he said.

The deep rich blue sparkle trickled back into her irises, and the candle-scented air parted to make room for her revitalized perfume, an odor that might induce a man to get married, or

130

at least to consider its pros and cons the way a whiff of baked pie will induce hunger, or the way the iron odor of foam on a short beer can start a man thinking about stepping through a pair of swinging doors.

"You're not yet thirty," Melanie said. "I can tell if a man has peaked thirty. You've got years left. It's a pity you have no use for your dream root." She smiled wide and swept out from behind the counter with a rustle of silk, moved to a side wall where glass-bottled and bag-packed potions rested on shelved display. She reached high into the woven bowl of a long wicker basket where cloth packets of colored powder lay scattered. "I can sell you a philter that I guarantee will make any woman take a practical interest in the fundamental comforts of your being."

She held up a powdery pink packet reeking of rose, which shaped on Draco's face an uncontrollable smile as he pondered the raging power that drives the velvet fist of romance.

"Got to make a living first," he said. "Got no time for a family."

Hammer a hornet's nest, poke a sharp stick at a rattler, but don't talk nonsense to this woman. Draco saw in her irises a quick flash of red run around the rims like a sunstruck rainbow trout leaping, though it was not so much anger as disgust. And was that not the faint odor of brimstone he smelled?

Melanie lowered the packet looking at him without expression, her thoughts strangleheld as she gauged again this stranger before her, this good-looking unattached male carcass unswayed by her pitch. She put the packet back in the basket.

"Naw," Draco continued, "if I can't unload this dream root in town, I got to move on," talking to a smile that was not personal now, was kept on her face for all her customers, and he knew it. Melanie walked back behind the counter, reached up a sleeve, and brought out the deck of cards. She began shuffling.

"You come back after you're thirty," Melanie said in a not-unfriendly tone. "I get lonely men crawling in here ten years after their first visit, pleading for my assistance." She tapped the deck square and said rather dryly, "Men like you got to learn the hard way."

Draco glanced at the door, then looked back at Melanie as though reluctant to leave. "You remind me of my older sister," he said. "And two female cousins, and an aunt who lives near Belle Fourche. Their existence is bitter with the knowledge that I am elusive prey."

Melanie didn't look up at him, attending to the winged blur of her quick shuffle, but a smile raw and pleased stretched her cheeks. With a flat-palmed, swift, practiced sweep she spread the cards in an arc across the countertop. Draco looked down at the fine white lines crosshatched on the blazing red rectangles. Melanie moved her right hand back and forth above the cards, and with a snap of her middle finger knocked one out of the deck. She lifted and looked at it, and her smile faded. The pleasant odors of the room itself seemed to fade along with her smile, until there was only the dank stink of aged wooden walls. Melanie looked at Draco and asked in a voice gone level, "Who are you, mister?"

"My name is Jack McCall."

Melanie held the playing card with its back to him, then turned it around so he could see it. A high card. A face card. A king.

Draco nodded. "Thank you for your time, ma'am." He touched the brim of his hat, then turned and opened the door. The batted bells danced and sang his exit into the night.

chapter sixteen

A top hat leans past the shoulder of a man fingering black soil packed into a clay pot, and the sharp eyes beneath the brim peer to watch a shadow darken, and then let light flow through, the doorway to Melanie's shop.

Delgado stands upright but stays hidden behind the blocking bulk of an interested customer as that stranger with odd barter on his back comes this way again. He watches the man, who enters the intersection and stands a moment scratching his chin with a single finger before moving north toward the high flat false front of one of Baxter's many loud saloons, watches until the man makes a shadow pushing the swinging doors open. Delgado raises a finger to catch the attention of two men who are loping slowly against the grain of traffic, two tall leather-clad, black-hatted men with hip-slung slug-studded belts and holstered pistols. Their long coats hang open displaying their armory, their stride is sure, and when they see Delgado's cue they part the browsing crowd unhurried.

Draco let the doors swing at his back as he stood a moment taking in the layout: long bar to his left supporting elbows wet with spilt hooch, the tables and chairs crowded with laughing women and men fingering dealt cards. At the far end of the high-ceilinged, dark-beamed, candle-chandeliered room was a stage made for dance-hall diversion, where a single man sat upon a wooden chair working the strings of an acoustic guitar. Long blond hair hanging across a bowed serious face, his hat lay upright near his right toe tapping out his tune's time as fingers pressed chords and a fanning hand stroked requested melodies.

The populated tables near the stage tossed coins and applauded, but the crowd at this end of the room, the rowdies splashing drinks and tossing bets, horse-laughed at their own wit and called for rags from a big-boned weary waitress pretty in the face, who hauled a tray high between card players as she attended to her job.

The bartender popped jug corks and filled tin cups with moonshine, and not far from him, swaybacked with damp elbows holding him upright, sat Parker, his crutches leaning against the bar at his side.

Draco moved off toward the wall to his right where a table was being vacated by a couple bound by the miracle of drink, who staggered past him waist-held toward the exit and their newly discovered romance. He pulled out an empty chair and sat down as the waitress wiped the table and slapped the rag onto her tray. "What can I get you?"

"Whiskey."

She grinned and poked a cheek with a tongue, rearranged the weight of her tray, and leaned close. "You can have moonshine or moonshine."

"Bring me a cup," Draco said.

She walked away. Draco lowered his bag to the floor and heard the delicate four-footed click and thin whinny of a horse. He turned to a table where three standing women hovered around a seated man holding a short stick leapt by a gimcrack steed no larger than a beer bottle. Its fine hooves struck and sprayed spilt hooch as it cantered, shaking the cotton fluff of its white mane. The women clapped and

The Legend of Carl Draco

moaned as the toy stallion trotted abruptly into the open doorway of a hand-carved breadbox of a stable. The owner snapped the lid closed.

"Dollar," the waitress said, placing a tin cup filled with moonshine in front of Draco. He reached into a coat pocket and pulled out two coins. "This is for you," he said. "And how are you this fine evening?"

"Tired," she said, scooping up both dollars.

Draco grabbed the bag off the floor and set it next to his cup. "If you've got a moment, I've got something here you might like to take a look at."

She sighed adjusting the balance of her tray, saying, "I got customers to wait on, cowboy," and started to move off. But as Draco opened the sack wide, the burning silver glow caught the woman's eye. She paused and gave it a second look. Draco reached in, chose a twig, and held it up. "Interested in buying some dream root?"

She glanced once at the bartender, once across the heads of the noisy crowd shouting for immediate service, and looked back down. "What is it?"

"An herb," Draco said. "You boil it up and make a tea. Drink it down and you can see your lover's dreams."

She looked up at the beams delighted, and laughed loud enough that a few heads turned to see what new business was coming down. Best joke all night, she shook her head and looked Draco in the eye, looked serious. "Sounds like a dangerous item to me."

"Could be, I suppose," he said with a shrug.

But she didn't go away, she looked at that pile of bagged light on the table and sucked at her cheeks, a vague and distant expression smoothing the bought lines of nightly labor on her face. Then she shook it off, shook her head fast, and reached to catch and place a sliding cup on her tray. "I don't need to buy any trouble, mister. I got troubles enough."

She walked away, grabbing the rag and snapping it like

135

a soft bullwhip at her side. The last thumbed wire stretched across a hollow wood hole shivered into silence, and coins spun into the musician's weighted hat. Applause strong at the stage-end of the room rippled lesser down the chairs toward the front door. A lull marked by the dull knock of tin cups tabled and muttering voices mulling over cards settled on the house. Draco sipped at the stiff room-temperature recent vintage and watched as old customers called it a night and stumbled outside past new customers coming in, including two men with gun belts exposed stepping up to the bar and looking the room over as they signaled for a drink each.

His cup sipped dry, Parker set it down and nudged it toward the bartender, who stood twisting a wet cup with a dry towel above a sink. Cheeks glowing with a buck's worth of hooch pink, Parker grinned at the man and said, "How about one on the house?" and waited with teeth gritted, desperate behind his smile.

The mustache in the apron glanced sidewise but kept on working. "Give it up, Parker."

A standard response, but the one thing Parker would not give up was his smile. It was his last medium of exchange. He raised one empty hand like a working man who'd maybe left his purse at home but was good for a tab anytime. "I'm bust," and his hand dropped on its back on the bar, the fingers spread showing his comic worth, but it was a pleading reach.

"Yesterday's news," the bartender said, setting the dried cup on a spread towel and dipping his fist into the sink searching for new tin.

"Hey Parker, I got two dollars for ya!"

Parker looked around, kept the smile nailed squarely onto his face showing all his teeth until his eyes finally roosted on a buckskinned bearded trapper slouched with impolite outstretched booted legs blocking the aisle. Partying at his table were two laughing females and a sullen man holding an unattended fan of clubs and diamonds.

The Legend of Carl Draco

The trapper dragged his legs in and leaned forward looking at Parker, then opened a cupped hand to display the candleshine of two silver dollars. He slapped the coins onto the table. "All ya gotta do is walk over here and get 'em . . ." Parker reached for his crutches and made to move off the stool, but the man continued talking. "Without," he said, setting his condition, "using your wooden legs."

Parker stopped feeling for the floor with his leather-cupped stumps and sat frozen—not counting the ceaseless DT trembling of his forearms and fingers—digesting the single condition of this challenge.

Notes plucked onstage faded into the silence of conversations abruptly stopped and the soft sound of necks brushing coat collars turning to see just what lengths Parker would subject his threadbare pride to for one more chance to indulge in his admitted weakness. Was there a person in this room who had not walked past that hungover wretch with his hat outthrust from a gutter at dawn? A man you stepped around carefully, and thought twice, and twice again, about dropping a piece of silver into his hat. Compassion came with a price in his case. The people watching counted the weeks since last they'd helped him out, mute faces fixed on the face of a man whose tongue tip finally worked his lips apart, thirsty and calculating the odds. The silver dollars glowed like promises beneath the wax chandeliers: two guarantees, two bucks worth two cups brimful, and two shorn legs to gather them up.

"Two dollars," the man said. "That's a lotta hooch."

Parker let the crutches bounce lightly back against the bar and slid his baggy pants to the edge of his stool. Gripping the bar with one hand, he stretched his right leg down to the sawdust-sprinkled floor, where the leather cuff touched and settled, its hand-sewn stitches bulging as his leg weight filled it full.

His eyes remained fixed on those two coins, which helped

ease all thought of the pain spreading at the balled base of his ankle. He let his left leg dangle until it touched the floor, sliding until the small of his back was braced against the edge of his stool. Chairs creaked and clothes rustled as witnesses leaned forward for a better view of his chest rising and sinking as he swallowed hard working up his courage and energy while studying the short distance to those two damn laughing minted eyes.

A woman shouted, "Fetch it, Parker!" and he kicked off striding on stumbling cuffs scraping floorboards in the silence with a lip-tight muffled whimper and traveled five steps with his eyes anchored to his payday, until pain buckled his knees with his final step. Arms windmilling wild, he fell face forward toward the howling laughter of the trapper, and as he toppled, Parker let fly a panicked squeal and grabbed the edge of the table.

And held.

Held himself braced with neither knee touching the floor, saying "I done it!"

The trapper's sublime amusement faded seeing Parker working both elbows like a drowning man hauling himself into the haven of a rescue boat.

The trapper slammed a palm down on the coins. "You fell, Parker. Sorry. You lose."

Parker's intake of breath lifted him a bit. It was the only sound in the room. Not one head turned, not one strut of wood glued against wood creaked. The only movements inside this room besides the shake of indifferent flames overhead were the eyes of the audience darting from Parker to this hairsplitting welsher and back.

Fists balled beneath his chest, the rate of Parker's breathing increased as he looked at the level dark glare of the trapper, whose face was still settling from its creased mirth with eyelids lowering wearily and growing disinterested. The game was over.

The Legend of Carl Draco

"But I done it!" Parker said with red watery orbs jerking from the trapper's face to the black-haired sunburned breadth of the man's masking hand, his eyes flitting up and down with new panic afraid that the hand, and the treasure beneath it, and the table supporting his shivering lame legs, might all disappear in one unbearable blink.

"Hit the road," the man said, leaning back and aiming his chin at the woman next to him, whose cautious eyes waited for a cue to break the silence. The trapper grinned, raised his eyebrows, and dropped a gap-toothed jaw, rolling a bubble of laughter around on his tongue.

Turning their heads away, afraid that this mountain man might catch an eye and take offense and call someone else out, the crowd went back to its own business, picking up cups and filling mouths gone dry, striking matches to light cigars or packed bowls, and fanning forgotten poker suits. The musician grabbed his chair and tugged it a few inches to one side finding just the right spot, then sat idly picking at the tied-off strings of his unopened songs. All this risen clink and chatter and card shuffling and cork popping muted the heavy sound of Parker's defeated body collapsing to the floor.

He gave up his smile then. He knelt like a dog, leaning forward holding himself aright with sawdust-encrusted fingers splayed. The feeblest cough hopped a few times from his slack lips, and two sniffs snorted to still something leaking from his nose or his soul were unheard too below the table and the sounds of the indifferent crowd.

Draco felt ribs shaken by sobs hanging fire in Parker's stifled throat as he lifted the man off the floor. Poleaxed by something more brutal than alcohol, Parker's head swung side to side, his world surrendered unequivocally to grief, his eyes focused vaguely on something beyond the walls of the bar, beyond the lights of the town, beyond the steepled peaks of the valley.

He wasn't much help holding himself aright as Draco

escorted him bodily back to the barstool. But when Parker felt the solid and familiar support of the seat, he finally hauled in his drifting thoughts and bundled his fading motor skills for one last minuscule wad of effort, and manufactured a motion almost too small to be categorized as a show of gratitude: a nod that went down but didn't quite make it back up. His throat gave up a feeble, well-intentioned "Thanks" that died on the vine. His eyes rolled up just high enough to stare at— reflected in the bar-length gilt-edged silver-backed mirror— the calamity that was his life.

Then he noticed the man standing right beside him, gripping a familiar hank of burlap. It was that dream root drummer, new in town, peddling hangover cures.

"Bartender, give this man a pint," Draco said. He tossed a gold eagle, which began spinning, and continued to spin, and kept right on spinning until the heads of a few curious people seated nearby glanced over to look at the flashing fuzzy globe of gold with its mosquito coin-ring song singing on the hardwood bar.

"Keep the change," Draco said as the bartender set a blown-glass bottle down and smacked the hard cash flat. Draco slid the bottle directly in front of Parker. "It's on me, brother."

Parker's eyes went into action as a team, focusing on the clear warped glass flask full to its carved cork. He reached out and touched the cool shoulder of the bottle, then looked up and shifted his focus, wondering why anyone in this town would waste a single moment of their time, much less a penny of their poke, on him.

He hacked a shot of air clearing his vocal cords, then nodded and lifted his chin, "Thank you, mister." His eyes were drawn to that gripped sack top. His hand crawled crabwise down his coat to a soiled slit of a pocket. A muscle on the side of his face lifted a corner of his lip with a grin of private business shared as he pulled out the complimentary twig and held it up to Draco. "Make any sales tonight?"

The Legend of Carl Draco

"No luck so far," Draco said, giving his head a mock sorrowful shake.

Parker smiled at the twig, contemplating its benevolence, a boon to his ilk. But time was being squandered on useless talk. He couldn't wait to give this gift a trial run. He pocketed the twig and the bottle of moonshine, grabbed his crutches and said, "Thanks again, mister," and swung from the barstool vaulting expertly toward the doors, ignoring a certain sonofabitch eyeing him with unconcealed contempt.

Draco collected his change and waited until the doors fanned with Parker's passing before he walked over to the table where that sonofabitch gripping his tin cup muttered at his silent companions and tried to ignore the newly arrived and uninvited visitor.

"You owe me two dollars," Draco said, pointing at the coins still lying on the table.

The man took a drink and set the cup down, refusing to acknowledge Draco's presence. But a new and even thicker silence settled over the room, until the trapper finally was forced to raise his head due to the drilling sensation of near a hundred eyes waiting on him to make his move.

He leaned back and looked up Draco's lean length. Boots and hat, clothing in general favored by sodbusters, and though the stranger's hands were tanned and scarred on the backs, they were oddly soft in the palms, which didn't look like they had ever been on very close terms with manual labor. "The hell you say?"

"Parker won the bet."

The man glanced around the revived arena, then shook his head no. "He fell. Everyone here seen it."

Draco raised his chin and indicated the far side of the room. "I was sitting all the way over against that wall, but I had a pretty good view of the action and I say Parker made it to the table without hitting the floor."

The man rolled his tongue against a cheek like chaw and

looked down at the tabletop, then scooted his chair in and proceeded to concentrate solely on drinking. But his snub was interrupted by the appearance of Draco's hand reaching for the two disputed dollars. The trapper followed suit and beat him to it with a hand-slam over the coins, barking "Hit the road!" while his face wrinkled like the snarled snout of a riled cur.

Draco's hand drove down and slapped flat against the back of the trapper's splayed ham. The crowd silence seemed to part to make room in the air for a sizzle of ozone crackling between the dueling men. Draco startled the fixated audience by making a snatching move, turning his hand over revealing the two silver coins nestled in his open palm.

The trapper turned his own hand upright revealing nothing but tabletop.

Draco dropped the take into his coat pocket, walked to the wing doors, and stepped outside. All eyes shifted to the seated man with his hand still hovering above the table, a frowning man wondering whether or not it might be to his disadvantage to follow up on a move like that.

Two cups settled on the bar, and four boots thumped the floor in Draco's wake, ending the silence. Two men with gun belts exposed headed toward the gently rocking doors.

Draco moved up the sidewalk past people standing outside shop windows gazing at tinkered kitchen devices new and used. He looked through a window at smoke-shop pipe and pouch accouterment on display, which made him recall Dunsmore's delight with the ritual of a properly packed bowl. But the image faded with the heavy tag of a paw on his shoulder. He turned and faced two mountain men crowding him with the reek of that ritual chewed leaking from their lips. He noted the odor of oiled gun barrels rising from their hips. "Evening, gentlemen."

"You selling something?" one man said, speaking with the dangerously polite inquisitiveness of all men who are blessed

The Legend of Carl Draco

with authority.

"That's a fact," Draco said, thinking he'd never stood so close to two wide-brimmed shadows who'd lived long afterwards. "What's it to you?"

The man's mouth smiled, but the rest of his face stayed out of it. "We been told you're new in town, so you wouldn't know. We're deputies. My name is Pike and my partner here is Hays, and I asked you a question."

Draco turned his chin toward the bag draped over his shoulder. "I'm selling dream root."

"What's that?"

He swung the bag down and worked the drawstring open for them to see. "It's an herb. You boil it into a tea and sip it like a medicine to get rid of bad dreams. It chases the bastards clear back to whatever private hell they came from."

The two deputies leaned in and sniffed the stock.

"You got a license to sell that?" Hays said, looking up squint-eyed with a doubtful voice.

"No," Draco said.

Hays drew back with a sigh implying affront. "You can't sell nothing in this town without a license."

The pedestrian traffic that had been nudging the sidewalk conversation began to flow out into the street, the passing people deliberately avoiding eye contact with Pike or Hays or the unarmed answering man.

"I wasn't aware that I needed a license," Draco said.

Pike grinned and gave his head a little acquiescent shake disposed to offer slack. "You can buy all you want in Chuckney, but you got to get permission from the high sheriff if you want to sell anything. There's a levy."

"Who's the high sheriff in this town?" Draco said.

"Baxter."

Draco nodded, chewed on the inside of a cheek thoughtfully, then leaned toward them and spoke with a voice muted toward conspiracy. "He probably don't know I'm in town. So

143

why don't you fellas just forget about it?"

Socking fists onto hips, Hays leaned into Draco's face. "Say what?"

"I'll even part with a couple of free samples just to set things right between us," Draco said, digging into his bag.

Hays grabbed his wrist. "What the hell you saying?"

Draco eased his hand out of the bag and the grip. "I'm just saying, why don't you let me off? What's it to you what I'm doing?"

"I told you, we're deputies," Pike said. "It's our job to see that all vendors are duly licensed."

Draco stepped back a pace and bumped up against the smoke-shop window. "If you're the law in town, how come I don't see no badges?"

Hays reached down and unholstered a long-barreled revolver. "What's your name, mister?"

"Jack McCall."

"I think you better come along with us, Jack McCall." He placed the muzzle near Draco's nose and gave the barrel a couple of sidewise twitches, indicating the desired direction of travel.

Struck planks echoed with the sounds of boots moving a little faster than the average stroll of shopping people, echoed against the wooden walls of a darkened alley between a saloon and a two-story hotel where Parker sat with his back against the soaked bulge of a water barrel, raising a blown-glass bottleneck to his lips. He lowered it, licking driblets tickling his stubbled chin, and looked up at three men passing by. Draco looked over at the upturned empty hat on Parker's lap as the panhandler stretched his neck to get a better view of the guns and the faces of the deputies, who, as they passed, saw discarded clothes stacked in a heap shaped like a man, a gutter bum engaged in his nightly habit. Parker's eyes did not turn away from those coldhearted glances. They locked on with a hatred that sparkled bold, unafraid, and impotent.

The Legend of Carl Draco

Just before Draco looked ahead toward his destination, he saw Parker's eyes drop, saw his head bow to the empty hat propped between his crossed legs, as though that afflicted scrounger could not bear to witness the sight of a man being led under the gun to the house where Baxter ruled the valley.

chapter seventeen

Moonlit cheeks ballooning among cattail stalks rustling along the steep banks of the creek, a concealed chorus croaked love-calls as tongues shot at winged things laying eggs in the slough. The damp crooked spine of the valley was the dominion of the frog, but the undirected chirrup of the choir ceased abruptly with the hollow thud of three men stepping onto the wooden bridge.

Draco crossed over glancing down the length of the creek, which curved toward the meeting of the two ridges south. He stepped off the bridge onto a naked fan of earth that sloped half a hundred yards up to a low fence demarcating the front yard of Baxter's mansion . . . and the moment his foot touched the damp earth, he heard the music of a frantic fiddle and stretched-leather timpani marking time behind the backup chords of banjos and guitars. Yellow candlelight scored a rectangle on the trammeled path leading to the open door where no guards were posted, a sincere and arrogant message to thieves.

Pike and Hays led him past a useless gate tipped aside. He looked up at the wide front face of the house with its yellow windows bright with that light which had bested the noonday sun. A steep roof hammered with squares of tin across rain holes among rotting shingles, it was a house maintained on the verge of ruin, shouldered by the immense tower of the black-barked tree, a malevolent species unto itself. He stopped to look up the length of that spike, but Hays poked him in the back with his gun barrel. "Right on through the front door, McCall."

They stepped onto a porch walled on one side with tree stumps chopped and stacked for the hearth, a twin-bladed lumberjack axe sunk into age-rings at the ready. A warm breeze blew from the open door carrying the heat of a house packed for partying, with odors that made Draco's mouth water appropriately, for this was the catered feast of a king.

They stepped into a foyer that made a lie of the facade decay, a log-braced structure of plumb right angles and solid floors. And it was clean, a rustic cabin overblown and built to withstand wind, lightning, earthquake, flood, and uninvited guests. Beneath the roiling rich feast odors he could smell the pleasing sawmill wood-sap stink of timber freshly cut and planed.

Two massive double doors stood closed upon the party. Hays stepped up and pushed them open. Pike poked his pistol once in Draco's back and walked him in.

Hays knuckled the shoulders of men crowded around the door watching the dance, who turned irritated until they saw the glint of muzzles aimed waist-level at a prisoner being led in. They parted mute and eyed Draco, who passed through to the edge of the dance floor where clog-clad men and women pounded heels chasing the rhythm of a band driving accelerated hill tunes home.

"Hold there," Hays said, grabbing Draco by the coat collar and giving it a yank. Dancers swept past sweat-riddled and grinning. Draco raised his head to look above the dancers toward the musicians quartered on a wooden bandstand in a far corner of the high-ceilinged room with their eyes closed aiming guitars, banjos, and fiddles at the crowd. Behind that wall of steel strummed, a seated man rattled drumsticks on a carnival chromium trap set with a sock cymbal pumping.

People began to take notice of the silent trio in their midst, nudging ribs and pointing at the drawn armory, but kept their smiles fixed below their curious furtive glances.

A fiddle man stepped to the front of the stage and brought the melody to an end with a rugged bowstring draw. The crowd spun to a standstill applauding, and as the guests moved off the floor, Draco got a clear view of a long feasting table set against the back wall. Holding court on a chair of throne pretensions at its center, full flagon gripped and bone-threaded beard curls caressed by laughing young women at his side, Baxter lifted his flagon high and threw his head back howling his approval of the dance.

Hays touched Draco's back and told him to get moving. The three men walked across the empty floor toward the table where Baxter was now engaged in ticklish business with the chin of a waitress leaning in to refill his drink. He took no notice of the men's approach. It was the surprised face of the woman seeing those guns, and the sudden hush sweeping around the room, which induced him to look toward his waiting deputies. He gave Draco a silent study, boot-to-hat, and spoke with a deep and disinterested rumble. "What'cha got, Pike?"

Pike pocketed his pistol and placed a hand on Draco's shoulder.

"Caught a man selling without a license."

A murmured groan of disapproval made its mandatory circuit around the room. Baxter tongued a gold molar and peered slit-eyed at the prisoner. He raised a finger and wiped a leaking drip of beef grease from a corner of his mouth. "Selling what?"

Pike pointed at the burlap sack, then frowned uncertainly and leaned into Draco's face. "What did you say you was selling?"

The Legend of Carl Draco

Draco lowered the sack and drew the top open, all the while holding his eyes steady, returning Baxter's searching stare. He reached in and pulled out a twig, held it high for everyone to see. "Dream root."

Baxter ignored the merchandise. He leaned forward, his gut lodging like a boat prow against the tabletop as his eyes flickered up, held, and worked their way down Draco's frame. "Dream root is one plant that I do not believe I am familiar with," Baxter said in a tone so benign that it nearly came across as amused. "What is it?"

Draco moved away from Pike's edgy hand, approached the table, and held the twig toward Baxter. "It's an herb. You boil it up and bathe in it. It makes a woman's skin as soft as that of a newborn fawn."

Hays ducked as if dodging a tossed rock. He strode forward and stood face-to-face with Draco. "That ain't what you told us!"

The throne creaked. Baxter eased his bulk back and pulled at a beard curl thoughtfully. "What did he tell you?"

Turning to his boss with teeth clamped containing his rage, Hays shook a thumb at Draco. "He said it cures bad dreams!"

Twisted hair strands snapped back to their curl as Baxter set his hands flat upon the table and began to smile like a man who'd finally come to understand the thrust of an obscure joke. Dropping one shoulder, he reached for something set handily out of sight on the floor beside his chair, then raised a burr-edged wooden mallet doweled with a grease-stained handle disclosing years of judicial use. He swung the tool flat on the table barking, "Court's in session!" and set it aside as people rushed the floor elbowing playfully for ringside seats to witness the proceedings. Instruments hot and losing tune were set aside as the musicians abandoned the bandstand to refill moonshine cups and take an unscheduled break.

Whispered conversations rose to a natural pitch of intrigue, then slowly dropped to a hush as the guests began waiting for

149

the judge-jury-and-executioner to speak. When the hall was quiet enough to hear the attic scrabble of mouse feet in the rafters, Baxter leaned forward and put a procedural question to the prisoner at the bar. "Selling without a license. How do you plead, vendor?"

Draco looked over his shoulder once, as if to ascertain whether or not the audience had vacated the building, so perfect was the silence. Solemn faces listening wide-eyed and eager leaned in to hear his plea. He returned his gaze to Baxter and made a resigned clucking noise and shrugged and smiled shyly. "I didn't know I needed permission to trade on the street, sir."

Fivescore heads pivoted to catch Baxter's reaction, but his languid black-beaded eyes gave away nothing. He held out a hand. "Let me see that dream root."

Draco leaned forward and dropped it onto his palm, then stepped back a respectful pace. Thumb and finger pinching the twig, Baxter rolled it over, turned it this way and that, and noted the odd manner by which the candlelight seemed to snag and hang momentarily on the silver-barked ragged ridges. He shoved the pretty thing against a nostril, buried it deep in black hairs, and took a long, loud whistle-sniff that rose to the beams and made the mouse feet scramble.

He lowered the twig and looked at Draco. "What's your name?"

"Jack McCall."

"Where you from, Jack McCall?"

"Mount Shasta, California."

Baxter took this information in and let his tongue poke a cheek as he pondered the facts. When he uttered his response, it came out a deep and guttural "Uh-huh" like the nocturnal groan of a hibernating bear smelling danger in his den.

He leaned forward and raised his chin to get a fresh fix on Draco's boots, pants, coat, and hat. "Your people didn't teach you much about common courtesy, did they, Jack McCall?"

The Legend of Carl Draco

Draco looked down at the floor as if embarrassed about the exposed shortcomings of his family and neighbors, and replied in a humble and nervous tone, "I'm sorry if I violated an ordinance, sir. If there's a fine, I'll gladly pay it." Then he looked up, took a deep breath, leaned toward Baxter, and spoke in a voice a bit too loud and lacking a shred of humility: "Because I shore would like to get outta here as soon as I can."

Floor stomped, jaw set, and fisted knuckles shivering eager to break teeth, Hays put his red face into Draco's shouting, "Who the hell do you think you're talking to!"

Draco looked around and noticed that no one in the crowd was looking his way. Every face was aimed at Baxter, heads turtled into collars like people prepared to duck and run. The hot smell of lung-blown moonshine heated Draco's cheek. He looked at Hays' puffed lips, then raised his chin and looked at Baxter, whose lips were drawn back revealing teeth in what promised to be the terrifying realization of Hays' pup snarl and growl.

But Baxter wasn't gathering a roar of insulted wrath. He was hauling in a bellyful of air to launch an explosion of rafter-rattling slack-jawed laughter that sent those mouse feet scrambling for another home altogether. A plague of smiles riddled the room fast on previously uncertain faces following Baxter's fist-pounding table-shaking lead. They guffawed like strung marionettes with every whip of Baxter's wet-eyed head.

Cup gulped, mouth wiped, and under control now, Baxter rocked on his chair chuckling and rubbed his nose with a thumb. "I'll tell you what, Jack McCall. First off, you leave your bag of dream root right here on my table. That's your fine." Then he leaned forward, all hint of mirth gone from his voice. "Second, you get your ass back to Mount Shasta and don't ever let me see you in my valley again."

"I wouldn't have it any other way," Draco said.

It was Pike's turn now, his rage manifestly less pyrotechnic and thus more ominous than that of Hays. He stepped up and leaned into Draco's face and spoke softly. "Damn, boy. You don't learn. You'd best start showing Mister Baxter proper respect and I mean right now." He pulled his gun out and stuck the muzzle against the soft flesh beneath Draco's chin just above the Adam's apple and gave it a push, a little tactile reminder.

"Court's adjourned!" Baxter shouted before any more pointless confrontation could take place. The show was over and too much drinking time had been purloined from the feast. He gavel-slammed the table, sending pewter pitchers rocking across the boards.

Caught unprepared in the middle of fresh grub chewed and flagons half-finished, the musicians hopped to the stage wiping crumbs on denim pants and grabbing their favored instruments. A hand struck six steel strings while another clawed the collar behind Draco's fined and sentenced neck. Hays kept his grip like a rein leading the prisoner back through the crowd filling the floor to square off for the dance.

The porch echoing with their boots, Pike, Hays, and Draco walked past the stacked cordwood and down onto the compacted dirt path that led through the open gate out onto the flats. Draco looked up at the full moon near zenith between the ridges east and west. He looked down at his own shadow and those of the men walking alongside him, flat black bundles beneath feet sinking into soil growing damp near the banks of the creek.

Pike looked over at Draco. "You got lucky, McCall. You tickled Mister Baxter. I figured you for a dead man."

They crossed the bridge, and the fast music and sweet odors faded into the practical work sounds and smells of the town beyond the creek. Pike and Hays, still in their official capacity but with pistols holstered, took Draco into town past the lit flickering-candled windows of Melanie's shop, past the slat-raised stand where Delgado sat on a high stool watching

The Legend of Carl Draco

strolling faces and noting sights and conversations that might be useful to the minions of the king. His top hat tilted with a nod as the three men walked by. He watched them turn at the intersection and move past the saloon where the music and laughter seemed less driving and wild this evening, had seemed so ever since the moment he'd seen that escorted stranger emerge from its swinging doors.

On up through the north end of town, they marched out onto the prairie road, which shot straight as a picket fence into the foothill where trees grew in the middle of the road that led to the pass that had helped Draco's parents best Baxter long ago.

The two deputies accompanied him up the hill halfway to the tree line, then Draco heard the weed crunch of their boots cease. He turned and looked back at them. "You finished with me?"

Hays took one more step upslope and raised his right wrist high. He made a slow show of curling each finger into a pugil ball and said, "I'd like about five minutes alone with you in an empty room, you lying bastard," spitting a chaw into the weeds at Draco's feet.

Pike pointed up the mountainside. "Start moving, Jack McCall, and don't stop until you get to California."

Draco hiked up to the tree line, then looked back down and saw Pike and Hays officially observing his retreat. He went on into the trees and hiked a little further until he figured he'd gained enough altitude that his shape had blended into the foliage. He stopped and looked downhill and saw his chaperones tiny and strolling the road back to town.

The first round of tonight's set-to complete, he turned away from the north route and began making his way along the slope toward the Draco family home, the headquarters for his upcoming moonlit toil.

chapter eighteen

Loose pebbles, toed by scofflaw feet skulking across dry weeds low and fast, rattled downslope near the graveyard. The grease-flared town lights below did not reach this high, but Draco remained wary even though he doubted that eyes were posted to report the comings and goings on this cursed and desolate plateau.

Pondering a vain woman timed by a trick of his eyes during that kangaroo court, he paused at the back door and calculated the minutes since his departure, calculated the time remaining until the culmination of his second hello. He went on inside and moved through the stone-dust stink of the empty kitchen and into the living room, where the picture window framed the unlit lamp.

He touched its glass chimney, which rattled with a scraping sound, while at his back a shape arose from the floor with fingers probing the fitted stone wall for balance. Draco swung around wondering how it could be that this ambush could have gone unforeseen and unscented, viewing without alarm but with surprise an arm raised with a short bludgeon hiked to hammer, and hearing a voice squealing "Who's there?" trembling with such feeble and impotent courage that Draco understood immediately why he had sensed no danger when he had come into this house—because there was no danger. His thoughts had been focused too intently upon the business of the moment to note the innocent scramble of a rabbit uphill, or the crawl of a silent cricket along a leaf, or the crumpled form of a dreaming drunk sleeping it off by the fireplace.

He touched the lantern, and a flame sprang from the fueled wick. He gave Parker a good looking over, but the little man's light-blasted eyes were too weak to do much of anything except drop to slits as he turned to one side like a stanced boxer raising his bottle-filled fist high. "Who is it!"

"Calm down, brother," Draco said, shrinking the lamplight to half its glow. Parker stood as straight as a man could in his shape, and his brain worked to put two strangers together until he recognized again the man who sells dream root—who is this feller who shows up every damn where anyway? But his brain was finished putting things together for the night. Parker rested his backbone against the wall and let his trembling legs and single crutch lower him to his stone-floored bed.

Draco pulled out a chair and sat down at the table, and felt his bedroll with the tip of a boot. He reached under and pulled it onto the table and examined it for tampering. But whatever this beggar was doing here, it apparently didn't involve pilferage. He surmised it had to do with drinking, as Parker popped the cork on the bludgeon and poured a little liquid down his throat. Eye-opener. The night was young again. "What are you doing here, mister?" Parker gasped, refreshed though not yet reassembled.

"I might ask you the same thing," Draco said.

Parker coughed a muttering sigh. "I hole up here sometimes when I got the need to get away from town." He took another precious sip from his diminishing stash.

"Do you know who this house belongs to?" Draco said.

"Baxter," Parker replied not losing a beat. "He owns every gat damn stick in this valley! He owns me, owns you, owns the dad blang moon when it crosses his sky!"—and poured the last wiggling pinch of white lightning onto his tongue— "Everything"—swallowed it licking the stinging walls of his cheeks—"The works!"—letting the bottle clink to the floor. He blew a sigh that Draco could have ignited with a match. "Baxter don't let nobody live here," Parker said, "even though the house is in good shape. I crawl in here some nights and stay till dawn 'cause I like to think it rankles him." He sighed and shrugged. "It probably don't."

"Where do you live?" Draco said.

"No place."

Draco looked at the scored leather bottoms of the ankle cups stretched out on the floor. "A man in your condition ought to have a place to live permanent."

Parker looked up and nodded with lips met in a contemplative smile, as if agreeing with the wisdom of such a benevolent concept. He let his smile open into a grin and picked up the bottle, held it between one eye and the lantern, and gave the trickling walls a last peek. He undid the cork one more time. "Baxter won't allow it," he said, tonguing a few reluctant drops off the rim.

Draco took off his hat and slapped it onto the tabletop, firing a ring of dust. He shook his head and said, "That Baxter is one surly man," talking the way a nonplused jailbird might pass judgment on a sheriff quick to knock heads. "He run me outta the valley tonight for selling without a license."

A choke stifled quick, Parker stopped licking the inside of his mouth in search of residue booze, and swallowed fast. "Whaddya mean, run you outta the valley?"

"Two of his deputies hauled me into court, and Baxter fined, sentenced, and exiled me from the valley. Told me to get the hell out and don't never come back."

Fingers touching his crutches, Parker remembered now, just before dragging himself out of the alley and heading up the hill to this place, Pike and Hays brandishing guns on

The Legend of Carl Draco

a man, this man, taking him to jail. "He run you outta the valley?" he said, taking hold of the crutches and sliding them onto his lap. "So what are you doing here?"

"I got further business with Baxter tonight."

That's all, brother. Parker stabbed the floor with the bristled ends of his wooden legs and started crawling up their lengths. He worked the rags under his arms and hopped around gaining balance—"Nice knowing you"—and swung his legs toward the door.

Draco watched the furious acrobatics of this man felled by booze and raised by fear, but just before Parker reached out to lift the crossbar latch on the front door, Draco said, "What happened to your feet?"

Parker paused and bowed his head and looked at the frayed cuffs of his trousers. "Baxter took 'em."

"Why?"

"'Cause he's a sorry sonofabitch!"

"You hungry?" Draco said—because a man driven by fear and alcohol is usually driven by hunger too, and the mention of something as simple and sustaining as slab meat sandwiched can sometimes freeze the chaos, put hell on hold, and elbow a little room into a man's troubles for a brief spell of something resembling sanity. Parker frowned at the mention of eats. A man who begs alms for booze tries not to think about food, because even if eating is on his list of things to do this month, it lies way down near the bottom of the page.

Draco stuffed a hand into the center ringfold of the bedroll and pulled out a paper-wrapped sandwich and a pint of moonshine. "You got nowhere to go," he said. "Fill your belly," shoving the meal across the table.

It's always there, that tiny animal of hunger hibernating just below your breastbone. It never gets any bigger, but it won't shrink neither, and all the booze in Baxter's stills won't drown the critter, so you stretch your gut with hillside springwater and try not to think about it. The mortar-and-stone room

Gary Reilly

smell was elbowed aside by the rising oven odor of bread and meat. And greens. Hell with Baxter. Parker swung over to the table and sat down opposite Draco, dropped his crutches, and peeled back folded layers of paper overflowing with lettuce leaf, with lips of meat hanging from the leavened slices.

He looked the fixings over, snagged a few hanging strands and tucked them neatly inside, then lifted the sandwich with both hands and bit down. Mustard dripped, he eyed it splashing the table dust.

Draco looked out the window. "Does Baxter ever come out of that house of his?"

Jaw muscles reborn working his chin, Parker swung his head and looked at the black house across the river.

"Nope."

"Why did Baxter take your feet?"

Parker swallowed hard. "Listen. I appreciate the feed, but if Baxter knew I was answering questions asked by a man he run outta the valley, he might decide to take my head, not to mention a few other unmentionable extremities."

"Baxter can't hear a word we say. I guarantee it."

Parker grinned and looked his sandwich over. "I wouldn't bet on it."

"Why'd he take your feet?"

Parker let loose the sandwich with one hand and pointed at Baxter's house, then raised his finger indicating a spot halfway up the hillside. "Baxter's got a moonshine still built up there in the woods. It's a damn factory is what it is, with barrels of hooch and a dozen stills. Who'd of thought he'd miss one tiny gallon jug? I didn't. Course, I was drunk at the time."

And speaking so of distillation, Parker set his sandwich down and worked the cork loose from the new gift bottle. He slugged enough to rinse stuck teeth meat and lubricate his tongue. "About five years back I was wandering the hills up near the stills one night drunk, as I said, and I'd just finished

158

The Legend of Carl Draco

the bottle I was sipping, and it seemed to me that Baxter's stills were a lot closer to where I was and much quicker to reach than my shack down on south creek. So I sort of snuck on over to the works and give it a little look-see. Weren't nobody present, I thought, so I crawled up behind the shelves where Baxter's brewers stack gallon jugs, and I removed one. I tried to remove the cork but the long arm of the law took aholt of my shoulder in the form of a bootlick toady by the name of Hays who put me under arrest and dragged me off to jail." Narrating, his eyes became vacant, gazing inward at every recalled second of that disastrous night. "Well, Baxter was partying as usual, the bastard never sleeps, and he put me on trial right there in front of that whole crowd of no-account unemployed dancing morons who kiss his ass night and day. Buncha saps is what they are. I was mad as hell, mostly about getting caught, but I got fed up quick with all those giggling simpletons gaping at me, so I interrupted Hays' delineation of my crimes including trespassing, and flat-out told Baxter I wasn't guilty of nothing 'cept touching one of his moonshine jugs, and that I was a free citizen and didn't give a damn about his court of law and said I was gonna pack up and leave his dad gam valley that night, and if he didn't like it, he'd better learn to live with it." Parker took a quick sip. "Well, he didn't like it. He wasn't even smiling when he took my feet. It felt like a pack of running dogs knocked me ass-over-teakettle and I found myself sitting on the floor staring" — swallowing, squinting to get a solid fix on that memory — "at round naked stumps on the ends of my legs. He took my boots too. Left me with no feet and no boots, and didn't even give me no crutches. My ankles didn't hurt, though. The pain was more in my heart, brought on by the certainty that there was no way in hell I was ever gonna make it outta this valley without my feet. And sitting on the floor in front of all them folks who was probably as scared as I was, I knew I was doomed to live here for the rest of my days. And if I know Baxter, he's gonna see to it that I live to be ripe and wrinkled."

He offered the bottle to Draco, who took a shot and handed it back.

"A deputy named Pike carried me outta there," Parker continued. "Took me across the bridge and told me I was on my own. Said I didn't have no shack down on south creek no more, and that I was through trapping critters for a living. Said I was gonna have to make it on my own any way I could." He nodded, giving a final affirmation to the remembered facts of the story. "That's how I become a panhandler."

"Pike and Hays are the two deputies who hauled me in tonight."

Parker nodded. "I know. I seen them escorting you down the street. I didn't hold out much hope for you. It's bad enough when some citizen of Chuckney crosses Baxter, my case in point, but when a stranger violates his ordinances . . . well, sometimes you just never see that feller again. But once in a while you do." He smiled and nodded at Draco. The new stash was kicking in, and Parker tipped it for another boost. But when he set the bottle down, a dull glaze of hurt crossed his face. He sighed, reaching down to massage the throbbing ankle of his right foot.

"Pain?" Draco said.

"Awww," Parker sighed, pressing his thumb hard against a tendon, "it comes on when the moon is full mostly, if I'm on 'em too long. Baxter didn't make these things for standing."

"Have you ever tried to get out of the valley?"

Parker sat up straight and looked out the window. "The next damn day after he crippled me I crawled up toward the ridge above this house at dawn. But I didn't get halfway there before I heard the grumbling of stomachs and smelled the stench of wolves. I seen three just above me peering out from the trees awaiting their breakfast. The hills are full of 'em. I turned tail. After I carved my crutches I made another attempt, thinking like a idiot that I could whump on 'em and make it to the ridge. Sheesh. I give up on that idear quick."

"When I came into the valley this morning, I was followed by wolves most of the way down," Draco said.

Parker's eyes lit up with interest. "Did they bother you?"

"No."

Parker nodded and sat back in his chair considering the reply. Then he turned off the light in his eyes and reached for the bottle. A drink, pound the cork back in, he nodded wisely and looked at Draco. "The wolves let people in. Getting out's another story, if Baxter don't want it."

"Are you a native of these parts?"

"Naw, I come here fifteen years ago. I got family down south, got a brother in New Orleans. He's a gambler." He began chuckling about this, pulling at his lower lip in thought, a gambling brother and a family down south, but the laughter slowly evaporated until the small light of the lantern revealed Parker's eyes sparkling with collected tears. Draco was startled when a bizarre honk of weeping rage burst from Parker's mouth—"Damn!"—fist plastering the table and then reaching for the bottle or maybe the crest of a mountaintop, but he slipped off the chair and hit the floor with a sound like tools tossed from a roof.

Draco slid his chair back and leaned down to look, but you don't always want to hold out a hand to a man long used to helping himself. He saw Parker grabbing his crutches and leaning forward on all fours, cuffs dragging and pant knees tearing bare on cold stone as he scrambled, screaming "Bastard!" toward a moon-tossed rectangle on the floor. His shadow joined him there, and when he saw its mimic mocking black crawl he sat upright on his tucked legs and raised his crutches like axes and tried to stave in that black head that swung black axes too.

Draco raised an arm to shield his face from splintered sticks flying as the hammered crutches broke spinning into the open-arched echoing hearth.

Gary Reilly

"Aaaah damn," a whispered lament as Parker stared at the ruined hand-carved work of days gone by. He tossed aside what was left of the broken sticks and worked his legs out from under him and began rubbing both ankles, shaking his head with unfettered sobs and moaning, "I want to go home."

Draco stepped over to the moonstruck mumbling man, squatted in front of him, and touched an ankle. Startled, Parker drew back a bit frowning, his tears drying fast as Draco squeezed the stump as if measuring its hacked length.

"What are you doing?" Parker said.

"Easy, brother."

Draco rolled up the pant leg and examined the leather straps crudely lacing tight a foreshortened boot top leaking cotton, and saw white leg flesh rubbed naked of hair. He yanked the dried, caked worm of knotted leather lace and undid the bindings and proceeded to drag off the cuff as the scream of a vain woman distracted Baxter, who was curious about an odd tug in his thoughts as if trespass were occurring, or thievery of an abstract sort, but the scream interrupted his musing, and Draco knew it, pulling the soiled cuff and stinking cotton bandage down over an ankle lengthened, over a heel pink and baby-bottom soft, exposing the concave sweep of an unfallen arch—Draco knew—drawing the discard boot away from toes spread shingled with toenails as shiny as newly minted coins.

Which wriggled flexed as Parker held his breath, watching Draco repeat this clinical sleight of hand on his other ankle.

Draco tossed the cuffs and cotton into the hearth and stood up as Parker leaned astonished to interlock his fingers between his new toes. He'd seen his own magic lure fur into set traps, had seen plenty of freelance tramp wizard enchantments cast, but he'd never seen anyone put a bona fide boomerang kibosh on a Baxter spell!

He craned his head back to scrutinize Draco's face, knowing this wasn't your average hobo warlock or nomad

162

The Legend of Carl Draco

conjuror standing before him. This was a man schooled in the black arts. A man . . . to be . . . reckoned . . . "Who are you, mister?" — his joy at healing giving ground slowly to uneasiness — except . . . why be afraid of a man who just gave you back your feet?

The stranger standing over him replied, "Have you ever heard of a man named Carl Draco?"

Speak of smallpox, speak of earthquake, speak of bad doings in a graveyard at midnight, Parker nodded acknowledging familiarity with the name that skip-rope children chant out of their mama's hearing because it's two words like "damn" or "hell" for which you might get whipped for saying, and not merely because decent folk don't use that kind of language but because you never know . . . when sheep disappear, when cattle trample fences, when crops wither without a frost, it could be that the bug-fleshed swamp-shambling Carl Draco has been listening in on your conversations and expediting his wicked agenda, shuffling death's deck and dealing stillborn babies, consumption, and the fates of souls known to have gone for a walk in the hills never to be heard from again.

And though most people discounted it, some said Baxter believed the legend, which asserted that one day Carl Draco would come into the valley and take over, depose him, and establish his rule, which . . . but here the legend grew vague and didn't give the believers and nonbelievers alike enough substance to speculate upon what sort of living conditions might afterwards be endured. It was all speculation, and speculation, like weeds, tended to grow wild, so that the legend of Carl Draco had taken root over the years in the hearts of the most gullible, and their neighbors, who believed that if this specter ever did come into the valley, it would be to establish a reign surely more dark and calamitous than Baxter's own.

Parker looked up and nodded, and said, "Sure," as if to say "So?" and waited for the shadowed face looking down at him to speak. Waited until his uneasiness broke with the sudden rush of dawning realization that can make a grown man feel like a duped and gullible rube.

*

As if he'd just been tapped on the back of the neck, Baxter glanced sidewise to see who might be interrupting his attention to the band's performance, but no one was there. He reached out to lift his refilled flagon and noticed the lumped and crumpled bag that Jack McCall had left behind. He snatched it off the table and hiked his arm back and hollered, "Throw this garbage in the fire!"

But before he could let fly toward the hearth, a hand twenty-four and favored at his side reached up and gently caressed his arm. "I'd like skin as soft as a newborn fawn," said the woman, whose name was Claire and who was seated at his side in party garb, a former servant and now an honored guest and paramour.

Baxter looked down at her young, sweet, black-haired, lovely head, surprised that anybody would give credence to the claims of that outcast levy thief. But the touch of sweet Claire, and those teasing pleading eyes and pouting lips, how could he deny her small request?

He laughed and handed the bag to her. "Give it a try, my dear. Let's see if that drummer was lying."

Claire took it grinning at the promise that every woman seeks, reborn youth and a maiden's fair face, arms, breasts, and belly, hefting the bag, a fair load, a cheap bargain, a free stock of dream root. She had listened and watched as that handsome shy prisoner at the bar had explained the function of these herbs, and though only twenty-four, unblemished and flush with youth, she did slick exotic creams into her pores each night, into her once rough and dishwash-reddened hands remade soft since she'd gained the favor of the king — a beauty who can see only flaws in the face looking at her from the mirror. Crow's-feet? Worry lines? Flesh sagging beneath the chin? Searching for imagined signs of age, twenty-four and unmarried, but all the while thinking of those rival females just eighteen invited from across the river who have no practical use for skin creams—just a bath and a comb, and those lithe limbs are ready for the dance.

She set the bag on the table and worked at the drawstring, a cache, like gold, it excited her. She opened it and looked inside, and was disconcerted that she did not see a silver glow like that of the prisoner's displayed sample twig. She spread the top wide and leaned in as Baxter again looked up wondering what that odd sensation was, like someone getting dangerously close, like the stealthy brush of a pickpocket.

Claire's shriek drowned out the music. When she jerked her wailing face from the bag, Baxter forgot whatever was distracting him and watched her rise from the table screaming with fingers splayed to protect herself from something inside the burlap. The band checked its music, suspending the dance, and the floor turned to look.

"What in the hell!" Baxter roared like a baffled father raging at a manic child's tantrum. Claire stumbled back from the table, and Baxter looked down at the bag with the word "stranger" suddenly boiling up in his mind . . . the appropriated sack of a stranger making one of his ladies scream. He grabbed the burlap and upended the contents, which dripped slick and slapping onto the table, a nest of thirteen dead black snakes.

The odds were small that two men in Chuckney would experience simultaneously the sudden rush of dawning realization that can make a grown man feel like a duped and gullible rube, yet here was Baxter kicking his chair back and rising screaming, "Pike!" and from the silent crowd plowed Pike hollering, "Sir!"

"Where's that sonofabitch Jack McCall!"

"We run him outta town like you told us to, sir!"

A felled tree trunk cable-hoisted, Baxter's right arm rose. He pointed across the heads of his wary guests. "Get him!

Ride! Bring him back to me!"

Stabled at the side of the house, two stallions lifted nibbling heads hearing bootheels sucking trough-splashed mud at the fenced entry to the corral where Pike and Hays, long-rifle armed, lugged saddles.

Strapped, bit-clamped, and rein-held, the bucked horses dog paddled empty air as their mounted riders turned them toward the gate and spurred ribs into a drumming run across the bridge.

*

There's always something electric in the air, Parker told himself, like the way your hair rises on a bald mountain peak just before the ground gathers enough swarming energy to detonate a passing cloud. The kind of unseen energy you can almost taste on your tongue when fear mounts, yours or your quarry's, when you meet eye-to-eye after a sprung trap didn't take and you encounter an escaped critter crouched bristling and razor-clawed. But Parker couldn't feel any of that ear-popping danger bell clanging every dull sense awake. In this room there was only a stranger walking across the floor and taking a seat on one of two chairs hauled in during years past from the trash of saloons after Parker had gotten sick of sitting on the cold stone floor. A man, even a drunk man, sometimes needs to just sit on a damn chair.

The stranger reached for the lamp and raised the wick until the room glowed a bright friendly-cabin yellow so that Parker got a good look at his own feet, those bent toe knuckles flushed red and white with pulsing blood tingling refurbished flesh and warming solid bone.

Draco watched Parker for a minute, having given him a sizable hint. You don't want to throw something like this whole cloth at a fragile individual without preparing him. But he figured the favor he had done Parker probably had broken all the ice before the coming deluge, so he said, "I'm Carl Draco," but spoke in a tender drone that might be employed by a man trying to calm a skittish hound. "I've come home to the valley to put Baxter out of business."

You heard talk in bars and back alleys, threats describing all the mayhem due a cheat vendor or a commonplace bully, only it never seemed to get past words. But there was something in the way this stranger spoke, this magician who claimed to be Carl Draco, that lifted the small hairs on the back of Parker's neck—this man's words didn't sound like talk.

Parker planted his feet flat and lifted himself standing ramrod erect and stomped the floor delighted at the twig and pebble pain shooting through his soft soles. He walked across the littered floor toward the door, grinning at the shock of chilly stone, then turned to Draco and shook his head with doubt. "Baxter's powerful. Nobody can touch him."

Draco paused politely, conceding the possibility, then spoke. "Tonight I walked into Baxter's lair and stood not five feet from him. He's been trying to kill me for twenty years, yet he didn't have an inkling as to who was on trial before him."

Parker began to breathe a little faster, as if the air in this high room overlooking the town was growing thinner with every incontrovertible fact that Draco uttered. "But he might have guessed!" Parker said. "Why'd you take the chance?"

"Because I wanted to see and hear and smell up close the man who murdered my parents. I wanted to stand face-to-face and let him take a good look so that the next time we met he wouldn't have any trouble identifying the truck that run him down."

Parker's saloon-cadge grin welled up authentic. He began rubbing the dirty bottoms of his feet against the insides of his calves. "What are you gonna do?"

"It's already started," Draco said. He leaned toward the window and pointed outside. Parker went to the window and looked out, seeing the equine sprint of two whiplash riders kicking dust devils along the town road north.

*

Sucking wind, separating squirrel fur and wolf from the reek of leather boots hiking upslope, Pike and Hays rode low off their saddles sniffing the path where they had last seen Jack McCall. Up the rocky road into the tree line where the moonlight nearly ceased, they slowed to a trot watching the ground with tracker eyes for twig break or fresh stone upturned, until finally Hays brought his heaving horse to a halt hissing, "Trail's end."

He pointed at a spot in the dark, and Pike hopped off his horse and struck a match. He held it close to the ground and looked at the place where the smell of leather still clung, a scrabble of pebbles kicked revealing damp earth and dry boot-flattened weeds half sprung back, the track of the vanished man. Pike peered higher into the trees, a dark wall with wolf eyes watching, but detected no sign or smell of Jack McCall. He looked at Hays. "Gone."

"Gone hell," Hays said. He kicked rib and drove his horse uphill. Pike led his own horse by the reins, walking bowed and squinting to read the unwritten earth.

The clucking pop of horse hooves grew dimmer. Pike listened to his partner's eager, vengeful search until the sound stopped high up. Stopped and didn't start again. Pike stood still, wondering suddenly who it was exactly that they were searching for anyway?

He stroked his horse's head and held his breath listening to the moonless silence all around, and listening for a sound from his partner, but Hays was either listening too or had vanished too, an idea that came sudden in the way gooseflesh blooms on a spooked neck. Could that stranger be crouched hiding somewhere poised to dry-gulch deputies that he knew would be back? Those thirteen snakes had been a sorry and sickening sight. But what kind of cut-rate charm hawker can make himself vanish without a trace? That sort of power is relegated to . . . high wizards and . . . men schooled in . . . things Pike would rather not dwell upon alone in the woods

The Legend of Carl Draco

at midnight.

He cupped a palm and hollered, "Hays!" and heard hooves start kicking rock. Pike hopped onto his horse and unsheathed his long rifle and held it pointed upslope until he saw the discouraged face of his partner coming back down. "He couldn't of got no further than this on foot," Hays said, reining in and watching curiously as Pike put away his rifle.

Even though they understood the requisite next move, they waited listening, frustrated, knowing that their man ought to have been run to ground, bound, and dragged back to jail by now. Pike understood that Hays would prefer to continue the hunt, Hays being the sort of man who took things personal and couldn't be satisfied until brute justice had been executed deputy-style, because vengeance wasn't his business, it was his art.

"Let's go give Baxter the news," Pike spat, yanking rein and aiming his horse downslope. They took it slow in the break-ankle dark until they emerged from the tree line into the moonlight, then plowed unspurred heels and made tracks.

*

Parker listened to sedition ricochet off stone walls until Draco paused speaking to nod down the hill. They both watched the riders streaking toward town. Parker felt a chunk of satisfaction as real as a satisfying meal resting solid in his gut, understanding their mission, having now been told about Draco's snakes, and contemplating with glee the lame excuses that must be spinning in those deputies' lame brains.

Draco pulled a brief sip of hooch and set the half-full bottle on the table. "I intend to draw Baxter out of his house. I want the whole town to see it when I finish him off."

"He never leaves," Parker said. "I've never seen him come outside in all the years I been here. He's got plenty of men willing to do his dirty work on the outside."

"I expect Baxter never had a good enough reason to come outside," Draco said.

Gary Reilly

"I bet the bastard's just scared," Parker said. "Scared some washout like myself might bushwhack him." He smiled at his joke, then his recollective gaze drifted out the window. "Every night I fall asleep drunk on Baxter's moonshine, and every night I dream about killing him."

Draco nodded, then studied Parker's face for a moment. "Killing a man is easy," Draco said. "Baxter deserves worse."

But before Parker had time to visualize various chilling alternatives to death, Draco set his elbows on the table and leaned forward. "Do you feel up to a little action tonight?"

Parker swallowed hard. "What do you mean?"

"I'm talking about a little vengeance of your own. You can help me on the inside the way Baxter's men help him on the outside."

Adam's apple accelerating, Parker ceased his noisy panting and reached for the bottle—but just as suddenly withdrew his hand, because alcohol and plans never mixed too well in his experience. He sat back in his chair. "Help you how?"

Draco leaned closer. "I want you to understand something. Baxter can't hurt you as long as I'm around. If you want to help me, then you've got to trust me. You've got to have faith in everything I say. You've got to do things exactly as I tell you, because I'm going to ask you to do something that's going to be difficult, something you might not want to do."

Parker sat awestruck, contemplating this invitation to partake in the prosecution of a bold scheme to dole out retribution akin to the improbable machinations of revenge that he had experienced only in his dreams.

Then he nodded. "I'm game."

chapter nineteen

The guests were already primed for the squeak and slam of double doors getting a night's workout when Pike and Hays burst in slapping road dust from their coatfronts and elbowing aside clotted onlookers and making straight for the feasting table. Their number, only two, heralded their message before they spoke.

"Sir!" Pike panted. "We couldn't find him. We tracked him up the north ridge but . . . he covered his trail. He must of hid out somewhere," getting it all in, covering his failure fast while wringing his hat. Hays was right behind him with his grim face petrified angry and silent so that Mister Baxter would see that he was not a fawning failure begging grace, that they were delivering a hard and strange truth.

Stroking Claire's backbone still trembling from that trickster's gift of snakes, Baxter sensed something odd about the presence of the woman seated on his lap, the subtle near smell of a cast spell mingling with the perfumes in her hair, except . . . who would dare cast a covert spell within these walls? That stranger . . . that stranger . . . he had some explaining to do.

"Hid out in my valley?" Baxter said in a voice so mellow that the rafters merely trembled. He eased Claire off his lap onto her own chair and looked through the doors into the foyer where he'd last seen the back of Jack McCall's departing head. He didn't kick back his chair as he arose this time, one show of strategic rage was enough. You didn't want to alarm the guests continually. He walked along the bench as feeding people leaned forward, that his splayed hairy fingers might not drag across their backs. Walked past the bandstand where instruments hung silent, poised, horsehair keening from the motion of the man who strolled toward the hearth where the sectioned trunk of a tree glowing red rested on a steaming length of skeletal steel. Guest fists tightened on flagon stems. They didn't see Baxter cross the room without a woman that often, and never toward a window.

Shutters clattered open as Baxter heaved his shoulders through the frame and looked up at the traveling moon. No clouds threatening his town, the constellations burning in their assigned latitudes, he sniffed the cold night air the way an animal might explore the confines of his burrow before entering.

Then his broad back expanded with a hissing that the guests could hear, the vacuum of his spreading lungs sucking wind with a mean sound like a rattler vexed. And just when it appeared to the guests that the wood frame confining his girth might crack, Baxter hauled his head back and snapped it forward unleashing a bestial vocal load.

Which sets cattail stalks clashing in the slough as if blown by a hard wind, though at this moment the air in the valley bowl lies inert. They bend rustling away from the source of this piercing wail toward the town on the far bank still in business though the hour is growing late.

The children are the first to hear the sound, to notice the shift in shadows on the backs of parents browsing the stalls. They begin to stare curiously at greased pole flame leaning level above the streets where men and women finally raise their heads with a vacant gaze listening to a call to congregation

The Legend of Carl Draco

emanating from the mansion across the creek—a sound like that of a man imitating the long-drawn warble of a wolf—and begin looking around to make certain that their spouses and children are near.

While above an understood demarcation like a timberline, jaws nibbling mouse marrow cease, and lupine ears leap erect. Pup wolves at play interrupt their false bite and claw, and watch as their elders rise from slumber and lope toward the cry coming from the valley floor. The younger wolves fall into a lumbering line behind the hoary pads breaking trail downslope.

Parker looks out the window toward the far range where small shapes emerge from every rill and burrow pale with full-moon light, scattered shapes drifting downhill like a siege of ticks toward Baxter's mansion, from which that eerie cry, not like a man's and not exactly like a wolf's, begins to fall from its menacing klaxon crescendo . . . and Parker's skin, erecting hair, it crawls.

Not a single guest had moved, though the musicians one by one had sat down on stools to splay uneasy hands against strings singing in sympathy with Baxter's beckoning call. Guests gripped cups and watched Baxter's back until the spent wolf cry's mountain echo faded. Relieved but not understanding, the guests looked finally to one another during the space of silence between the last echo and the first stirrings of something felt in the floorboards accelerated by something coming fast, recalling to those who had experienced it in other locales the first tentative vibrations of an earthquake.

Baxter returned to the table, grabbed the burlap bag, and strode to the center of the floor as the first wave of wolves broke into the room billowing hot breath that devastated the sweet odors of the feast. Guests pressed screaming against the walls as a river of wolves began rampaging ceaselessly around its central axis: Baxter.

A brute head dominant and sailing above the pack

stopped directly in front of Baxter, who knelt and grabbed the animal's jowls, digging fingernails deep into the bristled flea-nibbled neck eliciting a throaty canine moan of pleasure. Baxter crushed the burlap bag against its ebony leather snout. The beast breathed deeply of every sweat stain and skin flake therein.

Baxter stood up. "Bring him to me!"

His favored pet threw its head back and howled, evoking a death-knell chorus from the pack running muzzles-to-the-rafters. Men threw down their cups and covered their ears as women busied themselves fainting, as the wolves diverted their clockwise channel toward the double doors, intent upon fetching alive their master's enemy—who took a sip of bottled lightning to cool his overworked throat while thinking that it seemed he'd talked to more people during the past week than during the past twenty years.

*

"They're coming," Parker said.

"I see 'em."

Saw that those who couldn't fit between the railings of the bridge leapt the bank and churned creek water crossing.

Saw those grassy banks shimmering with the popcorn hop of routed frog life.

Saw the wolves make town.

*

Delgado bagged a sale coin and drew the drawstring tight. A good night so far, good sales and good profits. He tucked the bag inside a box below the counter with the bone-deep satisfaction that comes from storing cold cash accounted in the black, a feeling almost unassailable, a feeling unaccountably diminishing as the first marauder crossed the creek.

He leaned across the counter and saw along the road a riotous torrent of wolves charging the outskirts of town. He raised an arm watching folks scattering into doors opening and closing in panic, raised a hand and deftly knocked a hook loose from its mooring and took the weight of the front slat in his palm. He lowered it and let the slat lodge closed, wondering, what is going on here? Why would Baxter send these animals to chase off my paying customers? As bodies bumped the thin walls of his booth, as dust drifted gently from the rafters clouding his eyes—why are these animals running tonight? He closed secure the three remaining slats.

Melanie licked her thumb and pinched a wick dead, and from the thin hiss of snuffed punk seemed to come a tumbling clutter of sounds so odd that she had to stand in the silence of her shop listening for a moment to determine that it was in fact the distant yelp of running hounds. She moved to the front window keeping her eyes off the scattered deck on the counter, the shuffled numbered cardboard that she could no longer bear to look at because she could not understand the intractable resolution of her random choices. Five times since those chimes had rung good-bye above that stranger she had failed to pluck other than a king from the deck, which was but one pack from a cellophane-wrapped gross ordered indirectly from a manufacturing house out of Chicago.

Cheek pressed against the cold glass of the front door, she saw across the road a prone man crawling fast beneath the soft wall of a tent closed for the night, saw a wolf leap over his scrambling legs, saw the pack invade the main intersection where men and women, and children too, took flight diving into the safety of saloons.

Tin bobbing among clouds of soap bubbled by fists plunged into a murky tub, a hand paused searching among cups as a bartender, listening, knowing without seeing what his customers standing three-deep at the windows saw, thought with a recalcitrant conscience of that burden known only to himself and his brother barkeeps who must of necessity associate with (and thereby incur potential consequences) the broke and disheveled hank of hair who begs outside establishments until enough lucre has been acquired to allow him to step inside and purchase at least one honest cup—and as always after Parker has licked the last dreg and can no longer justify holding the tin to his lips, he sets it down a little too hard as a signal to the barkeep (and his brothers) that the time has come once again to reject a favor.

The squawk of wonder and gawking heads leaping to see above ringside, and the rabid incessant howling of wolves, stayed the hand of the bartender thinking of the huddled shape seated each night outside the door who was always there when the bartender came to work, crutches straddling knees with ankles tucked. A man in his shape can't travel fast, and what with this rampage out on the streets, how would such a man fare? Ripped to shreds?

The bartender sank his fists deep to his elbows, grabbing up a dull flagon lying sidewise on the bottom and jamming a fresh rag into its mouth, thinking he ought to edge over to the door and ask someone if they can see whether or not that cripple has made it safely inside, that cripple who makes demands upon saloon owners that he will not or can not make upon others, always, and without fail, asking for one more drink on the cuff. But how can you give free drinks to a recipient of Baxter's wrath? You have a job here, you make your living in this place, you make good money. Why risk annexing a piece of that wrath just to slip something as pointless as alcohol to a deadbeat?

He set the rinsed and polished flagon on a spread towel and closed his ears to the fearful chorus outside as Melanie peered through the glass pane at the flanks of a beast crouched snuffling at the crack beneath her door, muscles rippling on its ribs with a snout now jammed here, now jammed there, the window rattling as the beast's fur-lined skull hammered the door seeking the fountainhead of some elusive scent, an elder beast emitting a pup whine of confusion. It looked up at Melanie, who met those two deadly almond eyes with her own eyes gone red. She stared him down, until the beast with

The Legend of Carl Draco

a last whimper scuttled into the ponderous flow past the shack where Delgado leaned to strike a match on the counter to fire his cheroot, and noticed the gold-leaf plant, and recalled that dream-root drummer whom he had reported and then saw later being escorted under arms to jail. As he sucked a coal onto the tip, he thought "Some connection?" between that stranger and the running of the wolves? But he shut off this train of thought fast because you never can tell, Baxter might sense some disapproval, so forget those lost profits and that stranger too, who sips on a sideshow seat viewing the gray shapes of a pack charging the hillside just below the plateau.

*

Parker was tense. He leaned so close to the window that his panting breath shot a growing mask of fog.

"They're here!" he said.

"Easy, brother."

But the small man shuddered as the first animal rose clawing its kicking body onto the plateau followed by tracking snouts hovering on the run, sniffing the yard with tree circle and weed scratch and baffled wails. Parker eased his visible head and shoulders away from the window, crept to the center of the room on feet refurbished just in time for running, and looked reassured at the barred solid wooden front door. But windows were made of glass. There was no getting around that, and he started thinking about a new and practical purpose for the spice root cellar.

"Baxter's worried," Draco said, as if to turn Parker's mind away from the immediate problem. "He doesn't know what's come into his valley. He doesn't know who I am."

But Parker wasn't having any of it, his nerves unraveling like bootlaces with every door paw scrape as the frantic pack probed the yard. He slowly sat down on the floor. Then the futile yipping began to diminish as the pack as one began scrambling off the plateau into the higher trees. Parker shook his head and told Draco that he had known there was a mess of wolves in the hills, but if he'd known that this many might have come after him on one of those desperate days when he'd tried to flee . . . well . . . he let the dire and single consequence dangle in the air unspoken.

Draco studied the empty streets of Chuckney. The only motion now was the whipping lick of flame on staggered poles, shops closed for the duration, yellow windows gone black, the subtle rumble of foot traffic and talk, tangible even up here, silenced.

He got up and stood in front of the window watching the lights of the black house across the creek where Baxter would be calling off his dogs about now, their scorched-earth quest proven fruitless.

"I imagine this may be the first time Baxter has ever been bested in his own valley," he said in a voice so soft that Parker wondered if he might be talking to himself. Then, "It's time for you to go to work," turning to Parker sitting knees-hugged in the center of the floor listening to the last yip fade.

Parker looked up and blinked as if waking from a dream or contemplating too late the outcome of an impulse buy. He unbuckled his fingers and stood up looking beyond Draco into that rectangle of night where he supposed this hard work must take place. "What do you want me to do?"

Draco reached into the fireplace and pulled out the discarded slammed and busted crutches strangely made whole again, and rested them on Parker's right shoulder.

Parker reached up and gripped the familiar weight. He listened as Draco explained the plan, and as each maneuver crucial to the success of tonight's bold scheme was elucidated, Parker felt an unexpected, unwanted, and unpleasant twinge of sobriety tick inside his skull.

chapter twenty

Pondering the doubtful benefits of this blessing as he walked alone along the bleak overgrown north road toward the flame-lit silence of Chuckney, Parker leaned into a nonexistent wind balanced by his crutches shouldered like rifles.

He passed among the first silent outskirt tents with their entrances tied off, walking with a white stride, his new naked brown-bottomed feet eating up the ground. But doubts accompanied him like so many insistent and irritating gnats. "I have seen Baxter's power thwarted, I have seen his emissaries turn tail confused, seen what was taken given back . . ." Thus ran his thoughts as faces peered from behind the dark panes of shops closed early, worried heads still hearing within their fear the snarl of marauding wolves but harkening to a soft sound of feet traveling the street.

Candles snuffed in crowded rooms, women crouched with weeping children hugged into the plumes of bundled skirts, while men gripped rifles and peered past drawn curtains at the sight of some fool hiking alone, whispering among themselves, "Who is it?"

He passed his landmark of confrontation and victory, the saloon gone dark now, the larger door closed against

179

the swinging ornamental butterfly slats, but he could hear footsteps and the whispers of worried drunks beyond the windows. Coming up on Delgado's establishment he made a hard left and walked east on the approaching prints left by those scavenger pads toward the creek now quiet after its riotous frog departure. "I have seen a man hauled to jail and come out of it clean, heard him state his profaned name, and watched him get down on his knees to work an uncommon cure . . ." And even though Parker was oblivious, it seemed, to what was going on around him with all his internal struggle between doubt and fierce determination, he did notice on the dirt road a squared patch of candlelit earth crisscrossed with shadow. He recognized it but still looked up with something bordering on surprise at the shop where Melanie plied her magic of love. That woman had dropped her share of silver into his hat. He saw her now, standing at the door within the confines of her shop jewel-bright with what must be every candle she owns fighting against the night. So bright that her head was in silhouette, thus he didn't see her eyes until he walked abreast of the door. He couldn't tell what color they were, but they were watching, meeting his eyes briefly as he marched out of the rectangle of patchwork light and on toward the sloping earth bordering the silent creek.

"I heard a deadly scheme orchestrated as if it were nothing but a childish prank, and therefore I have to turn my back" — the wood of the bridge was warmer than the damp creek earth, and his tender soles noted every crack in every trod plank as he drummed across the bridge with people back in town stepping gingerly out of their doors whispering, "Did you see that? It's that feller who sits in front of saloons all day with his hat in his hand begging money for booze! It's Parker! He's got his feet back!" Doors throughout the town began to squeak open after the headstrong passing of the unaccountably rejuvenated man who dared to walk in the wake of the wolves.

The Legend of Carl Draco

And the people began to follow.

A fresh slick deck was shuffled as balled cellophane uncrumpled itself slowly in the trash box below the counter. Melanie cut and shuffled twice and twice again and dragged the cards across the countertop in a long stairstep and closed her eyes and picked fast. She plucked a waxy card from the deck and lifted it, looked, and let fall again to the countertop a high card, a face card, a king.

Pawprint trails were fanned across the barren plain, pouring from the single-file width of the fence gate that Parker walked toward clinging to his crutches—"on my doubts because if a man has endured all the tyranny and benevolence that I have, and is still alive to bear witness"—determined to wrestle his fear down choke-held and spread-eagled because a man walking toward annihilation has got to collect every ounce of courage real or fabricated within himself to put one foot in front of the other if he expects to pass through this gate uninvited and step up onto this porch, which he had thought he would never tread again in his life, and pass into the foyer of Hell's cathedral to lift one leg and with all his strength kick that hinged wood open—"THEN THAT MAN HAS GOT TO HAVE FAITH!"

And because a mournful ballad executed by the band had just ended, and because the guests had not been invited to partake in any slow dancing by Baxter, who sat slouched sucking the rim of his flagon, the room was exquisitely silent when Parker's apparent act of insanity exploded in the form of flung doors.

Emotions nearly sapped by the seemingly endless dramatics disrupting the feast, the wary guests turned to watch the shape of a man familiar to most striding into the room on naked feet slapping the slick cotillion floor.

Seated sidewise and alone with one elbow hiked disgruntled on the table, Baxter held steady the sloshing pewter near his lips and looked over at Parker, who, because Time is held in such low esteem within these walls, might have been hauled out unceremoniously by Pike only one minute earlier shorn of his feet. And though that now belligerent face eyeing him squarely had been exiled glazed and bemoaning a terrible-bought fate, it was not the perceived attitude of the small man who strode with long knotted lengths of wood held above his head in the manner that a soldier might hold rifles fording a waist-deep stream, it was the alabaster glow of new feet that attracted Baxter's serious attention, the smell of fresh skin coming toward him and stopping in the middle of the floor as Parker leaned back gathering all his skinny coiled strength. But it wasn't even the infant reek of feet reborn that made Baxter sit up and recall something he'd dismissed deliberately, as Parker snapped his arms heaving the crutches that flew through the air and hit the floor like unearthed bones bumping Baxter's boots beneath the table. It was the odor of a foreign brew.

It made Baxter scoot his throne around and sit straight ahead and lean with both elbows on the table and indulge in a good long study of those pale splayed toes rocking after that insolent crutch toss and tumbling clatter.

Something palpable, dim, a shadow crossed the furrowed, frowning flesh of Baxter's studious brow, something that could have been interpreted during its brief appearance as either anger or foreboding. But a smile rendered that interpretation irrelevant as Baxter began to nod and open his mouth with a split-cheek grin revealing tombstone teeth and vanity gold. His body rocked with contained chuckles as he rubbed his furred face and peered at those feet. Then his nostrils flared, and those furrows increased in depth, as the bouquet of a moonshine that he had drunk more than once in his youth blossomed into full remembrance. There was only one woman he knew (Grace) whose hand tilled those mean spirits, but he could not make a connection between that odor emanating from Parker's snarled lips and the stranger

The Legend of Carl Draco

he had dismissed deliberately (Jack McCall). It rested outside his comprehension. He could not quite piece it all together, as if a thin fogged windowpane stood between himself and understanding. So he phrased his inquiry gently. "Who . . . gave . . . you . . . back . . . your . . . feet?"

Parker panted from the exertion of long hiking and crutch chucking, from the excitement of knowing that at any moment now he'd probably be dead. He swallowed hard, grinned, licked adrenaline spittle from his lips, and thrust his head forward to articulate valley blasphemy:

"Carl Draco."

While among bulbous steaming boilers hissing above glowing shoveled pits, among coiled tangles of sweating copper tubing, the man in question waited on a moonshine plateau shut down but simmering for the night. On the mudflats below, one or two members of the curious crowd from town filtered across the wooden bridge following the path of that lone soldier who had marched determined, insectlike, brazen, and undeterred toward the black mansion, Parker, who'd gotten his feet back in inexplicable defiance of the man who lived on this side of the bridge. Draco looked up at the moon now descending toward the west ridge but hanging motionless in its exit as if to catch tonight's climactic performance, its fully rounded crater-painted face spotlighting the cloudless valley's curious residents shuffling sheeplike toward the gate of Baxter's house.

He felt it first through the soles of his boots, a shiver in the mountain rib, heard treed leaves twitch startled by something capable of launching wild sparks from a chimney on a shake-shingled patchwork roof, something roaring the single word "Draco!" drawn out long and raging, giving form to the speaker's vague foreboding at last.

He turned his back on Baxter's conniption fit and walked up the hill a little ways above the machineries of drink, past wooden shelving where staved barrels and corked gallon jugs stood in even rows. He removed his hat, coat, and shirt, and tossed them above an angled spot of ground at his feet, which he began to study. Baxter's raging rube lament diminished up the valley as Draco leaned down close to the ground, listening until he could hear the rush and trickle he was seeking. He sniffed the air, and a clean, fresh, odorless stink cooled his nostril hair. He knelt bare-chested with one knee planted in the soil. He brushed scattered leaves aside.

He picked his spot.

The white naked flesh of his upper arm rippled as muscles flexed and bunched themselves hard on his shoulder and back and chest. He curled each right-hand digit until a fist was raised high and held momentarily motionless. The barren circle of ground waited like a pug face already stunned and sleeping. With a throat grunt Draco punched the waiting earth, breaking surface and plowing his fist, wrist, elbow, shoulder, and prone cheek against the earth. Augered fingers penetrated silt and struck damp groundwater that washed his fingernails clean.

His arm came out of the pumping earth like a snake tossed by a geyser rising. He hopped up and grabbed his clothes and stood close to the waterspout letting the friction kiss the mud off his extended arm. Then he climbed a little higher, away from the mushrooming mist, and put his shirt and coat and hat back on, and watched with satisfaction as the fountain flow toppled earthward and began to flood the plateau.

Outraged coals hissed dead as pits filled and boiler walls cooled with the metallic music of warped steel popping unsyncopated across the hillside. The gathering waters rushed into a natural depression feeding toward the plateau rim. The first bulged momentum lipped, and the earth beneath it crumbled, and the floodwaters congregated to begin their journey down to the unadorned log-doweled mortar-plastered flat back of Baxter's house.

Draco circled the plateau to find a choice spot to watch

The Legend of Carl Draco

the tide go out, wrapping one arm around the lamppost of a stripling pine and feeling its age-rings shake from the cascade roar. The thin flow of the first moonlit breakers dropped foaming into gullies, came to full stops in ravines, paused to find new routes around thick trunks and tightly tangled undergrowth. And with this pause in its downward flow, water coming from above caught up and pummeled the crest so that ravines filled and gullies leveled off as the tide was kicked higher by the flow fed by the unflagging geyser with new water slapping the back of the old until it surged unstoppable, uprooting trees unable to withstand the blindside tackle of surf made steel by speed.

Impressed by the flamboyance of sluggard nature given freedom and opportunity, Draco stood away from the tree and began retracing his route back along the hillside.

Break time was over.

*

Upturned tabletop litter bounced and rang, and a single flagon rolled thumping against Parker's naked big toe. Baxter's shoulders still flexed from the effort of this furniture toss, he stepped over the fallen table onto the dance floor as memories flushed out by the smell of ex-wife Grace's tonic took a back seat to memories of a night when rain hammered the valley fierce and lightning stabbed, split, and burned a hillside tree. The memory of a child's successful evasion and deliverance now a thorn sunk deep into the heel of his thwarted soul. "Where is he!" he shouted.

As guests huddled against the walls looked to one another and whispered "Carl Draco?" with eyes growing wide with the fear of childhood nightmares, "Did he say . . . ?" setting drinks on tables or letting them drop to empty their fists for futile defensive fighting as Parker stood ever straighter with the acceptance of whatever fate he'd earned, his grin frozen and triumphant as Baxter approached with hammer-handled fingers driving toward his bony neck (Baxter can't hurt you

185

as long as I'm around).

"You seen him already!" Parker barked as he felt the first touch. "You held court on him tonight. Jack McCall! You had your man and lost him!"

Parker's brief bit in this indeterminate program might have ended ungracefully right there but for the plummeting sound of something large making its presence known at the back of the hall where there were no doors, no windows, only a flat-backed wall founded in the foothill rise. A loud . . . deep . . . thud. The house shook.

Baxter's fingers withdrew from Parker's neck and snapped closed, his head whirling to see whatever booted giant or relentless demon might be trying to burst through the wall to effect Draco's vengeance.

One frightened male guest who was crouched below a window felt a crumb of fear dislodged by a distraction near his ear, a rushing sound familiar to anyone who had lived his life outdoors, the steady plunging liquid roar of a springtime creek bank overflowed. He rose wary, watching Baxter's twisted upper body studying the back wall as another thud racked the building, generating gasps from huddled women. The guest leaned to look out the window but did not have to lean far because his face was tickled by a mask of mist painted fast. He pulled his head in and turned to Baxter, his fear shunted into the background by raw astonishment. "Floodwater!" he said.

This pronouncement reshaped the nature of the fear among the guests because, no matter that Baxter was a force of nature unto himself, there were few threats more indefensible than a deluge, and this being the inarguable case, the guests made for the window to ascertain the breadth of the incomprehensible calamity looming.

Tree bob and rock tumult scattered horses unreined out along the flats as the wary guests fought to view their own doom raking the mountain naked, heads erupting from

The Legend of Carl Draco

the window only long enough to spring eyelids wide with horror and duck back for another shouting, scrambling rubbernecker to fill the vacant space. Shored by untouched pine upright, a river of unaccountable source spilled down the mountainside toting uprooted trees that broke against the back wall straining the foundation—the dancers could feel it through the thin soles of their Sunday shoes. The house was being shouldered by an avalanche of water, a massive nudge. A woman screamed "Carl Draco!" and broke for the double doors presaging a rout as Baxter strode to the window snatching shirt backs and tossing guests aside, who turned their rolling lost balance into a dash for the exit.

Baxter cleared the window frame and leaned out into the night to see for himself whitewater forging a cruel clear-cut on the side of his mountain rising ever narrower like an accusing finger toward the copper gleam of his factory exposed, where, from this vantage, a thin waterspout fueled the torrent unabated.

Impressed by the simplicity and malevolence of Draco's salutation, Baxter backed toward a table set with uncooked meats by the hearth, ignoring the insult of guests here and there, now and then, slipping out the front door like leaves sucked by a passing wind. But the bulk of his admirers stood rooted and watching as he grabbed up a gallon jug and punched the neck off with a fist and upended the hooch and drank it whole. Pike and Hays dashed front and center armed with long rifles loaded, cocked, and aimed high awaiting orders.

Baxter lowered the empty and threw it aside, wiped his lips, and spoke with a wet breathy hiss. "Draco. He's here. He's in the valley."

"Where?" Hays said, squeezing the oiled trigger-housing of his weapon like an eager lover primed for gratification.

But no matter which way Baxter turned his shaggy head and listened with every ounce of valley ownership in his shaman being, he could not . . . quite . . . see where his enemy lay in waiting. But there was one man who did know, one whose defector's traitorous soul awaited its reckoning. Baxter turned to Parker, who had remained on his spot throughout the flood rumble and jump-ship scramble that was still taking place in small increments near the double doors.

Baxter walked up to Parker and grabbed his neck and pressed flexed thumbs gently against bony cartilage, and said, "You don't know nothing about real suffering," and gave a brief poke with a thumb to kindle Parker's confession. "Now you're gonna learn."

But Parker held steady (can't hurt you as long as I'm around) even though that thumb business did shoot a little pain through his gagging neck (you've got to do things exactly as I tell you, because I'm going to ask you to do something that's going to be difficult).

"Where's Draco?" Baxter demanded, clamping down on Parker's windpipe so that even if the little man did have a change of heart he couldn't have croaked a word.

But maybe Baxter didn't really care about the secrets contained in the voice box hidden beneath the clutched flesh of that scrawny neck, because he suddenly brought his fingers together like you'd crumple a napkin, anticipating with pleasure the sound of Parker's neck snapping like fresh celery, except the small man wasn't there anymore. All that remained was the infuriating reek of Grace's brew and the fragrance of a spell fashioned by Carl Draco (a man has got to have faith).

chapter twenty-one

The slap of fast feet fleeing the house was muted by the sanding hiss of a new bed being gouged through the flat topsoil fronting Baxter's mansion.

Guests ran parallel to the whitewater channel curving down the barren plain to the creek struggling to contain and carry south the flood, which swung with a vicious dogleg at the north corner of the house where water dipped and splashed scooping out dirt around the roots of the black tree that gripped crumbling, sandy sinkhole walls, slowing the flow and hurtling it out of its natural path off the mountain the way the stalled mass of an avalanche boulder will redirect the appointed current of a river. And with every pass of new wave, the sinkhole lost another few chunks of earth, the steady flow washing roots naked, the massive barked monument to Baxter becoming enfeebled inch by ungenerous inch.

This ominous erosion was lost on the patent-leather-soled, cuff-linked, petticoated and perfumed women and men scrambling with the grace of terrified rats toward the creek where their only exit, the wooden bridge, lay on the far side of that newly gouged bed.

The crowd began to amass at the creek bank, and not only guests but half the uninvited from town found themselves

189

commingled with those whose lives had been blessed by an invitation to the dance. "What's happening!" the uninvited screamed—"Where did the flood come from?"—at guests running past answering "Carl Draco!" without slowing. "He's in the valley!" their voices muted by that earsplitting scrape of sanding, log-jammed, bush-toting, rock-rolling current plowing a deeper riverbed into the topsoil plain.

No one was near enough to see the first ground-shift and branch-shake of the black tree finding its new gravitational mean. The only ones near enough to hear it, Pike and Hays standing in the abandoned foyer, dismissed without understanding the odd creak and rumble of the foundation succumbing to first strain. It sounded not that much different from the back-wall slam of mountainside trees, not that Pike and Hays were listening. Their alarm at the thought of floodwater taking out this whole building was almost as intimidating as the thought of tossing their weapons and joining the cowards at the creek.

So the movement of the black trunk tilting sluggishly in an unnatural direction caught first the eye of a woman at the tail end of the fleeing crowd, a woman who didn't have the ground speed of the gentlemen highballing past, giving her plenty of uninterrupted running room. Being the last guest out of the house she heard the repeated pop of roots snapping. The sound drew her up short, she stopped barely halfway to the creek and wheeled around to determine whether or not she ought to flop belly-down because the rapid fire of something like guns getting louder every second was coming from the corner of the house where she supposed Carl Draco might be dug in for some kind of turkey-shoot ambush. She looked back scanning for the flash of gunpowder, but all she saw was the lone black trunk gone naked at the base, and damn if that trunk didn't look askew to her eyes. She'd lived in the hills all her life, and it didn't take a genius to judge the correct plumb of trees. That tower was plumb skewed, and getting more skewed every second.

She saw the first splash of something like flat rocks in the spiraling sinkhole at the base of the tree, saw water leaping where dark objects rained down. She looked up to see what new abomination had come to harrow the valley, and was momentarily rendered breathless by the sight of the treetop spike tip bullwhip-snapping as it leaned with the trunk sending sidewinder waves snaking up and down its length denuding bark shards fomenting a rainstorm like coal, the stripped tree now blazing moonlit-white against the sky and leaning ever faster and further with people hollering at the woman, "Get out of the way!" above the louder sound of the strongest roots giving up their grip until the stone foundation of the house was shoveled underneath by tree-trunk leverage upending the north wing and igniting a flameless explosion of cannonballing log, mortar, and stone.

The triggered impact sent half the creek crowd diving face-first into their own footprints. The other half of the crowd, too frightened even to faint, saw the toppling timber roots lift the corner of the house, saw the white trunk lie down on the earth with a reverberation that sent shoe-shattering shocks knocking the last standing people to their knees, a reverberation of pure concentric earthquake ripple rising up the valley bowl to the naked tooth-ragged tips of the mountaintop ridge rock and vaulting into the sky.

*

The shake passed almost but not quite unnoticed where Parker sat. Its power was met by immobile living rock beneath the house where he watched through a circle of window glass, which he had rubbed clean with a sleeve so he'd get a good view of the spectacle unfolding below.

The upright tree had seemed from this promontory no more than a toy model figurine, denuded and leaning. He watched the timber lose its frail root grip in the scooped sinkhole walls, watched the naked length falling with a liquid slowness upending the north wing. Watched it all from a prejudiced perspective of physical distance that eliminated what he knew must be a bone-chilling moment for all them saps clotted facedown on the creek bank.

And like a struck baseball, the sound of that timber hitting, bouncing, and settling came a few seconds after the fact, the window membrane pummeled by air as if from thunder or dynamite lit far away. It was pleasing to see the tree hit the earth, and to see it a second time with his feet as it faintly shook the floor, and to see it a third time with his ears.

"You done good."

Parked turned and saw Carl Draco shaking fleck mud off his fingers in the doorway, gripping like a watermelon under his left arm the inspiring sight of a freshly brewed day-aged gallon jug of squeezings.

Draco carried it to the table and set it in front of Parker, who snatched the plugged cork and leaned in to get a good sniff of that hair-raising aroma. His ears rang as he sat back grinning and shaking his head with thoughtful recollection. "I swiped a jug like this five years ago, and Baxter took my feet before I got a single taste. I used to think on that a lot. I thought if I could've at least emptied the jug beforehand, it mighta showed there was some justice in this world. I was convicted without the opportunity to partake of the fruits of my shady efforts. But I see now that there is justice in this world, it just don't run on a gat dang train schedule," and he upended the bulbous clay and partook.

Draco sat down on the chair opposite and peered through the window at the tableau across the river, at the figures of fallen people rising, at the thinning flow of floodwaters emptying into the creek. The geyser was spent.

Parker's lips popped as he pulled his mouth off the jug and backhanded his chin dry and swallowed hard from the sheer exhaustion of having faced down Baxter as well as having taken a hitherto unexperienced trip from the insidious grip of

192

rabid fingers to a seat on a chair in a house within the blink of an eye. And also from the anguish of trying to avoid doing the one thing universally recognized as good for the soul.

"I got something to confess to you," Parker said.

Draco glanced at him. "What's that?"

"When I was down there in that house, and Baxter got his meathooks around my neck . . . well, right at the end there, when I felt his fingers testing the give of my throat . . . I started to feel a little bit of doubt. It was just at the very last second though. When he started to show he meant business by pressing especially hard I suddenly got this terrible feeling that . . . maybe I'd made some sorta mistake by putting my faith in you and . . . well, shoot . . . I just feel kinda bad about doubting you."

Draco shrugged. "Doubt is okay. It keeps a man on his toes."

Then he reached up and wiped the window where moisture had begun to gather with the subtle changes of temperature and humidity both inside and outside the house. He couldn't see the moon resting its chin on the west peak behind the house, but the long edge of a shadow the size of a mountain born of that moon's reflection now covered half the town below.

"This isn't over yet," Draco said, watching three figures darkening the yellow light of Baxter's doorway.

Parker looked out the window, preparing his lips to slug anew, and said, "It's a rare courtesy to let a man know ahead of time that he's about to get blowed outta the water." He smiled at Draco and lifted the jug. "If it had been up to me, I woulda just dry-gulched the bastard."

chapter twenty-two

Beached, a schooner hoisted and tossed aground, its flanks stripped and sprung, its hull lodged in a final sand-bed dry dock, the long tree groaned and splintered under its own settling weight as gaseous eruptions bubbled from the slick naked riverbed underneath. The broad trunk was skinned white, but its sparse branches still maintained their black bark like ripped coat sleeves hiding cocked arms. The wreckage dripped floodwater, blocking the last wash streaming down the mountainside now carved thoroughly clean of trees revealing a shining brown silt path from the warped stills to the back of Baxter's house, which had taken the brunt but stood.

Silhouetted in the doorway, Baxter studied the tree toppled across his property crushing the ramshackle meaningless boundary-line fence. The music and laughter of the feast now extinguished and the deluge abated, a suffocating silence settled in to take their places, so that as Baxter finally stepped out onto the porch, his boots echoed on the wood.

Pike and Hays at shoulder-arms followed Baxter to the edge of the porch, where he stopped to take inventory of the damage. His guests were huddled far down the mudflats lit by the moon top sinking below the west ridge. The flats were now halved by the floodwater scar running to the creek, which had taken the new infusion of water, held it, and hauled it south.

Baxter stepped down into the mud with his boots sinking deep and sucking air as he approached the tree at the corner of the house where the foundation hung raised by a clawed hand of fanned roots. The worst kind of devastation imaginable to a man of his stature, the withering devastation of bald-faced insult. He reached out and placed a palm on the chilled, smooth white wood. "This is my valley," he whispered.

Pike and Hays looked at each other worried. "Sir!" Pike said. "I'm sorry, did you give an order?"

Baxter swung around—"This is MY VALLEY!"—and saw out of the corner of an eye a tiny square of yellow light hiked high and unfamiliar. He walked three steps and stared across the valley above the town where that beacon flickered on the black sweep of the west slope below the white sky glow of the sinking moon—the abandoned Draco house.

Baxter pointed. "He's there."

Pike stepped alongside to spot with a squint-eye the direction indicated by Baxter's shivering extended finger. Baxter's whole body shivered, but it wasn't the cold, and it wasn't fear, and Pike didn't need to squint. He saw the target and barked, "Hays!"

They made the corral where their still-saddled mounts chewed trough meal with flood-shied hung heads breathing hard.

*

"Riders coming."

Draco looked out the window, nodded, and shoved the jug one last time across the table toward Parker, but Parker didn't drink. He corked the neck and stood up. "We better get."

The pock of hooves striking naked rock echoed up the slope.

"You make tracks," Draco said. "I'm gonna let them take

me."

"Take you? Why, you could hang those two sonsabitches out to dry with a snap—" But he stopped, recalling quick who he was talking to. This wasn't some bindle stiff plotting chicken-thievery in the night. Parker unplugged the jug and sucked a warming dawn snootful and recorked it. He started to turn toward the rear exit but stopped as Draco dug into a coat pocket and pulled something out.

"Take this," Draco said, holding up a long thin object, gray in the last ambient light of the gone moon. A steel nail.

Parker took it.

"You're a worthy man," Draco said, looking Parker in the eye. "I'm gonna let you do it."

"Do what?"

And with hoof leaf-crush growing loud in the front yard, Draco told him.

*

It was a fast and easy ride along the north road flats, but when the horses made the grade they had to slow. It was slow going up the hill to the Draco place, so by the time they breached the plateau, it might have been a race to see who got there last, Pike or Hays, guiding their mounts reluctantly, carefully, toward the white stone house with its brightly lit front window.

They unsheathed their rifles, thumbed back the hammers, dismounted, and crouched behind the protective bulk of heaving horse flanks. They peered across the slick creaking leather of saddles, each waiting for the other to articulate a strategy to assault the man who had unleashed that hill deluge.

"This is Baxter's valley," Hays finally said. "Get the rope."

Pike unslung looped rigging from his saddle and held it out to Hays.

"You do the honors," Hays grunted, running low toward the front steps. He stopped to check his breech, then mounted the steps and lifted his boot and stomped the front latch, knocking the door open. He stepped back startled at the ease of this move, then held the muzzle gut level and strode into the house. Pike followed but couldn't stop the fear-launched alto howl that leapt from his throat as he dove through the doorway and rolled.

Elbow on the table, legs crossed, Draco sipped at the jug and glanced over to view this sudden door-bang rebel ruckus. He nodded at the two badges lifting long rifles taking aim at his heart.

"Get up!" Hays shouted.

Draco set the jug on the table, which upended when, frustrated and driven by fear-become-rage, Hays crossed the room and planted a kick on its underside. Draco sat still, giving it to them, letting them take it, sitting without looking at the outrage twisting the cheeks of Hays who, standing so near a thing feared by children and discounting lying men, held the gun barrel between himself and the thing he feared most, held it like a forked stick pointed at the quick neck of a poisonous snake, and yelled, "This is Baxter's valley!" but was drowned out by the shattering jug drenching Draco's boots.

Rifle and rope gripped together, Pike came lasso-jiggling, crouched and circling, watching the motionless back of Draco's head.

"You're a dead man!" Hays shrieked, plaintive, wishing, thumb-stroking the hammers and sighting on the quiet eyes of Carl Draco, who gave it to them whole cloth and irritating. Hays unleashed his spring coil and tipped Draco's chair over with another kick.

Draco fell easy and rolled onto his back. He looked up at both men leaning cautiously over him, then started to rise, but Hays grazed his ear with the muzzle. "Hold steady, you sonofabitch! Tie him!"

Doing the honors, Pike whipped the lasso around Draco's neck. He rolled his prisoner over and fastened his hands sailor-yank tight until the wrist flesh gathered in bloodless ridges.

The two deputies crept back a step and grinned at the detainee. They were breathing hard and not from exertion, but the way that men at a lynching breathe hard.

"Carl Draco my ass," Hays exhaled. "This ain't nothing but a jerkwater sideshow freak."

Pike's fear suddenly manifested itself in a girlish giggle as he grinned with his mouth wide open showing chipped chaw-brown molars, though he trembled, taking it all from Draco, who got up on his knees and gave it to them in silence and disinterest. Pike moved in and let an icy muzzle mold Draco's cheek. "Where's Parker?"

But he wouldn't give them that, would give them only silence. He stared at the floor until Hays signaled Pike to back off. "Don't worry about Parker. He belongs to me." He poked Draco's shoulder with his rifle—"Move!"—and walked him out the door like that quick snake held on a forked stick with the muzzle nestled in the sunburned flesh of Draco's neck.

Pike raced ahead and pointed a finger at the treetops. "I say we don't waste Mister Baxter's time! I say we string him up right here!"

Hays looked up at the trees and considered the motion on the floor, a necktie party, as you might discuss the impending disposal of a jailbird cuffed to a cot on a slow night just to josh him and keep him from getting any sleep—for laughs. Hays had two druthers. One included Pike's proposal, which was out of the question, but his other could be written off as in the line of duty because everybody knows that a detainee will bolt if he thinks he has a chance and will doubtless attempt to fight back during the subsequent recapture.

He handed his rifle to Pike, stepped up to Draco, and leaned into the face of this liar who had shamed him in court: "Dream root," he said with his mouth and then with the balled bony comet at the end of his wrist, a follow-through uppercut that made the horses jump.

Draco took it and gave back some blood, put it all over Hays' stinging knuckles, and knew the man wanted to come back for more. Knew by the eyes and the sigh of pleasure, knew by the way Hays grabbed his rifle and mounted fast before things got out of hand.

Pike mounted, holding the end of the rope and lifting Draco's rigid arms wrist-bound behind him. He gave a tug, and laughed with that uncontrollable girlish giggle, and shouted, "Ridge runner, how fast can you run!" He reined his horse around, and Draco stumbled facedown in the plateau detritus and vine.

He struggled up dirt-faced and spitting blood. His captors guided their horses toward the plateau edge. They picked out their trail, not seeing the manshape emerging from a bush alongside the house in the fading dark of approaching dawn: Parker, standing upright, infuriated at his own uncertainty.

He could not believe that anyone who could foment a deluge would not have cut those two morons off at the knees as he himself would have done, avenging those five years of hate hoarded in his heart. If I had that magic, this valley would be mine already, but I have to believe my own eyes and ears and my further instructions, no matter how outrageous they may seem. I got to believe. And furthermore, I got a reason to believe—I got my feet back.

The bush shook as, backtracking, he made the hillside behind the house and began his journey along the brightening slope, clutching tightly in his palm that thin ridiculous gray length of flat-headed forged steel.

chapter twenty-three

Frogs spoke to the paling sky. Along the grass-banked creek bed formerly abandoned but now repopulated and croak-riddled, amphibian lips burped a consternation chorus of alarm. The chatter reply of flashing breasts hopping branch to branch in treetop clusters at the mountain base muddled the chorus with an odd pre-dawn tweet-roar, birds scrutinizing with skeptical eyes the population of Chuckney congregated on the damp mudflats watching the only motion, which briefly quieted the frogs in the vicinity, of two men on horseback leading a single man by the thin leash of a taut rope across the wooden bridge.

Far back and following, emerging past the last outskirt tent, walked Melanie, a shawl on her shoulders held at the neck by hands clutching not only gathered folds but the stack of a slick deck newly cracked. She kept her distance, having waited, having watched through the lit glass of her front door the two riders leading the man who now limped with signs of rough handling. Bloodied, dirtied, head bowed, he stumbled past the shop without looking at the woman who clutched at cards that had spoken to her whenever she had made an inquiry, but had never lied to her before.

Now she followed at a good distance, studying that

humbled bum in tow, about whom she had consulted those cards, which had turned up royalty each time, bar none. She gripped the deck and walked down the slope to the horse-hoof and boot-drummed bridge. She watched and watched hard. Even when she had seen the town sheep stalking Parker she wouldn't come out to join them, she had better things to do, but she was with them now, walking down the slope toward the wooden bridge, holding tightly to her deceitful deck.

Still standing where he'd stood when his deputies had departed in the full dark, Baxter watched a smaller crowd of latecomer citizens following at a safe distance behind the felon leashed as the trio came off the bridge and began the walk up the mudflat slope. And beyond the crowd, the lone figure of a woman crossing the bridge and letting something flutter from her fists, playing cards twisting in the soft dawn breeze and scattering along the bank. Baxter saw her but wasn't interested. He was working up a grin as the prisoner plodded ever closer, stumbling, weak, beat, and his.

"You dumb bastard," Baxter said, stepping forward with his boot bottoms sinking in the mud. "I mighta let your parents live if they'da stayed," and the creek croak and tree chirp ceased.

Pike and Hays dismounted pointing their rifles at Draco, but more for show than safety. The crowd slowed its approach, and a few people remarked to others in subdued voices that they'd never seen Baxter outside his house before in their lives, and certainly had never seen Baxter strut studying a man bound like prime beef, looking his prisoner up and down seemingly disappointed. This lean prisoner was his nemesis? This head-bowed, bound, unshaven tramp the subject of an outlawed legend who had killed scores of assassins in a score of uneasy years? This was Carl Draco?

Who finally lifted his eyes and asked in a quiet voice, "What are you going to do with me?"

Gary Reilly

This was too good. This was too funny. This loser talking like a souse collared in a coal bin by a cop on the beat. Baxter started making low chuckling noises like a stove dragged across a stone floor. He looked at the silent crowd for confirmation. Is this good? Is this ripe? Is this truly Carl Draco?

But nobody laughed with him. Maybe they did think it was funny, but those faces in the dawn poised sober and expectant only watched. The laughter went out of Baxter's voice and he stopped smiling, stepped up to Draco nose-to-nose, and spoke with a rifle-shot finger snap that made the treed birds jump to new branch seats. "Did you think you could just walk into my valley and take over like that?"

But the loser in this lifelong duel didn't bite. He just raised his head and looked above Baxter, looked toward the white dawn glow growing along the east ridge.

Baxter's feast-rotted booze breath ballooned, "Exactly how many of my men did you kill during the past twenty years?"

"Not enough."

Baxter was tickled by this insolence. He had fully expected some lame lie or beseeching denial. Stepping backwards he raised his bushy grin to the paling sky smiling, then turned fast and walked toward his fallen tree as if to walk off absolutely immaculate amusement, shaking his head and slapping one leather-clad thigh, then turning and socking his hips with bristled knuckles and roaring to the crowd, "To think I was concerned about a pissant warlock like this coming back one day to take me out!" not ashamed of admitting it now in his amusement. He pointed at Draco—"Look at him!"—and pushed off fast, gathering momentum. His flat-handed slap delivered a sting sending a heart-stopping ring into the air.

Draco's head snapped to one side, blistered and misting new blood. He spat red and kept looking to the side, giving the impression to the crowd that maybe he no longer had the guts to look Baxter in the eye, that he would take his sentence

202

and execution like the whipped cur he was.

Baxter got close again, nearly grazing Draco's averted face, leaning from the waist up with fists again socked, speaking so low that only the front row of the standing audience could hear him. "A two-bit magician like you ain't good for nothing 'cept knocking down trees and murdering garter snakes." His voice sank even lower, like it was a breed of insult to even speak of such petty things. "I oughta keep you around to sweep and mop my outhouse once a week—wizard."

It wasn't just the front row now but the whole crowd fanned out along the mudflats who turned to one another, appalled and embarrassed at the degradation of the bound man humbled at the bar, bowed in complete subservience and refusing to even speak in his own defense. Can this be the man of the legend? Our unknown demon whom children sing about at play? No. This cannot be him. This is a pretender, a sham. Some scandalmonger with time on his hands has spread hearsay among us. This is not Carl Draco.

Among the rising mumble of crowd musings across the flats there were those already sizing things up and thinking to themselves, Baxter is going to take an accounting when this is over, he knows who among us showed the white tail and fled his feast unexcused, he knows the guests whose fear sent them fleeing from even a rumor of Carl Draco's existence and thus insulted Baxter's dominion over the valley. He knows, and there will be an accounting.

Thus the guests began to suffer a pain akin to that of the prisoner, the pain of judgment anticipated, and the justice that would be forthcoming.

Meanwhile, throughout all this trial and vexation, below the ridge rimmed pale blue and driving back the night, one lone man struggled through the tar of knee-deep silt dragged down from the face of the mountain—Parker, gasping for breath and planting naked feet sinking deep in the mud as he crept along the flat-backed east wall of Baxter's battered mansion. In his fist he held high the sliver of steel proffered by Carl Draco, putting one extended and determined leg in front of the other while glancing up at the glow of dawn. He plowed his way to the corner of the building and peered along the north wall toward the massive dripping black roots of the upended tree. He could hear the crowd mumbling from here, and the cock-strut crow of Baxter having his day, walking in satisfied circles around his prisoner.

Ducking low, Parker pushed off and hopped through the runneled mud toward the base of the tree. Tiny whimpers pumped from his throat as he leapt up and began climbing the dripping roots arranged above him like a crazy ladder, his feet slipping on the slick wood. But he held on, gaining altitude with the nail now clamped between his teeth. He came up top between the fork of two enormous roots and slithered on his stomach along the barkless white trunk and saw Baxter's shaggy head shaking with the kind of pleased disbelief that a long-shot horse player victorious might display as he tramped back and forth grinning down at the mudwash sucking at his boots.

"Dawn's coming," Draco suddenly said, his head cocked and aimed at the bright east ridge.

Baxter glanced uninterested at the indicated natural phenomenon, then grinned big and stepped up close to Draco and pointed at the sky. "Take a good look, Draco. It's your last."

Sentence passed. The crowd went mute comprehending the grim end to this quick trial, but no one dared turn away. Some looked up at the ridge glow as if to appreciate fully the depth of the prisoner's loss—last dawn—and to understand with a sickly unease the nature of justice meted out in this valley. They'd never witnessed an execution before. Dark dealings like that took place at night and far away, excepting the minor punishments of men who had violated an ordinance, as this drummer had done. His dream root had been confiscated and

The Legend of Carl Draco

his exile mandated, yet he'd thrown it all away. Why would a man do such a reckless thing?

But then, watching the bleak gray light of dawn brightening the mudflat retrial, a few in the crowd noticed something moving out of the corners of their eyes, something moving fast along the trunk of the tree at Baxter's back. A wolf? A cat? Some critter belly-down and sliding along the top of the trunk.

Then it rose running low, knees bent at a hobbling dash, and the people in the front row finally got a good look at the puzzling shape in motion. It was a man, and those who'd seen the dance-floor confrontation prior to the flood recognized the ragged panhandler clothes, and they gasped "Parker" in hushed realization, nudging their neighbors and pointing discreet fingers.

The crowd buzz grew until Baxter sensed that his victory dance was no longer center stage. He saw heads lifted looking above and behind him, saw people whispering quick messages to one another, and he turned.

To see Parker rise full height creeping down the side of the white curved trunk with the heels of his soil-black feet slipping on the cross grain until he ran out of tree altogether and sprang high, snatching at sky and dropping to the new riverbed, where he hit with a meaty spread-eagled slap.

"Damn, Parker," Baxter laughed, studying the pathetic figure squirming in the slough. "This time I'm taking your legs and your arms. I'm gonna use you for a footrest!"

But Parker wasn't listening, he was moving, elbows, knees, and feet struggling through the mud toward Baxter, who couldn't take the sorry sight any longer. He threw his head back and tossed his solitary laughter at the sky. The crowd kept quiet, watching with a gloomy sense of sympathy—Parker was doomed. The little man who had spat in Baxter's eye and paid the price was now low-crawling toward his own demise. What in blazes was going on here? Things were happening in the valley that had never happened before in their memory: Baxter's vile and inappropriate all-encompassing amusement at Parker's desperate struggle—and bound and silent, the sentenced man awaiting execution. This would be a night to remember.

A few men stepped out of the crowd to get a better view of the impending moment but saw instead a cessation of Parker's movement not five paces from Baxter, saw Parker rise to his knees whimpering and gasping for new wind, and reach toward his teeth.

Saw a single piece of steel plucked from his clamped jaws held high for everyone to see, including Baxter, whose mirth settled into a rib-bouncing, tear-wiping chuckle.

Parker leaned forward and held the nail above a single footprint that had been stamped into the mud during Baxter's victory stroll. He placed the sharp tip of the nail squarely in the center of the heel print, and with his right fist balled, hammered that short spike home.

Then kneeled upright grinning like a man who had just done it, looking Baxter right in the eye and breathing deeply after all that skulk and tree-climb leap and mud-struggle. Sat back on his freshly minted toes and grinned.

There wasn't a sound. Not from the amphibian-lined creek bank, not from the studious treed birds, and not from the crowd who had just witnessed this baffling exercise in futility.

But Baxter's chuckling ceased too, ceased with abrupt premonition. If this was Carl Draco's sidekick in the night pulling invisibility pranks and undoing magic spells, then there was more to this puzzling business than he suspected. The time for talk was over. The time for suffering fools was done.

He turned and took one catastrophic step toward Draco— and felt his right foot nailed to the earth. Riveted. Bolted solid and immobile, and in that brief moment of attempted step and full-blown realization, his heart took one hard beat and

The Legend of Carl Draco

froze.

Baxter gripped his muscled calf and yanked at it the way a man might heave to uproot a small tree. And when he found he couldn't do it, he knew.

"Sonofabitch!"

He saw the bonds unravel from his prisoner's body, saw Carl Draco step out of the limp rope spiraling at his feet and move in slowly, tugging his hat brim low. Pike and Hays swung their guns and aimed at Draco thumbing hammers back, and felt a ferocious tug grab and toss the guns unfired across the yard, where they hit the porch posts and splintered coughing up bullets that rattled across the porch.

Baxter swung in a helpless awkward turn against that welded boot to face his enemy head-on, but Draco suddenly cut right and veered out of Baxter's reach. He walked up the trammeled path toward the porch as though the show was over and he was already intent upon taking possession of the house. The crowd as one began a curious parade-step backwards, a few of the men with arms spread as if to shield the women behind them from the awesome battle fomenting within the half-moon ring of retreating people and the white back wall of that portentous tree.

It was too much for some, already the wooden bridge was drumming with fleeing naked feet unshod by sucking mud, women mostly, though a few lesser men pumped arms sprinting for the illusory safety of the town.

Draco wasn't seeking the door of the house though. Rather it was the stack of bark-ringed cordwood piled high along the porch wall. Sunk deep into a stump with a long, polished, hand-carved ash handle, the lumberjack twin axe-blade squealed as he worked it free. He tested its weight, gave it a few practice swings to get a feel for its center of gravity, then worked his palms into a comfortable grip and stepped to the edge of the porch.

This brought the crowd up short, the ones in the front

anyway, who could see what he was doing. The others far down the mudflats either didn't have a clear enough view or else just weren't interested, still peeling off one by one and moving out fast. But Baxter had a clear view. He saw the machine-honed double-blade as he crouched tugging uselessly at his useless leg.

Draco rested the axe on his shoulder like a rifle as he strolled back down the path. The entire crowd ceased to move, row upon row like an accordion stretched to its limit and stopping. A hush so intense settled over the crowd that the sound of Draco's boots scuffling along the path could be heard even by Melanie at the creek.

Out of shape after a fashion, and unused to the toll of serious confrontation, Baxter lifted his head and stared Draco down. He may have been hamstrung and handicapped, but he was ready. He crouched, cocked his arms in a wrestler's embrace, and spread his grappling fingers. This would be a standing brawl.

But he was refused the opportunity to manhandle his enemy, who stood just out of reach twirling the axe-head slowly and glancing up at a skyline starburst, the sun itself mere seconds from making its appearance.

"You're finished, Baxter," he said. "Sun's up." And no sooner did he say this than the sliver of the sun's top arc tossed light down through the ridgeline pines, spreading a sparkle across the mudflat deluge runoff. The trees shook with dawn birdsong, accompanied by bass-fiddle bullfrog backup in the swampy bank-growth. Soaked mud heated into a mist rising from the damp earth and gathered into a roiling ground fog nuzzling the ankles of the people stirring now, waiting and wondering how much longer this terrible mute battle was going to last. It had been bad enough when Baxter held the upper hand and his prisoner's fate was understood, but now with this man (maybe he is Carl Draco) standing there idly watching the sun rise with that bold, flat, rotating axe-blade tossing handfuls of mirrored light across their stupefied faces, it was becoming intolerable.

Draco studied the crowd as though he could hear those thoughts of desperate impatience. He saw faces he had seen the night before, men from the saloon, the bartender, and Delgado, and down near the bridge standing aloof hugging herself within a knitted shawl, Melanie, who had plucked that telling card. He turned and looked at Parker kneeling with his damp hair drying wild in the morning sun. The little man had caught his breath now and was just taking it easy, grinning and wriggling mud out from between his chilled toes, watching like a little kid eager to witness something great and shameful. He was the only person here who didn't look worried.

Baxter's worry was buried beneath his rage though, his eyes moving with comic rotation as he watched those honed blades spin. Draco moved slightly, and Baxter's arms twitched to ward off an expected blow. But Draco was just shifting his weight to the other foot. He smiled at Baxter. It was a small and friendly smile of pity, and when he spoke, he said only, "You're a waste of my time, Baxter."

To hell with the soft combat of talk! Cranked tight for impending battle, Baxter snarled, "Die, Draco!"

Carl Draco turned his back on Baxter and looked over the crowd with that axe-blade hovering infuriatingly just beyond the reach of Baxter's flailing fingers.

"Anybody here care to step up and slap Baxter's face!" hollering like a sideshow barker. "Take your best shot! I give you my personal gaar-an-tee he won't hit back!"

Baxter's head swiveled to see who among the crowd might take Draco up on his offer, as if genuinely worried, for no matter how deep down he reached, he could not ignite his magic. It stirred inside him like a bubbling pool but would not rise to effect, not as long as that damn shaft of steel was sunk deep into the mudprint of his boot.

"No takers," Draco said. "All right." He faced Baxter and spoke loudly. "This man had me in the palm of his hand tonight! He had me where he's wanted me for the past twenty years, and yet this all-seeing and all-powerful and almighty fool didn't even know me!"

Death bought in a fair fight was preferable to this rain of ridicule, but all Baxter could do was stand frustrated and livid, gathering together all his human will just to stem a black tide of ordinary embarrassment as the crowd finally began to understand the extent of his impotence. He was gutted, and about to be unhatted.

Unarmed and no different now than the store clerks and farmers and guests cowering together, Pike and Hays listened with unbelieving awe as Baxter spat his last command. "Pike! Hays! Kill him!"

They sank back into the crowd.

Draco placed the axe-head on the ground between his feet. He hawked and spat a good friction gob onto his palms and rubbed them together. He snatched the ash handle and worked his hands tight getting a good solid grip, then hefted it again onto his shoulder. He turned to get a new fix on the sun, which was now halfway risen on the crest shooting its white shafts of light down the mountainside, down the naked flood scar below the stills, down to the base of the hills and out across the flats where the fog was beginning to burn off.

He turned and raised the axe high and positioned himself the way a man would to split kindling on a chopping block. Just before making his final move, he peered directly into Baxter's squinting black eyes as if to ascertain whether or not there might be something worth saving inside that skull.

Baxter read the look and crouched, his throat noisy with air sucked and blown, his flexed arms wrestle-ready, his sights fixed on the axe-head, his thoughts and impending muscular motion focused solely upon the catch and yank and wielding of that vicious weapon.

The Legend of Carl Draco

Draco swung.

And in that final moment Baxter saw an odd shift in direction and understood . . . between the grunt of Draco's thrust and the slap of the blade sinking deep . . . understood what Draco was really after . . . and his comprehension launched from his chest a pitiful shriek of despair.

The crowd had seen worse, but never anything quite as mysterious. And they'd never in their lives heard such a yell come out of a human being as came from Baxter's jaws. For there wasn't much doubt on the mudflats: the consensus was that Baxter was now merely human. His wailing and howling, and especially his weeping, confirmed it.

But it was that axe business—that was the truly unique and interesting aspect of this semi-execution, for the blade did not slice into Baxter's neck as anticipated, but rather missed him entirely and sank deep into the earth so close to his boots that the immediate surmise in the mind of more than one man was that Carl Draco intended to lop off Baxter's feet and make a sort of Parker out of him. But because this business didn't end there, they had to shelve their conclusions and wait a little longer for the truth.

For the blade had struck two dark elongated pillars tossed the length of a wagon by the sun along the ground, sinking through the shadows of Baxter's legs near the tips of his boots. The flat dark horizontal twins were severed clean, were no longer connected to the white-faced owner who felt this thievery in his soul.

He dropped with the wet sound of knees socking mud and slapped his hands across his mouth to stifle mortifying sobs as his screaming denial "Nooooo!" dwindled like the dissipating ground fog.

They saw that, the men in the front row, as did the women hopping up on dance-shoe toes to see over their protectors' shoulders. But they peered with far more interest at the still-standing shadow on the ground. Baxter's face was hidden in

Gary Reilly

disgrace, though the crowd had yet to understand the depth of the disgrace, the unseeing guests growing noisy behind them eager to get up front to see the blood-splattered ground that they were envisioning, not yet having seen the odd and mysterious upshot of Carl Draco's expert heave and chop.

What they saw was Draco fling the axe aside with disdain, as though he wished he'd never had to touch the damned thing at all. It flew toward the porch skipping across the split shafts of the destroyed guns. He tugged at his pant knees and squatted near Baxter, giving rise to a new surmise that he was going to finish the job with his bare hands (it passed quickly through the lurid minds of a few men that this was fitting), but Draco did not reach toward Baxter's naked white neck turning red in the morning sun. He reached to the ground and gathered into his hands the shorn shadow.

The crowd leaned as one to watch Draco gather the flimsy black shape devoid of even a paper's thickness into his palms, rolling it as a kid might pack a snowball in winter, squeezing together the barrel chest, spread wrestler arms, and crouched legs as they had lain cast by the sun just prior to that cleaving swing.

The shadow now balled in Draco's fists, he stood up and looked down at the shivering, powerless, meek, and disabled form kneeling on the ground. Baxter refused to look up to see the thing that he knew was coming, refused to witness the simple sight that astounded the crowd as Draco raised his cupped hands and opened them, revealing a blue-black feathered head with blinking yellow eyes, a quick shape hopping with wing commotion and caw beak squawk launching itself off his palms and pumping hard into the sky. The flapping blackbird flew above Baxter's mansion, drove for the east ridge, and disappeared into the globular shimmer of the fully risen sun.

The white shape of the sun was burned onto the eyes of the party-dizzied guests who hadn't seen that star in ages. They

212

blinked, unable to see much of anything, as one lone man took off running. They heard his slapping footsteps and peered dismayed, blinking fast to rid their eyes of the abundance of light, the whole crowd blinded as one but for the few who'd only glanced at the departing flight of the blackbird, who saw the man run five steps, the precise distance between Parker, who had been kneeling, and Baxter, who knelt now receiving a swift kick of curled toes on an unguarded rib.

Draco looked the other way, giving it to Parker, letting him vent those five years of injustice. But he allowed Parker to indulge in only one kick, because a satisfying punt is any vengeful man's due, but two is getting greedy.

Draco stepped over and plucked the hammered nail out of the mud and pocketed it, then walked up to Parker and put a hand on his shoulder and said, "Easy, brother" just as Parker was winding up anew. Parker held the aching but satisfied nodules of his reddened foot in mid kick, then backed off.

"You're right. He ain't worth crippling myself again, and never was worth a hoot in hell nohow," he said, but let his foot kick a wave of mud splattering Baxter's back before walking toward the porch to wipe his toes clean of Baxter's cooties.

Draco stood with his boots nearly touching Baxter's knees. He looked down at this former shaman's bowed broad back devoid of its magic and thus translucent to the extent that the sunlight passed through him unheedful and shadowless. He stood so close that Baxter could have grabbed him around the legs and dragged him down. Stood close to let him know he was beat.

Draco gave Baxter one brief and softly spoken order: "Get out of my valley."

Baxter reached out and steadied himself with trembling fingers and heaved himself groaning and shivering upright. When he stood, the crowd was amazed to see that, though he still wore the same feathered leather clothes, this man, whose maliciously benevolent rule they had endured for so many years, seemed somehow diminished in size and thus fearfulness.

He staggered into the crowd. They made a path for him, standing back with men perhaps out of habit spreading their arms against the rubbernecking women leaning in to look at Baxter one last time. No epithets, no mud slung, the tyrant's retreat went unimpeded and silent, until a bit of rustling parted another small path as two men hurriedly elbowed their way into his wake, Pike and Hays trotting a few discreet paces behind Baxter as he headed for the bridge. The people took their eyes off the retreating trio. Heads began turning back toward the mansion, for Baxter had been deposed and thus already was forgotten. Another man had risen to rule over the valley—the legend of Carl Draco had come true.

chapter twenty-four

Draco turned his back on his people, walked up to the porch, and grabbed the flung axe. He raised it over his head and slammed the blade into its previous practical hold. Job done.

He turned and looked across the sunlit flats, saw Melanie down at the creek bank stooping and picking up muddied playing cards and stacking them in her hands.

Coolies flicked clean, Parker strutted back and forth across the spot where he had planted his victory blow.

"You're free to leave the valley, Parker," Draco said loud enough for everyone to hear.

Parker stopped slapping his feet in the mud and looked up. "What about the wolves!" he shouted, pointing at the hills.

"They won't pester you," Draco said.

Parker appeared to be setting some kind of record for grins manufactured in a single night. His cheeks were surely destined to ache for days.

But speaking to Parker was easy. It was easy to focus on a single man if you had something worth saying, but for all of his courage and worldliness, Draco found it arduous to look into the faces of hundreds of expectant people only to tell them what he believed they already ought to understand.

Instead, he stepped down off the podium and went to walk among his people, but no sooner did he approach the front row than the whole mass of spooked geese began stepping backwards as one. He stopped, understanding that they didn't know what kind of new hell or heaven was in store for them.

But he was saved from having to speak impromptu by a parting of the crowd where Melanie walked against the retreating flow. She sidled among men who stepped aside observing her steady progress, men who began removing their hats with the realization of her intention.

She emerged from the front row clutching that dirtied deck and walked right up to Draco with her trembling lips pinched on a firm jaw. She looked him in the eye and spoke with a kind of fear-born anger alloyed with determination. "What are you going to do with us?"

Easy enough, too, to focus on a single woman if you have something worth saying. "You people are on your own. I'm leaving the valley."

The voices of the favored guests turning to the uninvited erupted as though there never had been one ounce of rancor among those who had been chosen to leave the hardscrabble labor of town to partake of Baxter's feast and those who for obscure reasons hadn't received an invitation. For now that Baxter was gone, it was as though their ancient jealousies had been carted away, the entire valley swept clean of senseless resentments.

But this sole store-owner and businesswoman didn't seem to be buying what Draco claimed to be offering. Melanie had been burned by offers in her time. You don't dole out cash or sign papers without some tangible evidence of a product that you can see or touch in some fashion, which you cannot do with promises because promises are made of words, surely the cheapest stuff on the face of the earth. Nevertheless, she proceeded to use a little of that unrefined crude to communicate what everyone else was thinking. "You're Carl Draco." Nailed it, didn't flinch, drove on. "The legend said you would come here one day to take over the valley."

Draco nodded, acknowledging the fact. "Maybe I did take over the valley for a few minutes here, but I'm leaving today," he said, talking loud enough for everyone to hear, all those people who had been standing packed tightly for self-preservation during that conflict but were now spread out across the flats talking, with a few peering south along the creek road where Baxter, Pike, and Hays dwindled seeking the exit of the south ridge gap.

But Parker bought the poke sight unseen. Draco had credit in his books. He grinned. "Where are you going, Mister Draco?" saying it that way so the whole crowd would cease their jabbering and listen up.

"Home," was all he said.

"I'm going home too!" Parker said. "Getting outta here! But I'm coming back next year, for good maybe." He held up his ten proud fingers, all of which had taken equal part in this latest harrowing near massacre. "I got my magic back!"

"I'll tell you what, Mister Parker," Draco said, hiking an extended thumb toward the vacant mansion. "If and when you do get back, this is your place to reside, if you want it."

Parker turned a dubious eye upon the architectural monstrosity.

"The rest of you people can pick up wherever it was you left off before Baxter took over, and get on with your lives," Draco said, speaking finally to the crowd. What with all the mudflat tension and unfounded fear gone, these were now people just milling around after a good show and open to suggestion. They smiled, leaning intently to hear his words. There were a few faces in the crowd who had been around a hundred years previously when Baxter had arrived to depose the former regime and impose his own law. Old men and women who did not look so old, who had been young when Baxter had set up shop. They remembered. There were no badges in those days. You worked the earth and traded without a levy that bled you dry, and if you wanted to leave the valley forever or a day, the hills did not harbor wolves to run you to ground.

But there were a few people here who didn't like the sound of this proposition, invited guests whose skills had been eroded by the dance, who had quit their jobs and homes long ago when Pike or Hays or one of the scores of deputies past had explained that an invitation from Mister Baxter to come and join his party was a rare act of grace not to be scorned or ignored. And they did come, came immediately, and did have good times, and the music had never stopped. Until now.

"What am I supposed to do?" called out a rare man trading in his ballerina shoes for a real pair. "My house is fallen into ruin and my field has been washed away! I got no trade or craft! I got no money!"

Draco didn't look to see who'd said it. He knew how things had been, but they were no longer that way—so why did he have to clarify that which he believed they already ought to understand: you are free, and a free people can pick up again and make it anywhere.

There was one man here, though, who had lived free for five years under the most debased definition of the word: free to scrounge and beg, free to sleep under bushes, free to drink rainwater, and crawl the streets unmolested. "Root, hog, or die!" Parker shouted. "You got no choice but to do it!"

And with that statement coming from one of their own whose story needed no clarification, the people finally looked around at where they were and what they were doing, which was nothing, listening to mere words, what a waste of time. The bridge began drumming as the crowd turned their backs on this scene of emancipation and began crossing toward the town.

Whatever his stature might have been in the valley a few moments ago, Draco now walked at the rear of the crowd, accompanied by Parker, who hopped over sharp rocks and the pedestrian wreckage of dancing shoes submerged.

"We got to fix you up with a new pair of boots," Draco said, looking down at Parker's mud-splattered extremities.

But Parker looked up fast and shook his head no. "Not today. I got to nurture me some calluses. Got to make my soles as tough as leather. These are the feet of a city boy. I'm embarrassed to be seen in 'em."

They crossed the bridge, which was so trammeled that a sprung cloud of ancient wood dust drifted above the liquid frog-road south. They hiked past the outskirt tents toward the main intersection and got there just in time to see a lone and lonely man struggling with the front hinged wall of his shop, desperate to get it shut before the new laird arrived. But damn if the eyehole somehow didn't jam the hook.

Delgado's desperate fingers began to sweat as Carl Draco came along at the tail end of the last bunch of residents going to open their businesses or shut them down for a morning's sleep after that fracas across the river. He didn't have the guts to join in with Pike and Hays scrambling behind Baxter's exile, and why should I, damnit! I'm not a bad man, I sell good product, and if I can pick up spare money and favors watching out for new faces in town and letting the high sheriff know, it's not as if I wished harm to come to anyone, I'm just—damn this eyehook—a man trying to get along in this miserable world—hell with it—letting go the overhead wall that wouldn't budge and standing away from the counter as Carl Draco strolled up to the booth like a potential customer.

With her thumb flicking dried mud dust off the shuffled corners of a short deck, Melanie stood beneath the marquee of her shop and watched Delgado's shivering top hat and downcast eyes and arms hung rigid at his sides fist-balled like a little kid awaiting penance, Delgado, who had earned more than a few enemies on this block. Melanie wasn't the only one looking. There were plenty of people watching

Draco's stroll like fans eyeing a celebrity askance. Subdued whispering ranged around the street now that Draco stood before Delgado, who had been Baxter's eyes and ears in town. There were scores to be settled with that double-dealing turncoat talebearer. People stopped opening doors or locking doors or policing litter in front of their establishments, just to stand and view with relish these just deserts about to be dished whole.

They watched as Draco lifted one hand and leaned over the countertop and clapped Delgado on the shoulder. Delgado's body gave a quick shake and proceeded to shiver with eyes shut tight and shoulders quivering as Draco kept his hand laid firmly in a kindly how-ya-doing sort of pat to show that whatever had gone on in the past, it's now forgotten. This is a new day, and I just know you're a changed man beneath that overworked sweatband.

Draco removed his hand and walked away. Delgado opened his eyes with a nervous sidewise glance following the man down the street until he finally understood in his spurious soul that this wasn't some hoax, that Carl Draco had given him a reprieve, and maybe even forgiveness, for being the stool pigeon who had set the law on him the night before.

Melanie watched the crafty busybody and lothario sit down on a low stool, his head and threadbare top hat barely showing, a man so depleted by a near-lethal encounter that his knees could no longer support his skinny cadaver, removing his hat and running his fingers through his oily hair, though not for the reasons he would do it when on the prowl. He'd come knocking on her door a few times, until he'd learned that she wasn't in and never would be for him. And seeing him sitting there with his hat off and his fingers plowing furrows in a scalp soaked with sweat, she actually felt a modicum of pity for that pompous Casanova.

But it was the man who had deflated him who interested Melanie most, watching him move past the saloons on the

The Legend of Carl Draco

north road with that little ex-beggar, Parker, to whom she had never been afraid to toss a coin every time she passed him on the boulevard, although she'd never sought him out on purpose. She knew his story. But she had never let the thought of Baxter's wrath deter her from offering charity, not only because she had believed Baxter was finished with him, had taken his toll and didn't care who tossed Parker nickels, but because this town had so damn many spineless cheapskates afraid to give up a few of their own coins, while taking full advantage of the benevolent economic atmosphere of a community of this nature and stature among the people who came from the outside to purchase their icons and brews, that if she hadn't tossed Parker alms whenever she passed him, the sorry little drunk might never have gotten to tip back any cups at all.

She began counting the cards, fully squared off though lumpy with crusted mud in her hands, her fingers flipping the edges of what she had not known until now was a short deck, for she thought she had retrieved the entire pack off the wet creek bank. She riffled them one more time, and they toted fifty-one. She flipped them faceup and took a quick read until she realized which card was missing. It was the same card that had harangued her all through the night.

She looked up fast, but Carl Draco had walked out of sight. She could not see him now walking the north road out of town with Parker at his side, could not see through the crowd converging in the dawn streets to gossip and fabricate impromptu personal heroics supposedly performed during the events of the preceding night.

With dried mud flaking off that deck's edges, she turned back toward the creek and looked at the spot across the bridge where she had scattered the cards after she had come to believe that the deck was no longer credible, to believe that after all these years her own magic somehow had been corrupted, only because she had seen a bum bound with rope being towed by two deputies. Bullfrogs were back burping proper in the creek grass, calling to the ladies, and the water level was customarily low. The only evidence of Carl Draco's passing consisted of the fallen tree and the ugly flood wash scarring both the mudflats and the mountainside. But nowhere could she see the sunlit slick reflection of that missing card, that king.

She decided that, though she would keep this particular deck among her personal things, she wouldn't bother to go back across the bridge and make another search. It didn't matter. Maybe the card had been swept down the creek, or had been eaten by a king toad bullfrog. What did matter was the fact that she had momentarily lost faith in her magic and had lost faith in that stranger, even though that one particular card had been bawling and bellowing at her all night long, thinking, I am not really all that different from Delgado. I'm not so noble or knowledgeable that I'm exempt from enduring the deflating needle of a hard truth.

She turned her back on the frog-leapt lost-card creek, stepped inside her shop, and blew out the display-window candles, erasing from the street the patchwork checkerboard cast from the only window in town that had remained lit throughout the nocturnal run of those marauding sentinel wolves.

*

Below the sweep of the path leading up to his home, Carl Draco stopped walking and turned back to look at Chuckney. In twenty-four hours the place had changed forever, but you wouldn't know to look at it. Tent-busy customers and rain-silvered saloon false fronts buzzed with new trade, though missing from the picture was a man seated cross-legged with an upturned hat begging the price of a drink. That particular fellow shuffled alongside him with a dance-like skip, scuffing the soles of his new feet on the dust of the road.

Draco told Parker that he had a couple last chores to finish up, and that he was heading back up to the house before moving on. Parker asked if he might be allowed to accompany him, and though Draco preferred to be alone, he decided that Parker had earned just about any indulgence he desired.

They hiked up the slope that Draco had descended only an hour earlier bound and bleeding, up to the rimrock yard where squirrels scattered off the shake-shingled roof at their approach. Draco went inside and grabbed his bedroll and took a quick look at the vacant bedroom where he had been conceived. Not a sign of that event, not a scrap of bedding, chest, or chair, just four well-crafted stone walls. He closed the door tight and walked to the kitchen, where he glanced at the root-cellar plank door in the floor, but decided he wouldn't bother to go down and take a look because he had never been down there more than a few times anyway when he was a kid, and had never gone down alone at all because, as he recalled, the basement had spooked him. Whether it was due to imaginary predatory critters or the bleak tomb-like solitude, he could not exactly recall. But it was a good feeling to know that he had once experienced pure clean fear untainted by reality or consequence.

Parker was seated outside in a leaf-shadowed splash of sunlight letting his city-boy toes redden. First thing out of his mouth when he saw Draco emerge slinging that sleeping roll over his shoulder: "What about the moonshine stills?" pointing above Baxter's former lodgings.

Draco replied that it was no concern of his. "I don't have anything to do with the municipal functions of Chuckney's government, if and when they get around to forming one. But if the folks in town want to keep the stills running, that's up to them. There was a bit of water damage, and the boilers might have trouble functioning, although I can't say for certain, not being a brewmeister myself. But I do believe there's enough moonshine stocked and aging in those kegs to keep a thirsty town wet while repairs are undertaken."

Parker sat giggling and tossing pinecones in the general direction of town. Then the grin faded into a look of sobriety and seriousness as he asked a question that a lot of people had wanted to pose when they had finally realized he meant it when he said he was leaving the valley.

"Where's home for you, Carl Draco?"

Draco glanced north. "Over the ridge. I was born here, but this isn't my home. It's somewhere over there."

"You ever coming back this way?"

"I don't expect to. I got no reason. But I've always been a traveling man, and if I pass this way again, I'll be sure to stop in."

"I'm going south to see if I got any family left," Parker said. "My parents might still be alive, and I got that worthless brother down in New Orleans, if he ain't been shot yet for cheating at cards. But I'm coming back here, and if you ever pass through, you got a place to stay," pointing at the inherited house east.

"Done deal," Draco said. He motioned Parker to follow. They walked the yard toward the family cemetery, where Draco set his pack on the ground.

"One last chore," he said, dropping his hat and coat onto the pack and stepping across the sawdust fenceline. Wading through weeds bug-ragged and waist-deep, a routed mouse scrambling out the back exit, he grabbed a handful and yanked a root-clod stem and tossed it over the fence.

Parker hemmed and hawed feeling slightly useless standing there with his beggar-soft palms empty, then made an offer to help. Draco paused momentarily in his grab-drag-and-heave and told Parker that this was something he wanted to do on his own.

Parker watched for a while, then offered one piece of unsolicited advice like a good observer of manual labor. "Why don't you just . . . you know . . . snap your fingers and . . . make all this rubbish disappear?"

The Legend of Carl Draco

Draco bent into his work noting with pleasure his own honest sweat dripping onto the face of a tombstone he was clearing. He shook his head no, and said as far as he was concerned that method of dealing with problems was finished. "This world wasn't put together so tough that you need magic to get through it."

Headboarded by slab granite, uneven rows of resting ancestors lay exposed in a primitive arrangement. Not lined up and squared off neat, like in a few cemeteries that he had cut through usually on the run, the ground here had sunk in upon the breasts of all his kin. Two children too, whose markers were made of wood, giving rise to the speculation that perhaps they'd died of plague and had to be buried fast—maybe the parents had planted the markers and lit out frightened. And though all these markers ran from simple wood to filigreed marble, he didn't know in what way the buried related to him, and probably never would. Mary and William Draco, Sarah and Benjamin Draco, Agnes and Obediah Draco, a gallery of simple names describing a clan of few words.

In the center of the fenced place was a square of barren ground just large enough for two, and beyond the fence, up the hillside in a shaded spot between two tall pines, a suitable plot of ground. Draco tossed a last pulled stem across the fenceline, then called to Parker and said he had a favor to ask.

Lying toe-splayed and dozing by the bedroll, Parker hopped up and came to the boundary line.

Draco pointed at one of the four still-standing cornerstones, which had been chiseled through for the placement of dowels. "Someday, if you've got the time, I'd like you to cut some lumber and put up a new fence around this place."

"I'll do 'er."

"And there's something else."

"Name it."

"If there's a stonemason in the valley, I'd like you to have two headstones carved and set up right there," he said, pointing toward the center. "And I want another stone placed between those trees," indicating the hillside plot.

"We got us a good stonemason," Parker said. "What words do ya want on 'em?"

Draco looked at the patch big enough for two. "No words. Just place the stones. Those two are for my mother and father. The one uphill is for a lot of men who didn't have to die."

Draco stepped over the fenceline, and Parker studied the boneyard calculating the time and labor involved in this mandate. Then he heard Draco grab the bedroll off the ground, and realized this was the finish and farewell of an event that his at-last lucid brain (he was now officially quit of bust-out dipso tippling) still couldn't quite grasp because too many momentous changes had come down during the night. He reached out fast to shake hands and to feel the heat of the magic fired broadside throughout the night still cooling in Draco's palm.

They shook, and experienced the universal moment in which the unlikelihood of friendship-eternal engenders regret. So long, friend. Glad to have known you.

"Thank you, Parker. You do good work."

"Good luck, Carl Draco," Parker said, and watched as the man turned away and headed north toward a break in the hedgerow that would take him to the high road home.

chapter twenty-five

Positioned amid stripped bark shedding pine curl blade-sliced with recent expertise, Professor Dunsmore kicked kindling aside and lifted a log shaved for a noon stove. He left the axe hammered into the chopping stump and, mindlessly enjoying the crush of leaves underfoot and the lid clash of pans wrestled in Aunt Grace's kitchen, carried the log around to the front porch where he stopped, hearing clearly another sound of leaf crush. He walked on past the porch to the far side of the house and saw Carl Draco coming down the path that he had ascended only one morning earlier.

Threw in the towel? Whipped and exiled? Or maybe the odds had been too monumental and the man needs reinforcements. These thoughts filled Dunsmore with a juvenile thrill of anticipation as he dropped the log and took a few steps closer to better study Draco, who looked a little banged up here and there. In fact, looked as if he had been wrung out twice and hung up to dry, his hands absolutely dirt-shot, his face swollen a bit, with something very much like dried blood shadowing his lower lip. Whipped or quit, he was back too soon.

"Morning, Professor," Draco said when he got within range, nodding and smiling not at all like a whipped man but more like a football player coming off a field of four hard quarters victorious.

Dunsmore heard soft steps at his back and turned to see Aunt Grace approaching with one hand supporting the bowl of a tooth-clamped pipe, the other balled at her waist as she looked Draco up and down.

"It's finished," Draco said.

Aunt Grace gave up a single nod.

Draco withdrew the boot shank and held it out to her, a souvenir. "You can keep this."

She didn't take it. She took instead a long puffing study of the thing. "I made them boots for that man a long time ago. He never knew what he was wearing." She accepted the nail from him and dropped it into an apron pocket. "But I did."

"Is Baxter dead?" Dunsmore said.

"He probably thinks so," Draco said. "I took away his power. He went south."

Aunt Grace nodded again at this once-towheaded child of her beloved kin. "It's your valley now," she said.

"I don't want it," Draco replied. "Those folks over the ridge can get along without men like me or Baxter hanging over their heads."

"Wash for lunch," Aunt Grace said, turning back to the house.

The men took their seats as Aunt Grace stirred pans on the stove and daubed plates. Dunsmore picked at his food, impatient to hear what Draco had seen and done over the ridge the previous night. But when Aunt Grace finally finished fiddling with the served food and took her seat, a businesslike silence settled over the table, punctuated by pewter scrape and cup thump that drove Dunsmore to distraction as he sipped his milk and glanced at the white flesh of his naked wrist.

As though Draco wasn't aware—asking for seconds and exclaiming at one point that toppling tyrants can foment a

The Legend of Carl Draco

keen appetite in a man, and if there's any of that pie left over from last night he surely would appreciate a slice, all the while beaming at Dunsmore, whose plate was by now bread-wiped and silverware-stacked, and whose chair was backed out half a scoot, eager to make the porch and those pipes and that talk.

When Draco finished gulping the last splash of milk in his cup, he set it on the table but kept his finger knuckled into the handle, staring blankly at his empty plate like a digesting man pondering whether or not to indulge in one more cup of milk, or maybe coffee, or even a snort of brew.

Dunsmore hiked his chair back another inch and made a restive show of folding his cloth napkin and draping it across his silverware and staring at Draco with a let's-get-moving glare.

It was all Draco could do to keep a straight face while asking Aunt Grace if the men present might be given the honor of washing and putting away the dishes so the womenfolk might take a well-deserved break, eliciting a peevish sigh from Dunsmore, which he transformed into a fist-shot cough.

Ignoring the proffered chivalry, Aunt Grace began gathering plates and carrying them to the sink. Draco shrugged and suggested to Dunsmore that "since there's nothing else doing around here, what say you and I go sit on the porch and have us a smoke?" But Dunsmore was already out the door.

It would occur to Dunsmore later that somehow Aunt Grace had already known the story in its entirety, which was why even after her suds struggle and plate shelving was finished, she did not come out to the porch until Draco had finished relating the details of his Chuckney escapade down to the most insignificant detail demanded by Dunsmore, who unashamedly wielded his notebook and ink. All the details except one, which Draco was saving for later.

The screen door swung open. Aunt Grace came out tamping tobacco. She moved to the edge of the porch and stood looking toward the noon-lit blue west ridge. She scratched a match on a porch post and sucked fire into her bowl. "What are your plans now?" she said.

Draco glanced into the mound of glowing ash heaped in his own pipe. "After I accompany Professor Dunsmore back to Los Angeles, I'm going to look for a place where I can live, and not just hole up."

Dunsmore stood up and stepped to the edge of the porch, and stood alongside Aunt Grace. "I won't be returning with you, Carl."

Just as Draco had suspected during the tale-telling, watching Dunsmore scribbling his scholarly notes as if drawing fast lines on a crude map—the intention had been obvious. This former Boy Scout, soldier, and cloistered intellectual was about to be unleashed upon an innocent and unsuspecting valley. "Giving up the Institute?"

Dunsmore shook his head no. "I am the Institute. Last evening Aunt Grace and I had a pleasant conversation"—he nodded toward her—"during which I was told that after this business in the valley was brought to its doubtless favorable conclusion, Aunt Grace could see no reason, barring your objection, why I should not be allowed to make a trip over the ridge in order to hobnob with the local gentry." He looked down upon his seated former patient, savior, and friend. "I hope you have no objection, Carl. I've spent most of my life searching for things in books." He turned and looked at the untended roadbed that led toward the ridge. "But they are not in books."

"I got no objection," Draco said. "You'll be taking your pencils with you, I suppose."

Dunsmore smiled. "During our conversation, Aunt Grace conceded that there is a proper place in this world for pencils. But I shall not be collecting notes for publication. I am going in there only to see it."

Aunt Grace spoke to Carl. "You like it out there in the flatlands, do you?"

The Legend of Carl Draco

"I never did before," he replied. "Maybe now I can."

Aunt Grace invited Carl to stay as long as he liked, but he said his business was finished and he wanted to get back down the mountain and bring this day to an end walking face-first into the setting sun.

With that said, he made the staircase and took five minutes to change back into his Dunsmore charity hitchhike wardrobe, then came thumping back down the stairs in city shoes that made his feet feel unshod after all that hobnailed hiking—although a man could run fast in this light footgear, if he had somewhere to run to.

He found Dunsmore and Aunt Grace pouring three cups of brew from a mason jar as he came out the door. They tipped the cups. After Draco had shaken his hand and had given him a little present with some advice and had said good-bye to the both of them, Dunsmore wondered why Draco did not kiss his aunt, or even shake hands with her. Wondered why Aunt Grace only jammed the pipestem into her mouth and watched her self-exiled nephew make tracks downhill to beat the sun.

It was something to think upon, the personal relationships between people who possess magic powers—but then isn't that just how a college-educated intellectual would view a thing that made him a tad uncomfortable? I shall have to dispense altogether with the debilitating effects of the university curse if I ever expect to fraternize effectively with people who are unfathomably superior to myself.

Dunsmore finally looked down at the odd, gritty gift Draco had given him with the remark that, when Dunsmore did take his trip over the ridge, he would most likely find Parker toiling in the graveyard. And, oh yes, there's a lady in town whom you might wish to drop in on, a refined and devastatingly attractive single businesswoman by the name of Melanie. You'll have no trouble finding her shop. Just ask anyone on the street. I've no doubt that she will welcome you into her establishment, and will take a practical interest in the fundamental comforts of your being. Provided, of course, that you mention my name and hand her this souvenir.

Dunsmore cupped the mud-plastered playing card in his palm and gently squeezed until its arching surface shattered, revealing the slick waxy graphic of a high card.

A face card.

A king.

The End